Anonymous

Life and Letters of Paul Seigneret, Seminarist of Saint Sulpice

Shot at Belleville, Paris, May 26th, 1871

Anonymous

Life and Letters of Paul Seigneret, Seminarist of Saint Sulpice
Shot at Belleville, Paris, May 26th, 1871

ISBN/EAN: 9783337029296

Printed in Europe, USA, Canada, Australia, Japan

Cover: Foto ©Raphael Reischuk / pixelio.de

More available books at **www.hansebooks.com**

LIFE AND LETTERS

OF

PAUL SEIGNERET,

SEMINARIST OF SAINT SULPICE,

(SHOT AT BELLEVILLE, PARIS, MAY 26TH, 1871.)

Translated from the French of the Second Edition

N R.

"Mihi vivere Christi est et mori lucrum."
—*Philip i., 21.*

NEW YORK:
P. O'SHEA, 37 BARCLAY STREET.
1875.

AUTHOR'S PREFACE

TO THE

SECOND EDITION.

———o———

THIS book was at first only meant to perpetuate in his family the memory of him whose life it is. It was written in answer to a lively desire that the friends of Paul Seigneret had expressed, immediately after his death, of possessing some memorial of a career of whose beauty they had already caught a glimpse, and which now appeared to them saintly and glorious as that of a martyr.

But soon the sweet and strengthening perfume arising from these pages, in which our young friend has written his own life, spread abroad. The little circle of friends, where the name of Paul Seigneret awakened such well-merited sympathy, has increased ; and the first welcome given to the simple portrait of his noble soul, encourages us to present it again, under a more faithful and finished form.

The letters which the affectionate youth addressed in great numbers to his father and mother, and which are the most confidential of all his correspondence, have lately come into our hands, and will furnish us many new and striking incidents.

At the same time, they will bring to light—and this is not their least charm—another figure, behind that of the young man who occupies the first place in this narrative : that of a father, who will reveal to us all the majesty and beauty of a Christian 'father—now-a-days, alas ! too rarely found.

The perusal of this life, we have reason to hope, will prove of advantage to the Christian youth of our times. Among those young men who now fill our colleges, and form the hope of the future, there are many whose minds are captivated by the beautiful, and whose hearts are yearning to do good. Paul Seigneret will be, for such, a valuable friend. His words will make their hearts vibrate, and purify the generous sentiments which animate them.

Those, above all, who aspire to the honor of the priesthood, will find a special attraction, and feel a resistless force in these pages, in which most lofty views abound, and which breathe forth a deep love for the priestly vocation.

The model here set before them differs, in certain respects, from many others which may have come under their notice. The ways by which God conducts His Saints are many, and no one soul exactly resembles another.

That which will charm them here will be to find, with all its eloquence and delicacy of form, that holy fervor, that noble enthusiasm, which make the days of the Seminary so happy and so fruitful, and which leaves remembrances in the heart that can never be effaced.

Paul Seigneret was, according to the expression he was fond of applying to himself, and which, in fact, admirably describes his character, a man of desires— " Vir desideriorum "—and one cannot listen to the vehement language of these desires, without feeling himself burning with the same fire that consumed his soul.

But there is one place, above all, which will cherish his sweet memory, and inhale the perfume that it spreads around : we mean the Seminary of Saint Sulpice, where this flower came to open itself out, and whence God deigned to pluck it for heaven.

May this humble work perpetuate the memory of the beautiful examples of the youthful martyr amongst those who have been his fellow-students and friends, as well as amongst those who will come afterwards to prepare themselves for the sacred life under the roof where he loved so much to dwell.

May also his venerated remains, kept as a rich treasure, draw down upon the Seminary of Saint Sulpice the best blessings from above !

PAUL SEIGNERET.

CHAPTER I.

AT COLLEGE.

PAUL MARY JOSEPH CLAUDIUS SEIGNERET was
born at Angiers, on the 23d of December, 1845.

He was, therefore, more than twenty-five years
old when death abruptly cut short his career.
His exterior was far from announcing that age.
His figure, tall and frail like the stem of a plant
which has shot up too rapidly ; his features slightly
stamped with melancholy, and rather mild and
gentle, than manly and bold ; his voice feeble and
trembling with timidity and embarrassment ; all
seemed still to indicate but a child. Nevertheless,
it was not necessary to have lived long with him,
in order to perceive that under this barely finished
frame lay hid, like a rich diamond in its crust of
earth, a soul full of life and energy. His voice
ordinarily gentle and timid, gave utterance, as the
occasion demanded, to things of such force ; his
looks, always bright, grew at times so brilliant and

animated, and discovered so well the flame that
burnt within ; the objects to which his heart became attached were so serious and elevated, that
those who had intercourse with him soon felt that
sympathy, which a youth of pure and noble soul
inspires, mingle itself with something of the respect due to a perfect man. Nay more ; they
recognized and venerated in him the manifest
action of the Divine Maker, who was preparing
for Himself an instrument and a witness.

God had enriched him indeed with gifts of nature most excellent in themselves, and most ap-
preciated by men ; and those most intimately
acquainted with Paul Seigneret are of one accord
in praising his intelligence, which was one of remarkable and rare elevation ; his rich and brilliant
imagination, the exquisite sensibility of his heart,
and, under an appearance of weakness, the altogether extraordinary stamp of his whole character.

Yet among all these qualities, there was one
which shone forth above all with more striking
lustre, and reflecting itself upon the rest, imparted to
them that peculiar tone which gave to his soul its
winning and characteristic expression. It has
often been said that " man's worth is in his heart,"
and it was by his heart that our young friend first
recommended himself. God had gifted him with
a wonderful delicacy of feeling, and a tenderness
of heart which overflowed on all sides during the
course of his life.

Hence sprang his deep and fervent piety, his
burning love for the adorable person of our Lord
Jesus Christ ; hence, too, proceeded his youthful

ardors, his admiration and enthusiasm, always new and sincere, for everything which appeared to him as a reflection of the beauty and bounty of God in His creatures ; hence those overflowing and affectionate feelings towards all who had rendered him some service ; hence that simple charity which, unwilling to believe in what is to blame, only looked upon the side by which we may always love our fellow-men, whatever their faults may be. Hence, also, those longing aspirations of self-sacrifice, which we shall see outstep in him the limits of a simple tendency, and become at length a passion. Hence, in fine, no doubt, that radiant serenity of countenance in face of a death, cruel indeed, but which faith presented to him under the grave and enticing aspect of a holocaust.

Yet that which made the ornament and the force of this beautiful existence might also have proved its danger and its ruin. An extreme sensibility is either a fruitful resource, or a grave peril, a force which spurs on to great virtues and heroic deeds, or a fatal weight dragging its victim to the abyss. And we ought to add, in order to give a full explanation of the life we are about to relate, that God, in giving this youth a heart full of ardor and tenderness, added also the inestimable favor of drawing it always upwards towards everything which bore a stamp of purity and holiness, and majesty, and above all towards Him who is goodness by essence, and supreme beauty. We shall see this heart—and there we may say lies its whole history—developing itself under the gentle yet powerful action of divine grace, gaining ever new strength, regulating its beatings, in fine, captivated more and more with God, up to the day when the young martyr will write from the prison, whose threshold he was never more to cross unless on his way to death, these words of irrevocable love : " I live all day long plunged in my Bible, in presence of the Eternal Beauty, which thank God, has ravished me forever."

And now to follow the progress of his ascent towards God ; to assist at the development and working out by grace of this happily gifted nature ; to see little by little the pure gold come forth without alloy, until the moment when our Lord shall try him in the furnace, and find him worthy of Himself ;—such is the true way of viewing with interest and fruit this altogether interior life of which we propose to give a sketch.

As we have already said, Paul Seigneret was born at Angiers where his father exercised the office of professor at the Lycée. This circumstance gained for the young Paul the benefit of a careful education, and of a classical instruction which, thanks to his intelligence and ardor for work, became at once extensive, solid and brilliant. But he received from his excellent family another blessing of a superior order, and a thousand times preferable : he was brought up in a Christian manner ; he learnt from his pious parents how to love and serve God ; he had under his eyes the fortifying spectacle of solid religious convictions confirmed by acts ; and his young heart received from them those impressions which it is impossible ever afterwards to efface. Thus he found himself from that very moment gently drawn towards God, as a tender flower turns itself to the sun from which it derives its life.

In this genial atmosphere of the domestic hearth Paul Seigneret passed the first fifteen years of his life. We know little about them. That which forms the charm of life at home is often the very calmness and constancy of the happiness we there enjoy. We find here no striking events which merit a place in a narrative, but a uniform succession of small daily facts by which the soul is prepared little by little, the character gradually formed, and the inclinations slowly declare themselves, up to the moment when, leaving this quiet retreat, the child shows what effect these obscure, but continual and powerful influences have had upon him.

When later on in his letters our young friend carries back his thoughts to the days of his childhood, he often mingles an expression of regret with their most charming reminiscences. His early years appear to him as a dark period in his life, when his soul remained too long torpid and inactive. He reproaches himself with not having then sufficiently struggled against his failings, with having had for God too languid a love; he often accuses himself of having given his parents more sorrow and anxiety than consolation and joy. According to the graceful comparison he loved to repeat, he was then sleeping at the bottom of a ravine, until it pleased God to waken him and discover to him the mountain-top where he should find invigorating air and pure light, and upon which ever afterwards his **looks were invariably** fixed.

There were, however, in **his young heart, the** most happy **germs,** and it was easy **for one with a** practised **glance to** foresee their rich **and speedy** expansion. **Such is** the **testimony of** those who **knew him best at that time.**

The life of Paul Seigneret opens for us at the moment of his quitting the paternal roof to go and complete his studies at the Lycée of Nancy. At this period he begins **a correspondence** with **his parents, which** is renewed **every week with inviola-ble fidelity, and** which **discovered to them his** inmost **soul, and has handed down to us** its faith-ful copy. **His father, "who** comes immediately after God **in his heart," is** the confidant of all his thoughts and **the true** director of his life. The young scholar **writes also as**siduously **to** his uncle, **a priest full of affection,** near whom **he had** passed **his childhood, and who,** besides **the** veneration **due to his sacred character,** inspired **him** likewise **with a lively sympathy. We** have been intrusted **with these numerous letters** which will form the **ground-work of this narrative,** and in which the **life of this youth, so full of** uprightness, is reflected **as in a faithful mirror.**

In the **month of May, 1861,** Paul Seigneret, **now fifteen years of age,** left Angiers. **His** father went to **undertake the direction of the** college of Epinal, **and** he, **in order to** be **near his** family, **was** to continue **his third** year at Nancy. As **far** as regards the **exterior,** he was then, both **in form** and **tone of** voice, **a mere child.** His **heart** was open to impressions in an excessive degree, and his sensitiveness was nearly a malady. Every emotion in any degree lively whether of joy, or sorrow, betrayed itself in the young scholar by tears which he had not the power to restrain; and a word which we find in one of his letters at that time paints to us his soul receiving unceasingly impressions opposite in their character, and alarming in their keenness: "I do not know," he says, in speaking of the joy of soon seeing his family again, "if I shall be able to bear the weight of so much happiness; for happiness stifles me, as sorrow consumes me."

One can easily form an idea of the effect which so sudden a separation from all his relatives would produce on a child of this character. He found himself all at once removed from that which until then had been his joy, and left to himself in a medium where his most cherished sentiments did not fail before long to meet with grating opposition. Thus his first letters are full of expressions of sorrow, and present him to us a prey at times to a gloomy sadness.

"Oftentimes," he says, writing to his uncle a few weeks after his arrival at Nancy, "black melancholy seizes me almost irresistibly. I have now before my eyes the minute details of those days of preparation for my departure, the remembrance of which will remain all my life, I am sure, engraved at the bottom of my heart. I see, as if I were yet there, the dining-room full of boxes, the whole house in confusion, my father's grave and mournful silence, my mother's feverish activity, my little sister jumping and shouting with joy. I hear the heart-rending adieus of our friends.   I see you, too, letting the big tears steal down your cheeks, whilst in person you take part in all these preparations.   And then, ere the morrow, my unexpected departure,—your last looks, your farewell words which are still sounding in my ears. Ah! how would you have it otherwise ? So many marks of sorrow have made too deep an impression on my imagination to allow me ever to forget them."

" My thoughts," he says another day, " are carried back to you all with incredible facility. ·I fancy myself still at Angiers.   We seem to be still walking together in its avenues, breathing with delight an air embalmed with the perfume of flowers.   Oh ! who will ever give us back again our delightful summer-evening walks, which Charles and I used to love so well ! "

Thus everything is for him an occasion of recalling and describing in a most striking manner that which made the happiness of his boyhood ; home and its deep joys ; the college of Mongazon, where his uncle was professor, and of which the young scholar, who always met with a cordial reception there, kept the most pleasant remembrances; the rich and broad landscape along the banks of the Loire, so well suited to please a soul ever wonderfully awake to the beauties of nature. But these remembrances will no more lose for him their poetry and their charms.   The bitterness of the first days of separation will by degrees be effaced, and he will always experience a lively pleasure in thinking of the places and persons which were the first objects of his love. A few days even before his death, from that prison in which they had so cruelly confined him, his imagination carried him back once more "amidst the splendid scenery of the banks of the Loire, with its rich verdure, and delightful sunshine. " Sweet peace," he adds, "and blissful harmony of nature ! What a bitter contrast this offers with the discord of men !"

At this period of his life, and under the circumstances in which the young scholar was placed, it would have been for him an irreparable evil had he yielded without restraint to these lively impressions, and to the wanderings of his ardent imagination. For a young man could not have a more pernicious counsellor than melancholy, which troubles the soul, and disposes it to acts which show both want of courage and want of strength. But God watched over this heart, whose most generous sentiments he had set apart for Himself, and the very event which would have disheartened and discouraged him was, as it were, the awakening to a new life. Away from home, like a bird from the nest, where till that moment it had found shelter for its weakness, he felt the danger of his position, and frightened at his loneliness he clung the faster to the strengthening remembrance of the counsels he had received, and sought in God the help of which he stood in need.

" I am frightened now, dear parents," he writes on the 7th of June 1861, "at feeling no longer your paternal direction. Here I am, only fifteen years old, with my character yet unformed, departed from you, and exposed to a thousand dangers from which you warned me when I was still under your watchful eyes. A mere nothing may lead me astray, and put me on a false track. I remember always with dismay, that you yourself, dear father, told me at parting, I had yet great need of your immediate direction. O how sweet it would be to find myself once under the guidance of you all! Would that you, my dear father, could always see me as formerly, and watch over all my actions, thoughts, and inclinations, in order to correct me when I did amiss. Where is now that time when every evening before retiring to rest you used to say, in bidding me good-night: 'Well, what have you been doing to-day? Have you worked hard?' Alas! in order to recall that happy time, I ask myself every evening in bed the same question. When I am content with all my day's work, I seem to partake of the same happiness as formerly, when you embraced me, saying, 'Well done, that's right! courage!' If I have something to reproach myself with, I try to recall your reproofs and encouragements on a like occasion. But all that is not enough, and falls far short of supplying the wisdom of your instructions. O my dear parents, if I am no longer able to receive your advice from your own lips, at least continue to give it to me in your letters. On Sunday next I am going to Communion. With so much before me to be done, who will give me the strength, courage and help that is necessary, if it be not God. . .! Jesus Christ has said so Himself: He has not come for the just, but for sinners, for those who suffer and have need of His help. It is this thought that encourages me and lets me presume to unite myself to Him."

God was not wanting in His part to good-will of the pious child, and made him find in his simple faith, in his ardor for work, and the love of several of his masters, the consolation and strength of which he had need in the first days of trial.

At first his timidity and extreme delicacy of feeling kept him, as it were, instinctively from all intimate connection with his young companions.

The atmosphere of the Lycée was so different from that of home that his pure soul could not but be strongly affected by it. He speaks of the Lycée with bitterness, and describes the hardships his piety had to undergo in terms so energetic, that at times his vivacity of sentiment becomes excessive.

"I have great need indeed," he writes, as the vacation of 1861 drew near, "of seeing at length all those I love, considering the long time I have lived alone in the midst of strangers. And most of all, I want to find comfort for my heart in the sweet intimacy of home. I am so tired of hearing everywhere nothing but coarse and revolting conversation. Ah! if you only knew in what company I find myself on all sides, blasphemies and horrors beyond all expression meet my ears, and wound my heart to its very core. . . Would I were alone! Such company as this makes my absence from you all the harder and more insupportable; and how could it be otherwise! Happy indeed the prisoner for he at least is alone ! In the depth of his cell he can, in full liberty and without fear of being disturbed, pour out his regrets for the past, reflect over the present, and hope for the future !"

As he was thus uttering his plaints there arose in his mind a contrast which rendered his reflections still more bitter. He recalled to mind a touching scene he had witnessed the year before in the college at Angiers. He had seen all the students gather around the statue of the Blessed Virgin before their departure for the vacation, he had heard their parting strains addressed to that house which was dear to them as another home. The remembrance of this pious custom afforded him the comparison of which we speak. "That touching adieu sung in chorus by your students has made an impression on me which will never be effaced.

"O happy dwelling ! How contentedly ought one to live under so Christian-like, so sweet, and so paternal a rule ! Morality and the good qualities of the heart are there preserved in all their purity, and within its precincts its inmates are strangers to that sort of emulation to evil which reigns in the Lycées, and which will always make their abode detestable to me."

He found, however, a real comfort for his affliction in the affectionate solicitude of several of his masters, who soon perceived the wants which so exceptional a nature demanded. So delicate a soul as his was soon filled with lively gratitude towards them, and it is with an overflowing heart that he speaks of those who had shown him kindness.

"M. N—— is a second father to me . . . Oh! who can tell him how I love him. Often, under the load of so much kindness, I leave his room as soon as I can, in order to go and ease my heart by a flood of tears . . . His very presence does me good. When my eyes, tired at beholding all around me, strange and unknown figures, fall upon M. N——, who always smiles at me, I am quite consoled . . . Then I feel how much more wretched I would be without him! After all I should be ungrateful to our good God, were I to complain. What would my case be if, instead of finding in our Prefect, our Chaplain, and Procurator such good friends and sage advisers, I had met with nothing but indifference on all sides? This thought consoles me, and calls forth my thanks to God, who has not willed that I should be exposed to the danger of being overwhelmed by melancholy. It is His own divine bounty that has given me all these excellent men for my consolation and encouragement."

His studies, also, were another precious relief to the young scholar. He had even then that love for work which always distinguished him. He applied himself with zeal to all his studies, and his active and serious mind gained for him the successes which were not wanting during the course of his college life. But from that time forth, he spurred himself on by high and worthy motives. Study, he felt, helped to drive away "his dark thoughts," and at the same time offered him the means of satisfying his desire to afford pleasure to his parents. The mere title of duty, however, would have been enough, for it always acted as a real charm upon our young friend.

An unexpected success was the first result of his efforts. He began by taking the first place in his class, a circumstance, however, which he announced with remarkable simplicity and modesty:

"You know," he writes on June 23d, 1866, "the good place I have had, and which I look upon as sent by God to keep me from losing courage. For that is certainly not the place I expected to hold in my class, far from it; as regards marks for study-room in class I have always had the best possible." But eight days afterwards a failure equally unlooked for, gave rise to the following reflections which reveal to us a charming feature in his character, and an ingenious brotherly love.

"I do not know if I have told you of my catastrophe in Latin versification. I was seventeenth in a class of twenty; that is deplorable! But what afflicts me most is the pain that place will cause to my father, who now, for the first time, will see one of his sons so disgracefully situated. However, do not think I am in despair, or altogether disheartened by the blow. No! as I offered up to God my good success, so now I offer Him my misfortune . . . Besides, in receiving this check, I have to thank Heaven for allowing it in answer to my prayer. Before the composition I had asked for all sorts of trials and mishaps, provided that my dear brothers were happy, and met with the success they so well deserved. And now I learn that Charles has come out first, and has been admitted to all the compositions of the grand concursus. The more trials God sends me, the more means I shall have of making myself less unworthy of Him, and of you all who love me so well, though I so little deserve it."

These last words show us what were already the truly Christian disposition of his soul. His piety, at this period of his life, is as yet no doubt single and inexperienced, like that of a child : it is nourished above all by sentiment, and seizes religious things mostly by their poetical side, but it is none the less real. It is truly the gift of God, and bears manifestly even now the inimitable stamp of that Christian piety which, later on in life, will make so glorious his loving acceptation and patient bearing of the Cross, after the example of Jesus Christ. This is the sentiment he ingeniously expresses in the following lines : " Our chaplain has lent me a small imitation of Jesus Christ, and every morning in bed I read one or two chapters of it. This book has taught me to offer up all my troubles to our good God. It is a treasure whose worth I have not known till now. How often, in the course of the day, when I was upon the point of losing courage, have I not felt strength revive in my heart, at the mere thought of what I had read in the morning ! "

" Even my sorrow and trials," he goes on to say, " become for me, a means of raising my heart to God, in the heart of Jesus, where one is so well. Pray God that I may always burn with a strong and holy love for Him."

But the best proof of the sentiments is the sin-

cerity of his generosity with which he fought against
his failings. It is easy to **follow in** his correspondence the progress of this **struggle** which did not fail
before **long** to be crowned **with victory.**

Every one knows that children are fond **of** deli-
cacies, and the **young Paul** was not **exempt** from
this weakness. He thought he had **something** to
reproach himself with on this point. But scarcely
had he set foot in the Lycée than **he writes** to
his father to tell him how, in order **to** punish **his**
greediness, as he called it, he **had taken** the resolution that, as long **as he** was at college, he would
not allow himself **a half-penny's** expense to pro·
cure **that kind of pleasure.**

"**You see,**" he says, "**I have** made this evil
inclination **my personal enemy ;** I fight against
it **unmercifully, and hope to be** rid of it forever,
when **I return home.**"

But **he did not stop there.** Some weeks **after,**
spurred on by his boundless ardor, he was taken in
the very **act of** committing **excessive austerity,**
and of **this he excused** himself in the **following**
terms :

" I ask forgiveness in all sincerity ; I beg **pardon**
of you above all, **my** dear mother, for the anxiety
I **have caused you.** I see that my ardor has **led**
me into an **excess, but it was** because I **desired**
completely to overcome my greediness. I imposed
upon **myself all kinds of** privations, **in order** that I
might **become indifferent about food.** I denied
myself **dessert and withheld from** dishes **which**
provoked **in me this evil** inclination. **All that,**
you see, was not bad at bottom ; unfortunately I

pushed it too far. Forgive me, my dear mother, in consideration of my good intention. Rest assured that I will perform faithfully all that you command, and will return to you quite fresh."

Another day, after a slight sickness which had made his parents uneasy, and had brought him a letter full of loving recommendation, he writes to his father : "As to your recommendation to procure myself some comforts, allow me not to follow it. I have done without them until now, and I shall do very well without them in future, and that willingly. Besides, on setting foot in Nancy, I came to the determination, that in order to punish myself for greediness, I should spend nothing to gratify it ; and this resolution well kept has always afforded me great consolation."

A foible, pursued with such energetic constancy could not long withstand his attacks, and scarcely had a few months passed by before the courageous youth could exclaim : " Now I am sure I am master of myself. I have fought so hard against this vile failing that it will not dare to show its face again."

His extreme sensitiveness was destined to cost him greater efforts. Nothing, indeed, was more lawful than the sentiments and affections which, according to his own expression, " swelled his heart." But it was necessary that he should learn to command himself more, and gain a greater mastery over whatever excess there was in the emotions which arose in his soul. Of this he was easily persuaded. He felt all the difficulty of the task, and asked pardon beforehand for the numer-

ous weaknesses into which, without doubt, he would
fall.

Accordingly, he threw himself with ardor into
the struggle, and applied himself with docility to
follow the recommendations made to him towards
gaining this end. " It is hard," he writes to his
father, " to overcome this weakness. But I have
already conquered other failings, and I will surmount this one, you may be sure . . . I feel that,
with God's help and spurred on by my love for you,
I shall end in subduing these emotions. . . . And
how could I help correcting myself when I see
what pleasure I give to all by doing so."

In the month of October, 1861, after the repose
of the vacation, the young scholar returned again
to the Lycée of Nancy, where he had still to spend
three years. He went back strengthened, and better prepared for the trial which he at first found so
painful ; and in his very first letter he hastened to
assure his parents that he had followed their
advice, and has so far "acted bravely."

He continued, until the end of his college life,
that " system of isolation," which his timidity and
the alarms of his delicate piety led him to adopt
with regard to his companions. Assuredly it was
not with him indifference or disdain, his soul was
equally incapable of either. He loved his companions, and his letters often expressed, with touching
warmth, the desires he entertained for their real happiness. But his thoughts and attentions were different from the thoughts and likings of those around
him, and the result of this naturally was, that without
ceasing to be kind and obliging to all, he was never

intimate with any, but remained solitary in the midst of the bustling and busy life of the College. Oftentimes, when he thought he could do so without being too much remarked, he would spend his recreation hour and play-day afternoons in some retired spot. He loved at such times to recite his beads, and later on, when the chaplain of the Lycée had gained permission for him, he would frequently go to the Chapel, whilst his companions were at their games, to pray at the foot of the altar.

This happiness he communicates to his uncle in the following terms :—" I am now at liberty ; " he says, " when I wish to go and pay a visit to our Lord in the Church, and pray there for you all and for myself. It is sweet, indeed, for me, then, in the silence and solitude of the Chapel, to plunge myself into thoughts of the goodness of God, to adore Him upon the altar, and ask His pardon for so many injuries that are heaped upon Him. O my God ! I wish to begin to give myself to You, and that for ever. . . . I have all this happiness at my discretion. How thankful I am to our chaplain for it ! "

" During the recreations," he writes again about the same time, " I pray for you, and the time passes quickly. They tell me I am wrong in remaining alone, and not allowing myself any diversion. But if I pass my time in thinking of God, and in praying for you and myself, is there anything wrong in that ? Is it not a means of filling the heart with consolation and joy ? They tell me I shall become selfish if I do not seek more the company of my comrades. I assure you I love them with all my heart, and would give all in the world to be able to do them all the good I wish them. What advantage would I bring them by mingling in their conversation, which I detest, and which, instead of that peace I find in prayer, only leaves my heart empty and disgusted. Am I selfish, if I pray for them? Oh! it seems to me, at least, that I am not?"

There was, however, one exception to the line of conduct that he followed with regard to his companions, and we mention it here in order to show with what jealous care God watched over the heart of this child, and guided him on every delicate occasion. When nearly at the end of his studies, Paul Seigneret discovered in one of his companions, a youth of his own age, that similarity of character and sympathy of feeling which tend to knit hearts together, and this afforded him, who was naturally so affectionate, a new unlooked-for pleasure. Close ties soon united them. Such friendships, however, are not without danger, and those who have devoted themselves to the education of youth know how easily they may become the hidden rock upon which simplicity and innocence are too often wrecked. But the uprightness and purity of his intentions and his child-like openness of heart saved him from a peril, which probably he did not even suspect. He adopted, as if by instinct, the true and effectual means of removing all danger, without depriving himself of the consolation he found in this friendship. Scarcely had he begun to enjoy the pleasure it afforded, when he hastened to make known his happiness to those from whom he had no secret ; and he did so with such simple frankness that they, on their side, could not but feel assured that a union of this kind would do no harm to either of the young friends.

"O my dear father," exclaims the affectionate youth in a long letter in which he tells him of his happiness with the greatest simplicity, "you know I have never yet hidden any thing from you. I have always loved you, and love you all with my whole heart ; and yet in this heart there was a void, which could only be filled by friendship. It is my dear N—— who has come to fill it up. Ah ! you will easily understand the joy this new found friendship brings me, for you know how painful it has been for me to feel myself for three long years alone, sad and desolate in the midst of the crowd of my indifferent companions, without one who could sympathize with me. . . This friendship has always found favor with the parents of N—— I hope it will please you also. . . Neither he nor I hide anything from our parents.

"From the bottom of my heart I have thanked God for this great favor, and I have begged of Him to pour His blessings on us both. Oh yes ! my dear friend, let us love all that is pure, simple, candid and innocent. What a happiness to be able to share each other's thoughts and likings ! may our hearts be like two pure vases, from which the freshness and innocence of our sentiments rise up to God as an agreeable incense in His sight. Let us strive with united efforts to keep our hearts free from every stain, that they may render homage to our

Heavenly Father, and let us try to be pleasing to Him in every thing. . . ."

The friendship of the two youths was in fact approved of by their families ; but, unhappily, it met with the same fate as more than one college friendship. It died out with time and separation, but not without having first given to Paul Seigneret the occasion of exercising in a touching manner his burning zeal for the good of those he loved. The youth, whose character had found its like in him, was a Protestant, and a short while after their departure from the Lycée, he communicated to his friend the state of his soul, which began to be invaded by doubt. To bring back a friend to the truth appeared so grand a prospect that the pious Paul could not help throwing himself with ardor into the work. " Help me to thank God," he wrote on the 20th of December, 1865, " for having deigned to bid me with my miserable science come to the aid of my poor N——. He wrote to me lately, telling me how he languished, plunged in doubt and incredulity ;—the natural consequence of the religion in which he has been born. From that moment my letters have become more numerous . . . I, who am ordinarily so timid in my conversations, am astonished at all that bursts forth from the abundance of my heart, and that I commit to paper in whole volumes . . . It is God alone who can thus inspire and enlighten me. All I have to regret is the scanty fund of knowledge which but twenty years have brought, and which I ought to have increased and enriched far otherwise than I have done.   Before each letter I recite a Memorare."

Unfortunately, the zeal of the young apostle did not meet with that success which would have made him so happy, and he thus makes known his disappointment in a letter to his father, January 11th, 1866:

"I am writing to you to-day," he says, "overwhelmed with a sadness which a few words will suffice to explain.   N——, my poor N——, who left me innocent and smiling upon life, has lost that which made all his beauty and all his happiness.   Doubt has taken possession of him, a spirit of skepticism has crept in upon him.   Oh ! were it only that noble and sublime research of a pure and respectful heart after truths which we love the more, the more we know them, and which had made of my poor Protestant friend my beloved brother in Jesus Christ !   But no ! . . . He forms part of a band of my old comrades of Nancy. These fine youths pretend to be affected with a great Byronic doubt, and thinking themselves capable of judging everything, reject or accept all at the whim of their wretched reason.   Oh ! what presumption in those who, just losing their boyish ideas and love of themes, come forth one fine morning philosophers, then, setting themselves up for doctors, dare to apply the ridiculous standard of their own reason to the incomparably beautiful verities of religion, to those divine and mysterious truths which ought only to be treated with a holy respect.   There, where they ought to seek in the evidence of faith their happiness and love, they find only a new field in which to give scope to their precious philosophism. It is such as these who have made me lose my friend. He was a Protestant, but he still had the simplicity and innocence of the pure of heart. For him God was everything, and to love Him was ever his greatest happiness. Now all is changed. Alas, too! all my letters have become like so much waste paper, and have been thrown away upon that heart, where the source of life is no more. To all my reasonings, to the proofs I thought so peremptory, he replies by subtleties which appear to me absurd, and yet behind them he dares to defend his incredulity. He is intent only upon the surface, without being willing to sound the depths beneath.

" Earthly friendships are but buds which are to be opened out beneath the rays of God's love. Alas, alas! must we then see ours fade away at the threshold of Eternity? Happy, too happy, would I be, were I able to consecrate my life to the love of a God whom so many weak-minded souls offend, and to spend it in praying for those who suffer themselves to be thus unhappily led away, the very thought of whom comes back too often to rouse my pity and affection."

In spite of the reserve which Paul Seigneret observed in his intercourse with those around him, and notwithstanding that his soul, somewhat inclined to melancholy, loved to take refuge in solitude, he won the esteem of his school-fellows, and amongst his masters he had the sincere and warm affection of those whose duties gave them the opportunity of knowing him and appreciating his worth. The principal of the Lycée of Nancy loved him as one of his own children, invited him every week to his house, and thus let his affectionate and grateful heart taste that happiness which he so much missed,—the happiness of home. More than once, the modest and timid scholar was astonished at the interest he excited, and the affection that was shown him.

"These gentlemen must be very good," he would say, "if they can love me a little who am always sad-looking, frowning, and weeping,—for, there's my portrait!"

But he was the only one who thought so, for no one who approached him could fail to discover the uncommon excellence of his nature, so happily gifted and full of affection, adorned with a piety as true as it was tender, and enriched besides with many amiable qualities, without feeling himself gently drawn towards him.

During all the time that he remained at the Lycée of Nancy, Paul Seigneret was remarkable for his application to study, and for the success that crowned his endeavors. He found great pleasure in the study of literature, to which he gave himself up with ardor, and he gained, by his conscientious and well-directed efforts, a broad and varied fund of knowledge, such as is not often to be met with in a youth at his departure from College. This it was that made his correspondence and conversation so interesting and remarkable.

He was looked upon as one of the best scholars of the Lycée, and was more than once the object

of flattering distinctions, for which he felt
happy, not so much on account of the pleasure
they gave him as for that which they afforded
his beloved parents. To procure them pleasure
was his great ambition, and his most consoling
reward.

One day, he announces to his father that the
Minister of Public Instruction had visited the
Lycée : " The principal," he says, " presented me
to the Minister, telling him I was the son of the
principal of the College of Epinal, and, notwithstanding my embarrassment, he continued to heap
praises on me before all those that were assembled. O my dear father ! how amply was I rewarded for all my efforts, in thinking of the pleasure
which you would experience. But stop,—to increase your joy, I will tell you all. Perhaps you will
think me very proud ; but pride is far from my
heart, and it is the sole desire of bringing joy to
you, my good and dear father, that urges me
to praise myself. The principal told the Minister
that I had not been punished once since my entering into the Lycée, and that every week I stood first
on the roll of honor of my division. Forgive me
this vanity, if, indeed, it can be called so. But no !
I can see no harm in taking pride at having done
that which forms the happiness of my conscience
and affords you pleasure. My reward is so great
that it seems to me to take away all the merits of
my labor."

This success which was the result of his study,
though always real, was not always complete and
invariable as he would have desired for the satis-

faction of those who loved him and took an interest in his efforts. He himself explains how his timidity and great liability to impressions cost him, on some important occasions, failures which would have discouraged him, had he not been well aware of their cause. His ordinary exercises, done calmly and without pre-occupation, were always the best. But sometimes the mere thoughts that he was undergoing a test was enough to disconcert him, and he gained nothing by his composition, as he says, but "a good-ache, and a bad place."

These trials and partial failures did not, however, hinder him from crowning his Rhetoric with a brilliant success, and passing with honor the usual examination for "Baccalaureate's Lettres." Some had expressed their fears that he was not sufficiently prepared, before his mind had been refined by the study of philosophy. He himself went forward trembling to stand his trial. How great was his joy to see his efforts rewarded and his prayers heard. His ingenuousness of heart, and the ardors and aspirations of his soul are beautifully set forth in the letter by which he makes known his success :

"Listen," he says, "to the recital of the favors which our good God has granted me. The subject of our Latin discourse was distasteful to all ; I alone was delighted with it. It was a letter of St. Basil to St. Gregory, inviting him to come and share his retreat in the Thracian Bosphorus, and communicating to him his joys and sentiments. With so fine a subject before me, my heart could not contain itself. I forgot that I was composing, and passed my four hours in **one of our** valleys of the Vosges, which **I** had taken **for my** model. . . In literature I **had** to appreciate **the** " Cid," **and in** philosophy to treat the question **of** Liberty **Lost** in these grand subjects, **and** thoroughly aroused **by** the lively **emotions** which have, during the last few days, sustained me, I forgot all,—examiners and assistants,—and gave vent, as **if in spite of myself, to all** that I felt **in** my heart. . . . Oh ! **I** really do **not** know how I could have done it,—I, **who** am so timid, and who trembled **at first** like a **leaf,** grew bold, and thought no **longer** of any thing but **of all these** beauties. I felt **that I grew** red,—that **I** grew pale,—but **that did not** unman me in the least. O, **my God !** it is **You who** gave me this force, it is You who, **then, for** the **first** time in my life, caused to flow from **my lips in public** a few of those words of burning **love, of admiration,** exhortation and consolation, **which for a long time past** I have felt spring up **within me, which swell and** fill my soul, and which **I would fain** pour **into the** hearts of those for God's glory and their own good."

One can see in these last lines a spark of zeal **which betrays** the serious thoughts of the future, **that** then absorbed his mind. And it was in fact **during** these years, wholly taken up **with** study **and** sport in so unfavorable a medium as was that **of** the Lycée, **that** those **ever increasing** longings after the priestly life took root in his soul.

His piety, far from growing cold, became every day **more fervent, and** admirably prepared his heart for the **call of God who** likes to make choice of pure and **loving souls.** It is touching **to see how** great a share of his college life is taken up by this simple piety. He resorts to prayer at every hour : in it he finds help in difficulties, by it he sanctifies his joys. He recommends to God and to the Blessed Virgin everything of any importance. He seeks assistance from God with promptitude and simplicity, and his recourse to Him bears that character of respectful familiarity which is the privilege of innocent souls.

"I have procured," he writes on the 8th of December, 1861, "An Imitation of Christ. It is such a long time since I have been wishing for this book. I read a little of it every morning during study, and find it teeming with consolation. I learn there to detach myself, as much as possible, from things here below . . . I pass my life quietly here thinking of you all, and praying a little from time to time . . . At night I have you all present in my thoughts ; I am with you, and talk with you all. Oftentimes God grants me the favor of waking during the night :—all is silent, everything around me plunged in sleep. Oh! how easily my heart then rises to Him! . . . It is sweet, then, to pray for your parents, as well as for the companions that sleep around you. Poor souls! they little know all the interest I take in them, and all the sorrow I feel for their faults."

He was astonished at first to experience at times a difficulty in prayer ; but soon, better instructed in the miseries of our fallen nature, which always requires an effort to raise itself towards God, he asks with his usual childlike simplicity : "Is it not true that we must not despair, though we often **feel** nothing but **dryness for** God, and cannot pray **with** love and **attention?**

" I read in **my** Imitation **that we** are not **even capable of** loving Him, **without His** help, and **that oftentimes He** sends us **dryness in order to punish us . . . What a punishment!** that **our soul** which **ever tends towards God, our** Father, **and** wishes **to love Him alone, should see** itself **thus** stopped at **every moment by thoughts of worldly** things. **But** such **is our condition** upon **earth . . .** O, my **God!** how **sad it is to** think **that, even** with the **best** good-will, we cannot **have** the consolation **of loving Y**ou perfectly, **and of** doing everything **for You! . . ."**

Yet, he loved Him already with a great love. One **can easily see this by the** sentiments that filled **his soul, when he drew nigh to the** Holy Table. **He then received Communion** once **a** month. **Every day on which he had this** happiness **was a feast for which he prepared himself a** long **time beforehand, and which left in his** soul a **precious remembrance that betrays itself in** his **more confidential** correspondence. **Nearly all** his **Communions are** mentioned in his **letters, and they give rise to** expressions of warm and **tender** piety.

Every year, too, the first Communions at the Lycée **awakened in his soul the most lively** emotions. **He never fails to give vent to** them with that **warmth which adds so great a** charm to all he writes. **In the following** letter he discloses the feelings **which the return of this** happy feast, in **July,** 1863, **occasioned:**

"Since I last wrote to you, we have had a very beautiful and touching ceremony, that of the first Communions. As server at the altar, I was invited to be incense bearer. You may imagine with what readiness I accepted the office. I was therefore able to assist at the ceremony quite close to our good God, and those dear little ones who were about to receive Him. Oh! what a happy day for me, and what gentle emotions! First of all I had the happiness of beginning the day by receiving Communion myself. And then, how can I tell you the joy that filled my soul, as I stood there near the altar, looking now at the accomplishment of the divine mysteries, now admiring the recollection and piety of those dear children, as, beaming with innocence, they approached the Sacred Banquet. N—— made his first Communion, too. I saw him, with a modest and composed look, receive the God who created him, his Heavenly Father. I saw him raise his hand to heaven, and in a voice trembling with emotion, renounce the devil, and then receive Confirmation, and at last address to the Bishop a small speech, simple and innocent as himself. But here his feelings got the better of him; the poor child began to cry and threw himself into the arms of his Lordship. This scene quite overcame me. Till then I had been able to contain myself, being too much exposed to view: but from that moment I was free for the rest of the day, and, alone with God, I gave vent to my pent-up emotions in a flood of tears. O God! a thousand thanks be Thine! N——, I am sure, has made his first Com-

munion penetrated with love, and full of the greatest fervor. Take pity on **him, O my** God ! Guide
him, and preserve him in the **midst** of the **dangers**
that **await** him. Grant that this child, who appeared
so beautiful, so pure **and** innocent, may **never** become a prey to the **enemy !"**

Two features, apparently opposed **to** each
other, are particularly noticeable in **the virtues** of
the young student of the **Lycée of Nancy.** To
a profusion of sentiment, **and a poetical** expression,
which might raise fears that imagination had too
great a share in his piety, he added **a** knowledge
of the supernatural beauty **of the** Cross, and **a**
love of suffering **which would** have drawn **ad-**
miration within **the Cloister, from a** religious **the**
most austere.

His troubles **and** moral sufferings at **the** Lycée
were not **his only** trial. **Illness often** exercised his
patience. **He** had **to suffer from** habitual head-
aches and **frequent sicknesses, but even** now he had
contracted that habit which **he never** afterwards laid
aside, of struggling on **in** spite **of them** till his
strength was at **an end.** When obliged **to make**
an avowal of the fact to his parents, he **does not**
fail to add such reflections as the **following :**
"Must we not suffer a little ? Besides these little
crosses have made **me think often of our good**
God. **Do** not be anxious **on my account.** I
support all my sufferings **with firmness,** I may say
even **with** pleasure, **because by offering** them to
God, they **will** merit for **me the** graces of which **I**
stand in **need."**

In **a letter** of the 1st December, 1862, he

makes known in terms stamped with a thoroughly Christian courage a rather serious illness which then confined him to the infirmary of the Lycée : "For some time," he says, "I could no longer keep warm in bed, and my feet were as cold as ice morning and evening, so that I passed a good part of my night shivering with cold. Yet I did not say anything, in the hope *that I might have the happiness of suffering without falling ill.* But eight days ago, I felt the cold seize my whole body, and at midnight most dreadful colics came on. I confess I suffered cruelly that night, without daring, however, to say a word for fear of disturbing any one. In the morning I had no strength left me, and they were obliged to carry me off to the infirmary." He then speaks of the precautions that were taken, and adds : " I am quite ashamed, my dear father, to avow all these self-indulgences. But God knows how I regret the bed I have left, with its sufferings, which moved me so well to prayer, and which, I am sure, were a great profit to me . . . Is not suffering, dear father, a happiness ? . . . "

It is the same youth, so generous in the face of the Cross, who appears to us ever gentle and affectionate, adorning Christian piety with the flowers of poetry, and directing as it were naturally towards God the flights of a charming and playful imagination. This can easily be seen from a letter, in which he describes in a touching manner the deep-felt joys that upheld him in the midst of the difficulties of college life. It bears the date of June 22d, 1863. For some time past the young

scholar had obtained what he looked upon as an
inestimable favor, the permission not to sleep in
the common dormitory.   He remained in a room in
the infirmary, and morning and evening could devote himself freely to his pious meditations ; . . .
"Yes, dear father, when I think upon the love which
you as well as all the others, bear me, I often shed
tears of affectionate emotion, and my heart pours
forth abundant thanks to God.   It would be ingratitude to complain of a little suffering, when com-
pensated by the love of such good parents.   This
thought brought joy and courage back to me yesterday when, having gone out, I was walking quietly under the lime-trees of the playground.   It is so
pleasant to walk thus alone, when the whole tide of
the Lycée has retired, and when the vast re-echo-
ing playground remains deserted and still.   I saw
the night little by little shroud everything in gloom;
I inhaled with delight the sweet perfume of the
lime-trees, and listened to the hum of the town
which came and died away upon my ear.   My
looks wandered from the beautiful starry heavens
to the mysterious shadows of the giant trees, over
the broad playground, where the silence was only
broken by the noise of the gravel crackling beneath
my steps.   I gazed upon the Lycée, that barracks,
that furnace, which, after having during the day
too often vomited forth blasphemies and corruption, now lay wrapt in darkness and slumber.

"Oh, the night is so lovely ! it is such an eloquent prayer to God.   Those thousand stars that
twinkle in the heavens, the long shadows of the
night waving to and fro with every breath of the

perfumed breeze, all nature seems plunged in silent contemplation, in unutterable thanksgiving to the goodness of God!

" Ravished with so grand a sight and filled with thoughts of God, I cast back a look upon my life, and love and gratitude took possession of my heart at the remembrance of the favors He had heaped upon me. It is He who has given me such parents ; it is He who came into my heart eight days ago, and who will soon again honor me with His presence. He has offered me all the joys of His love ; He has drawn me forth from the indifference in which I lingered, He is ever my well-beloved Father, and the soother of all my afflictions.

" The morning, when it is fine, brings me new joys. I rise at four o'clock, and have a good hour to spend in prayer, in delicious reveries in the garden of the infirmary. The morning breeze comes sweeping by bearing with it the sweet scent of flowers freshened by the dew ; the sun appearing over the tree-tops pierces with its vapory rays the golden mists ; all is yet quiet, sunk in slumber and silence, and the earth seems to come forth from a gentle sleep ; the birds have scarce began with their early carols to salute the Almighty, who gives them back the day. Soon, from afar, the morning bell announces that with the dawn men begin to adore the divine Creator, and its distant tolls, that reach my ears, are lost in the clouds along with the outbursts of love and gratitude which so touching a spectacle draws from my heart. O woods ! cherished retreats, fair nature ! how delightful

would it be to behold in freedom your awakening
with the morn ! O God, who art so good, and who
thus pourest down upon us Thy light and Thy
gifts, grant also this day happiness to all I love !

"Then my soul, full of such thoughts, hesitates
awhile, and casts a terrified glance upon the danger which awaits me during the day. Shall I be
able to keep myself without stain throughout the
struggles which I have to undergo, and the temp-
tations and bad thoughts that will assail me !

" But, at last, one must tear himself from their
sweet enjoyments, and throw himself bravely into
the bustle of the day, which comes too soon to
alter the purity and calm of the sentiments that
the morning inspires. Yet the soul, out of this
muddy torrent, against which it keeps on struggling like the stone at the bottom of the brook,
raises itself, ever and anon, to God with fervor
and love to ask pardon for the involuntary faults
into which it is allured, and to implore the
strength of which it stands in need."

"When at length evening comes, and finds me
often sad and grieved at the day's imperfections,
and tired with the strife, how gladly I run to shelter myself near our good God ! with what fervor
I read that touching Psalm : 'Quam dilecta Tabernacula tua, Domine virtutum !' Then, with my
soul refreshed by prayer, I finish thus my day.

" It is in this way, then, O my God, that you
heap your joys upon me,—joys, which the struggles, sufferings and sorrows that you send me only
help to make me feel more keenly. Oh ! blessed
be thou, my God, a thousand times blessed ! come

into this heart that loves Thee : come and abide there as in a tabernacle to receive my adoration and my love, in return for the scorn and injuries that are heaped upon Thee ! Make it wholly Thine, and above all, adorn this poor heart, so bare, so soiled with failings and weaknesses, adorn it with those virtues which will make it always an abode pleasing to Thee.

" But I perceive, dear father, that my paper is running short. What will you say to this flow of words ? Could you expect anything else ! my heart is full, and since I have no one to whom I can intrust its secrets I pour them out into yours, as you yourself have bid me. Besides, this will make known to you my disposition. Still rest assured that all this does not hinder me from working. . . . These joys are for morning and evening, or during the recreation time : the rest is reserved for my work. Thus, my dear father, a thousand blessings upon you for the love you bear me. Ah ! I love you all far more than I can tell you...... Farewell."

It will not seem surprising that God should have awakened in a soul, in which such beautiful sentiments open themselves out with so much ease and abundance, the thought of consecrating itself to His service, and living under the shadow of His altars. We see this idea dawn upon him at first as a faint presentiment, then take a more definite form, and become at length a burning desire which takes full possession of his soul.

At the beginning of his career in the Lycée of

Nancy, Paul Seigneret had no thought of the ecclesiastical state. The military career seems rather to have taken hold on his imagination. It no doubt also answered that secret instinct of self-sacrifice which formed, as it were, the ground-work of his soul. Later on we shall see him, in the midst of the last desperate struggles of his country, come back for a moment to this idea, and make hopeless efforts to fulfil that which he calls "the easy duty of giving his life for France in her agony." But at the time when nothing enticed him to the priesthood, he was astonished to find himself drawn towards it.

His brother having one day told him that he sometimes cast a look upon the ecclesiastical life : "How happy he is," exclaims Paul, "to have such a liking ! He will be able to live in the peace of the Lord, amidst the beauties of the country where all that we see leads us to adore and thank Him. What pure joy will he not taste in carrying help to the poor and sick, and in drying up the mourner's tears ! His noble soul is well fitted for all that .... Would to God that I were destined for such a vocation !"

Then, looking at the dangers to which his virtue will be exposed as a soldier : "Pray to the Blessed Virgin for me," he says, "that I may give up this idea, if unfortunately I should not have strength enough to keep myself pure and unsullied in the midst of all these perils."

We have already remarked how much his delicacy was shocked by that which he saw and heard around him on his arrival at College.

"And yet," he says one day, after having spoken of it with great force—"and yet, this is but a miniature picture of the army."

The young Paul, as can easily be seen, was, though unconsciously, much nearer the Seminary than the Camp. He was certainly above all fashioned for the worship of God, and the love of his fellow-men. Religious ceremonies enraptured him, and we have oftentimes heard him speak of the transports of joy which he felt in assisting at the beautiful offices of the Abbey of Solesmes ; and, later on, at the magnificent ceremonies of the Church of Saint Sulpice. And again, the mere thought of doing good to those who suffer sent a thrill of delight through his heart. Nor was it long before he heard in the depth of his soul the call of God, which manifested itself by his more frequent thoughts of the priesthood, and a more decided attraction for that which makes its greatness and its merit. From time to time we can detect in his letters a faint expression of these new desires, which shows that another horizon had opened before his eyes. From the beginning of his second year at Nancy, he speaks mysteriously to his uncle of thoughts that had been for a long time pursuing him, and which ere long he will discover to him. Another day, his imagination is seized with the thoughts of religious feasts, and he cried out, all at once, in finishing his letter : " It is so beautiful to listen to those hymns of the Church, mingling themselves with the mysterious noise of the organ, amid the glare of lights, and the smoke of incense ! Ah ! beautiful dream !

would that I could realize it ! But the drum is beating. Farewell."

In a letter written in July, 1868, he makes known to us one of those solicitations of divine grace, which God so sweetly adapted to the bent of his imagination and of his heart. This letter was sent along with a photograph representing the *Ecce Homo* of Enido Reni.

"For a long time I have had a religious attraction for this *Ecce Homo* of Enido. I had never known it until my brother made me a present of it, on my entry at the Lycée of Nancy. My prayers, my catechism, and some chapters of the " imitation " formed all my religious knowledge. This picture was a revelation for me, and was certainly one of the means that God employed to draw me from my love of military life. It taught me to aspire after other means of sacrifice. I often opened my desk to look with tears in my eyes, at that divine countenance which bore so deep an expression of suffering love. In looking at it, I learnt how sweet it is to love so good a God, in return for His love for us, and in order to atone for the horrors that I witnessed around me on all sides. I promised henceforth to consecrate my life to Him, —to Him who laid down His for us in the midst of bitter torments.

"I kept the photograph as long as I was at the Lycée, and have sent it since, as a last resource, to the only friend I had whilst there. He was a Protestant, and at that time in Germany, I had undertaken to convert him, and by that lost all my Rhetoric year. He kept my photograph, and never wrote to me again. I have given a copy of it since to many others with whom I was connected by ties of friendship or gratitude."

It was about the beginning of his third year at Nancy, that Paul Seigneret disclosed his new aspirations to his father, from whom he kept nothing secret.

"I am going to write to you," he begins, "the most serious, and what I look upon as the most important letter that I have ever written in my life. You show me so much kindness, and your heart is so often with me, that I cannot hide anything from you, and I wish to confide to you all those feelings which at any rate I should have to unfold to you sooner or later . . . My disclosure will nevertheless appear to you so strange, so unexpected, that I am embarrased, and do not know how to begin.

"Well, dear father, I want to tell you that for three years, though no one is aware of it, I have felt continually growing within me the desire of becoming a priest. But oh! what will you say at the mention of that word! I did not dare at first to speak of it. I said to myself that which, no doubt, every one else will say to me. What! you, so weak in mind and character, so wicked, so wavering in the love of God, you wish to be a priest! For along time this thought was enough to quiet my desires ; but they were always growing stronger. And now my dear father, this idea never leaves me, it is to no purpose that I try to drive it away, it pursues me everywhere,—in my prayers, during the night, at every moment. I feel the love of God increasing within me ; my heart is full of gratitude towards Him. I desire to give myself up entirely to God, who is so good, who loves us so much, who has died for us ; I desire to consecrate my life to Him, in order to honor a little by my miserable homage Him who receives so much contempt.   I desire to devote myself to the service of my neighbor, to live entirely for others, and to occupy myself with nothing but their interests and salvation.

" To this you will answer, that I only see the fair side of this life of sacrifice and abnegation. Oh! I know well how full it is of sorrow and bitterness ; I see all the contempt and neglect to which our God is abandoned ; I feel how painful it must be to see our neighbor, in spite of all our efforts and fervent prayers, grow hardened in wickedness, and turn a deaf ear to the voice of Him who would give all so willingly for his salvation. But for a Christian, can there be on earth a more profitable state, or one that sanctifies us better than that of suffering. And then, again, what a happiness to bring back to the fold a sheep that has strayed away! What happiness on our side to belong to God, and to be nourished every day with His Sacred Body! O my God! when I think of so much joy, of the holiness of the priesthood, and of the purity of soul it requires, I am filled with confusion. But then a cry bursts from my heart, a cry that gives me confidence and strength : Lord, I am not worthy that Thou shouldst enter under my roof, that Thou shouldst even deign to look upon me, yet say but one word, and my soul shall be healed, my stains blotted out, and I shall be spotless, and worthy to become Thy servant.

"Such are the thoughts that have grown up in my heart unknown to all, and almost in spite of myself. They have made me accustom myself to think of God at every moment of the day, to offer up to Him all my actions, and combat within me all desires that are displeasing to Him, and to find my greatest delight in blessing Him, and praying to Him. Up till now, I have never said a word of this to any one. It is to you, my dear father, that I unbosom myself. I throw myself blindly upon your affection, and intrust myself entirely to your heart, which is always open to receive me. It is my happiness to think that in three years, perhaps, I shall be able finally to consecrate myself to God, and enter the Seminary. But in the mean time I will do as you desire, and prepare myself till the time comes, when you can assure me that your fears are no more, and that you can see me with joy enter the ranks of the priesthood. I know well you will be happy to let me consecrate myself to God, as soon as, in course of time, you believe that I am really called to do so."

Without making any opposition to a vocation which appeared so strong, and announced itself in terms so touching, the father of the pious youth recommended him simply to give his ideas time to ripen, and, in the mean while, to keep them secret in his heart, adding that silence would be a test most pleasing to God. He accepted this rule of conduct with the utmost docility and filial submission. "My dear father," he writes, "it is a most agreeable duty for me to put into your hands the whole care of my future; persuaded that you have no other desire than for my welfare, I give myself up to be entirely guided by your experience and prudence. Now, that I have laid bare my heart to you, I am going to set to work with new ardor to render myself worthy of you and of our good God; to get rid of my many faults which every day I bemoan, which each morning I promise to avoid, but with which, too often, I have still to reproach myself at evening. Yet I am not disheartened. I have learned that life is nothing but a continual struggle between our good and bad inclinations, and that merit does not consist in living without faults, but in overcoming those to which we are subject. May God hear my prayers, bless my efforts, and reward me for them by giving me an ever-increasing love for Him, and making me more worthy of you all."

From this moment, the letters that are not addressed to his father contain no more direct allusions to his vocation to the priesthood. But his desire still remained deep-rooted in his soul, and is visibly brought to light when he has occasion to speak of the Seminary or the priesthood.

One day he informs his uncle that he is reading Jocelyn, by Lamartine, which had fallen into his hands. The perusal of such a book was less suited than any other to a youth whose extreme sensitiveness had rather need of some check, and for whom the danger lay in forming of the priest an ideal, in which the imagination would have too large a part. But, as he acted with uprightness and openness of heart, God changed into good whatever harm this book might have done. The pages which he relished most were those that re-called to him the thought which his soul was so fond of entertaining; and the description of the enjoyment Jocelyn found in meditating in the silence and retreat of the Seminary, or in praying in the loneliness of some church, inspired him with feelings of the most tender pity.

"Oh yes," he exclaims, "when at evening I wit-ness the majestic quiet of the church, and the gentle gloom against which the lamp is feeble, struggling as it watches alone before the taber-nacle of God, my soul seems to be carried away, to free itself from earth, and pour itself forth in torrents of love and gratitude to so good a God, who deigns to remain always amongst men! They leave Him, alas! lonely and forgotten, and still He is always there to counsel and encourage them. Then a mighty desire takes possession of my heart, a desire to consecrate myself to Him. One would wish, like that feeble light, to remain al-ways at the foot of the altar as a holocaust to the love of God."

They hastened, however, to turn him from a book which might have proved dangerous. The same advice came both from Epinal and Angiers, and in the letter which followed the one we have just quoted, the youth, with his accustomed sim-plicity, thus writes to his uncle: "Like you, my father has warned me not to read Jocelyn any more, and this double recommendation is to me a sacred and inviolable command."

Another circumstance gave him an occasion of showing in what light he looked upon the priest's daily life, given up as it is wholly to the ministry of souls. He describes the way in which he spent a day in vacation time, that had turned out a source of great pleasure to him. It was the solemn feast of Pentecost. Having arrived at Nancy the evening before, he had partaken of all the joys which so affectionate a heart as his experienced in seeing his family again. "The next day," he relates, "at four o'clock in the morning, I was awakened by the lovely bells of Epinal, and each peal drew fresh outbursts of joy and love from my heart. It was because that heart was pure, and ready to unite itself to God, my Heavenly Father, whose bounty is truly inexhaustible. After beginning the day so happily, we set off on foot at seven o'clock for a village at two leagues' distance, where Charles was to play the organ, and pass the whole day with me at the Curé's."

His playful imagination finds a singular pleasure in describing the charms of this excursion to the country. Nothing is forgotten,—" neither the fresh morning air, nor the perfumed breeze," nor "the thousand flowers of spring-time." A thrill of delight runs through him at the sight of " that beautiful little village, buried in verdure, beneath the shadow of the modest steeple of the village church." He sees with an envious eye "the charming little room of the Curé, with his library for study, and the crucifix, at the foot of which he lays down all his sorrows." Everything enchants and ravishes him on this feast, which offers so happy contrast to the many sad days at the Lycée. At his return in the evening, he talked with his brother. "Our conversation turned upon the happy life of a country curé. What happiness indeed is his! After having lived apart from the bustle of the busy world, solely occupied in blessing God, and in doing good to his neighbor; after having consecrated himself to the service and happiness of others, to pass unperceived, and die unknown to the world, regretted only by a few families, of whom during life he had been the consoler and the father! Thus separated a moment from eternity, he passes that moment in time, without allowing himself to be sullied by the vile things of earth, and whilst his eyes are invariably fixed upon his beginning and his end, he returns undefiled into eternity and the bosom of God. I know that troubles are not wanting. I have read and meditated in the book of the Abbé Bautin, 'The fine season in the country,' all he says about the curé. But still, for a real priest, is it not true that the more he suffers the greater is his happiness? Does he not receive with joy all crosses and sufferings? Has he not an inexhaustible source of delight and divine consolation in prayer, and in the presence of Jesus in the tabernacle? And then, what has he to fear? Come crosses, come sufferings, troubles, privations, and vexations of every kind; with God's grace, I despise you all, or rather, I accept you with joy, as so many favors from His hand!"

It is impossible not to see in such outbursts as these something more than the keen sensibility and generous enthusiasm of a youth of eighteen. They bear besides the deep stamp of truly Christian sentiments, and the mark of a real call to the priesthood.

In the young Paul's correspondence with his father, it is easy to follow the growth and progress of his vocation. Being more at ease with him to whom he had made known his secret, and who was, as he writes one day, "the mirror of his heart," he often recalls these thoughts which are the joy of his life. He strives, above all, to convince him that they are not the effect of some passing enthusiasm, but that God has engraved them in his soul in indelible characters; that he is drawn by a charm he cannot resist, and that the world holds out to him nothing but weariness and disgust. He weighs the reasons which might be urged in opposition to his desires, and tries gently to do away with the uneasiness that his too ardent nature was apt to provoke.

"O my dear father!" he exclaims one day, when writing on the subject, "I thank you for your strong and sincere love for me, which makes you endure so much anxiety on my account. But allow me to speak to you freely. If you see in me the form of a child, I think I can at least say that I have not the tastes of a child. I pass in review before me all the pleasures, all the joys of the world, and I find nothing in them but what fills me with weariness and sadness. God alone is all my joy, all my hope. Is it at all surprising that I should give myself up to this Father who is so good; who comes to seek me in my nothingness, and draw me out of the mire in which I grovel. You have here, dear father, the whole state of my soul. Though I am wretched; though I am unworthy to serve Him, God, who sees me, knows at least how much I love Him ; with what confidence I throw myself into His bosom, and how my only happiness is to pray to Him, and to hope that one day I shall belong wholly to Him. All this is not the fruit of a momentary enthusiasm : it has been my state for a long time past.

"If I am little and wretched, what of that ? The little will love me the more, and come to me with greater confidence. And if my body cannot perform anything but ordinary services, I have a mind which I will strive always to enlighten and enlarge, that by it I may afford others light and knowledge; I have a heart, which will find its happiness in sharing the afflictions and sufferings of others; I have a soul, in which God is forming by degrees thoughts of burning love, of charity, and peace; and last of all, I have a voice, by means of which I shall be able to pour those thoughts and desires into the hearts of others, and thus in-spire them with the love of God, and bring to them peace, consolation and happiness. O my dear father, what beautiful dreams of the future ! My God ! will all this ever come true ? Would you deign to call upon me to perform such grand things,—to scatter round me so much good ? Oh ! what am I saying ; let us throw the veil again over these sweet thoughts of future happiness, in order to let them ripen in silence and secret, in the gentle warmth of the heart."

In another letter, written later, we find these words: "Dear father, you bid me think well on my vocation. It is my daily thought, and that which forms my hope and consolation ; that which fills my heart with deep-felt love and gratitude towards our good God, and towards you all, my dearly loved parents, and that which inspires me with love for every one.

"I know, perhaps better than you imagine, the dark side of the sacerdotal life, and the sufferings which await the priest in his ministry. They will be many and great, I know. I shall have to undergo that which I witness every day, the contempt or disregard of so many, for whom the priest is a useless character, one who is entirely given up to good living, and many other crimes which I cannot mention,—for I hear all that. But when God is with us, the more men heap contempt and ingratitude upon us, the more we love them, the more ardent is our desire to soften their hearts by dint of kindness and gentleness, and thus gain them to God. Besides, where would be the merit, if we met with nothing but those ceaseless joys which it should be the lot of the true priest to experience. If his happiness is so great, is it not necessary that he should have much to suffer, too? Perhaps I shall be poor, and reduced to fight against necessity. But what of that? This will only add another joy: it is so sweet to deprive one's self of everything, in order to give something more to others."

And not long before leaving the Lycée, the

pious youth reports with touching simplicity the assurance that his heart could not set itself on any other but Him whose gentle call he hears in the secret of his soul.

"I seem to feel now more than ever an attraction for that future which holds out to me peace and happiness, and which appears to me serene as a beautiful summer evening. And I perceive with secret pleasure, I confess, that I am not made for this world ; that I am embarrassed when in contact with it, and that I in no way love it. I even feel that I shall never be able to have other desires than those which now swell my heart. I should require perfect creatures, in order to attach myself to anything here below, and even then I should fear to injure them by the contact of my coarse nature. We can only love God in this manner without doing Him harm, because He is above us by His whole infinite nature, and because He showers down upon us His graces, without our wretchedness and corruption being able to reach Him. It is for this reason that I give myself up to His love without reserve, and abandon myself to Him with the most peaceful unconcern."

While these beautiful thoughts and holy desires were expanding in his soul, his studies were drawing to an end. After having passed the examination for the " Baccalauréat ès Lettres" in the month of November, 1863, Paul Seigneret had finished the scholastic year; he had studied the little philosophy that the system of bifurcation, now condemned, had let creep into the colleges of the

university.   But his tastes led him, by preference,
to literature.   *

    *   A soul such as his found, as may well be imagined, an
enticing charm in poetry.   He read the great poets, and composed verses himself.   From these attempts, which were not
continued longer than this year, he acquired nothing but a facility
for happily composing a piece suited to the occasion.

One day in the month of July, 1864, Monseigneur Lavigerie,
Bishop of Nancy, honored the Lycée with a visit, and Paul
Seigneret read to him, in a voice trembling with emotion, a com-
plimentary poem, which he had undertaken to compose, on condition that another should read it.   Such a distinction was too
much for his timid modesty.   But when the moment was come,
no one, as was natural, wished to rob him of this honor, and in
consequence, he was obliged to bear, as he himself says it, "that
formidable array of eyes intent upon him."   The piece, which
was very well liked, ended with these happy lines :

    Quelle que soit pourtant la volupte secrete
    Que versent dans nos cœurs l'etude et la retraite,
    D'autres biens savent plaire a notre age enchante ;
    Deux surtout, Monseigneur, repos et liberte.
    Maintenant que l'ete, sur la nature entiere,
    Epand si chaudement la vie et la lumiere,
    Dans les champs, dans les bois, nous irions volontiers,
    Infideles, un jour, a nos vieux marronniers,
    Benir Votre Grandeur, dout l'heureux privilege,
    Nous peut ouvrir, d'un mot, les portes du college.
    Au repos, nous dit-on, Dieu lui-meme a songe,
    Cet exemple fait loi ! Monseigneur, un conge !

Which might be translated :

    Whate'er be the joys that we feel in our heart,
    From the pleasures that study and quiet impart,
    There are others, my Lord, and the two we love best,
    And which suit most our nature, are freedom and rest.
    As now the hot summer spreads o'er nature's face
    New warmth and new life, and bedecks it with grace,
    To the fields, to the woods, with our hearts full of glee,
    Deserting for once our old chestnuts, we'd flee,
    And thank you, my Lord, who have but to command,
    And the gates of the college wide open will stand.
    Rest ! Rest ! then we ask :—if God rested, we may ;
    His example is law,—my Lord, a holiday.

His correspondence, during this last year that he passed at College, is particularly striking. He was now a young man, and his soul spread itself out before life, like a flower under the first rays of the sun. Feelings of a force such as he had not till then been sensible of, now filled his heart, and caused him joys wholly unknown before. His literary studies captivated his lofty mind more and more each day. He worked with indefatigable ardor, and took advantage of the exceptional privilege granted him in the Lycée, of prolonging his studies sometimes far into the night.

When the week was at an end, Sunday generally brought him, besides the deep-felt joys of Holy Communion, the consolations of family life and friendship. On that day he left the Lycée, and was received as another son by the parents of his friend, and shared with them the happiness of their home. Very often, too, an excursion into the rich country around Nancy added another charm to those which he had already experienced, and awakened anew his lively admiration for the beauties of nature.

His letters of each week reflect with wonderful fidelity all the impressions these things made upon his heart. That which affords him the greatest pleasure is the love of his family, his keen sense of nature's beauties, his books, poetry and music, which last, he said one day, "awakes in me indescribable emotions." But that which he loves above all, or rather that which he loves in all, is God, whose name comes under his pen at every moment ; God, his supreme delight ; God, to whom he will be able one day to devote his life.

"It seems to me that I have very much changed of late," he writes on the 10th December, 1863. "Imagination, sentiment, love of poetry, of music, of nature, of all that is beautiful, and therefore of Thee, O my God, who art beauty and goodness itself, increase and expand within me in a surprising manner. I now feel my heart touched in a thousand different ways, and a thousand new flights of thought come to fill me with delight. Is it not that my soul is emerging from the darkness and coldness into which it has been plunged, and rises towards regions of light, warmth and life? Oh! if it is indeed thus, then thanks, my God ; thanks for the joy You give me by this happy change! This state of soul exercises its influence on the faculties of my mind. I told you last year I worked but slowly, and had a sluggish imagination. The ideas were not, indeed, wanting, but they passed quickly by, were confused, and wrapped in darkness. In the midst of this disorder, I did not know what to settle upon ; I hesitated, grew embarrassed, and composing was very slow and difficult. This year it is no more so. It seems to me that this confusion has disappeared ; my ideas are now clear and precise ; I can choose and render them at will ; when I recollect myself, they burst forth and spread themselves out before me, and I have only to take the simplest or most brilliant, as the occasion demands."

Having thus made known the state of his soul, he speaks at some length of the plans he had conceived for putting to profit these happy dispositions. The thought of the future comes before him of its own accord, and ere long he is beyond the gates of the College.

"At times my imagination carries me off. I say to myself, I will go and see Paris and its monuments; travel through Switzerland and Italy, in order to become acquainted with those beautiful countries, before renouncing the world for ever, and binding myself to the service of others. But no! that would be so much money wasted, which might have made some one happy. No! I will deny myself these pleasures, and will not see these fine things; I will strive, rather, to make my crown for heaven. Ah! God will be there, if I can only reach Him, and He, out of His infinite bounty, will turn the little privations which I shall have imposed upon myself into joys without number. I desire to be a hidden and unknown drop of water in that public fountain which pours out on all sides its health-giving streams. Why delay longer?"

His Sunday walks furnished him an ample matter for descriptions, and simple accounts which are full of most choice passages; some examples of them cannot fail to be read with pleasure.

He was very fond of flowers, and oftentimes he would bring some to adorn his room at the Lycée. One winter's day, he relates how he went with his friend to visit the conservatories of a nurseryman at Nancy. After having described the rich treasures they contained: "We chose," he adds, "two simple primroses, gentle and modest little flowers, that charm one by their sweet perfume. How happy I was that evening as I carried home my precious flower! On our way back we met a poor old man shivering with the cold, and we gave him all that remained in our purses. We were so happy, and it was but just to share our happiness with others. We were well repaid for it. The poor man was so touched that the tears came to his eyes. As he held our flowers whilst we sought for our purses, he admired and caressed them, so that afterwards they appeared to us all the more beautiful. At present, I have my primrose in my room. What a happiness each evening to see it again, to gaze at it, water it and watch over its development, to muse over this charming little creature which seems to smile at me and love me!"

"N. . ." he says, another day, "has given me a charming flower called 'Androssa,' which seems to have quite a virginal innocence and purity. Its snowy calyx opens itself out gladly and modestly to the day, and at night closes again for sleep. Each evening I see it thus go to rest. Oh! how lovely, then, are flowers!

"My room begins to be quite ornamented with them. I have now a vanilla, an androssa, a fern, and a charming tea rose. Every morning I water them, I attend them and inhale their perfumes; they are my little creatures, innocent and pure, to whom I bid good-day before returning to our dismal studies, in the midst of so many poor comrades who, I fear, alas! have no longer their purity and innocence."

"I do not know if everything is growing green around you," he writes April 27th, 1864, "but I cannot tell you how beautiful nature is here, or describe the joys with which it inundates me. No doubt you expect a long letter. Oh! if you only knew what delightful moments one passes in our playground, under the chesnut trees in blossom, amidst the silence of the evening, contemplating the soft moonlight which fills the heart with peace and soothing calm! On awakening in the morning I am moved with love and gratitude to bless our Heavenly Father, the Lord of this beautiful nature, when, opening my eyes, I behold the pure heaven above, and the sun rising majestically through the golden mist! .. O God! how beautiful is life when spent in your love! O my dear father, the happier I am, the more I love you, and feel myself borne to love every one. Ah! life thus passed would be a continual delight, and from it we would take our flight towards the land of endless happiness!"

One of his joys in his Sunday excursions was to go and hear High Mass in the villages round Nancy. There his favorite ideas found their way back to his heart.

"At seven o'clock," he writes, "we set off for Rosiére. The weather was dull, but calm. Our hearts were light with joy as we felt the fresh morning air blowing against our faces, and bringing to us the sweet odors of the country, which spread out beneath our eyes its meadows waving like the sea, and its fields with the corn already high. Then came the joy of assisting at Mass, and during the sermon I abandoned myself to fair and happy visions of the future. Oh! is it possible that I should one day have the care and direction of a little flock, in a village whose every roof would be dear to me, whose every inhabitant my son : that I should live wholly devoted to them, directing them and making them better and happier in this world and the next! Ah! there are moments when I, who am so weak and timid, feel as if I should be able to pour forth into the hearts of these men in words burning with love, tenderness, and entreaty all that I feel pent up in my own. It seems to me I would often forget my timidity and my embarrassment, in order to give myself up wholly to them.

"Does there not exist an eloquence, that of the heart, able to touch and soften even the most ignorant and the most hardened, and to win them over to follow the path which is pointed out to them? O my God! could all this come true! During these years of expectation, fill my heart with sentiments of love, with wise counsels, with those words which, coming straight from the heart, it is impossible to resist."

"Is all this," he says on another occasion, after having spoken at some length of his plans, and explained how he hoped to be able to gain souls, "is all this a dream, a simple vision of a guardian of souls, and can it not be realized? It seems to me that, though it be hard to accomplish these things, the end can always be gained by means of gentleness, love and perseverance. And with what love ought we not to surround these dear souls intrusted to our care, whose hopes and dangers are before our eyes, whilst it depends upon us to insure their arrival at the sovereign good, or to allow them to fall into everlasting misery."

As on the one side, the sentiment of nature's beauties and the love of God enlarged the heart of the pious youth, so on the other, he found no charm in the pleasures to which those of his own age give themselves up so readily.

There was a holiday at the Lycée on Shrove Tuesday of that year, 1864. A vaudeville was composed and acted by the students : songs, dances, and other noisy pastimes had each their turn; but all this had few attractions for the young Paul. He relates himself how he was then only too glad to pass that time at the bed-side of a sick person in the exercise of charity. "I had," he writes on Ash Wednesday, "another kind of happiness, which lasted the whole of yesterday. This poor Mr. N. is attacked with rheumatism in the joints, which causes him most cruel sufferings. He is confined to bed, and I have had the pleasure of being his companion, and watching by his side. Not having gone out yesterday I passed the whole day with him, talking and reading to him, in order to cheer him, and try to divert his mind from his sufferings. Thus Shrove Tuesday has been a happy day for me, and the uproars, that from time to time made themselves heard from without, rendered me all the more sensible to my happiness."

"This morning another joy. It is Ash-Wednesday, and happily it was our turn to assist at the ceremony. I took part in it then, and with tears in my eyes I have begun Lent, that beautiful season when we repent, and strive to purify ourselves in the eyes of God, when we love to ponder over those weighty words : 'Remember man that thou art dust, and unto dust thou shalt return.' Ah! Where is now the time when we were at Angiers, and used to take part in the striking ceremonies of Lent; when we listened to the chant of the penitential psalms, those cries of a repentant heart, so touching, and so full of consolation ; when we followed the retreat, when amid the glare of lights which surrounded the altar we sang God's praises and received Benediction; when, in fine, we assisted at the ceremonies of Tenebræ, full of such deep emotions. I was then, alas! almost insensible to all that : now, the very recollection of those things is sufficient to send me into raptures. Here we have none of these joys,—no hymns, no psalms, no retreat, no Benediction, with the lights tinging the clouds of incense with gold, no Tenebræ. It is always the great noisy heartless barracks, pursuing ever its old routine at the sound of the drum! But no matter, it is the last year."

The last days of this year, in which he had experienced so many different impressions, soon arrived, and then came the moment when the young student must come to a decision.

He had not as yet reached the physical development ordinary at his age, and though he would soon attain his nineteenth year, he still wore the look of a child. Besides, there was reason to fear that his ardent nature was deceiving him with regard to the difficulties of the life towards which he was aspiring. His family demanded therefore a time for trial. He yielded respectfully to so reasonable a wish ; and it was settled that he should employ the interval at a country-seat in Brittany, in forwarding the education of the young children of the Marquis Du Dresnay, to whom Paul Seigneret had been recommended by kind friends. The prospect of this new life, so unforeseen and yet so near at hand, gave rise to all sorts of "confused and contrary thoughts and feelings which crowded tumultuously into his mind." He knows that Christian faith and piety are in honor at the hearth where a place has been offered him, and this affords him great joy. He promises that he will be like an angel by the side of the two children, who are soon to be intrusted to his care, and will have a most sincere and tender affection for them. He will see Brittany, " that wild, poetical land of Brittany, so rich in remembrances of the past, from its Druid monuments down to the traces of the late bloody revolution ;" and his imagination tells him that this will be the place to read during the winter, whilst the storm is raging, " the gloomy poems of Ossian." He will be quite alone, far from his dear family, which he loves so tenderly. Nevertheless, he will be nearer Anjou,—Anjou which calls back such sweet and lively reminiscences.

"And then," he adds, "this will be for a year or two at the least. After that my life will be free ; I shall be at liberty to give myself up to Him who, in days often clouded with sorrow, sent me at times such soothing joys, and who has always been my hope, my life and my happiness."

At length, the time came to leave the Lycée forever. The last letter that Paul Seigneret wrote from Nancy, on the 29th July, 1864, contains his touching farewell to that house in which he had gone through his first trial in life,—a trial which was hard, it is true, but rich in sure and precious fruits.

"Truly my life here was not a joyful one. . . . Nevertheless, the sorrows that I have experienced in this Lycée, where I have lived for three years, the solitary joys I have so deeply felt, have formed so many ties, unknown till now, which bind me to it ; and to break them suddenly causes me a real pang. . . . Farewell! abode where I have lived in sorrow and in the pleasures of solitude ! Farewell, dear companions, who in the relations I have had with you have always shown me a kindness and condescension which have at times so much touched me ! We shall now soon be launched on the sea of life, to cut our way through it at the mercy of every contrary wind that blows. Which of us will gain the port ? Great and sad question, that comes often to my mind, and which urges me on to pray for the happiness of all. I feel that I love them, for we cannot help loving those with whom we have for some time lived and breathed ; and now on the point of leaving them forever, I would like to fold them in my arms, to bear them off with me, that being stronger united we might, all together, follow the paths of virtue and happiness. "Farewell to you all, my favorite spots ! Farewell to the bench beneath the trees, on which I sat listening in the darkness and still of the evening, to the wind sighing and the leaf rustling! Farewell to the corner where, in view of the mighty expanse of heaven, I gazed at the magnificent spectacle of a beautiful night! Farewell to that stall in the chapel, where I shed so many tears of regret and love! Farewell to my window where I loved so much to sit and muse, as I watched the clouds flying past: farewell to my room, where I passed such pleasant evenings in reading or in making verses! I leave all that to embark on the ocean of life!"

He was in fact about to begin another stage of his short pilgrimage here below, and as he advances, we shall see his noble soul increase in virtue, and gradually rise towards heaven where God was soon to call him.

CHAPTER II.

THE CHATEAU DU DRÉNEUC.

TOWARDS the end of September, 1864, Paul Seigneret arrived at the chateau du Dréneuc, situated at a distance of two leagues from Redon, in the parish of Fégréac, the name of which recalled to his mind the fearful scenes of the Reign of Terror.

The two years which the young student passed under this hospitable roof must be numbered amongst the most fervent of his life. There, in the midst of his solitude, God was everything to him, and heaped upon him His sweetest consolations. At this period of his life the ardor of his desires grew more intense, while his love of God increased to such a degree as to become, according to his own startling expression, " a love ready to burst all bonds."

He set himself, at once, to the task intrusted to him, full of that zeal with which he ever worked when duty held forth its claims ; and knowing how to look at things from their highest point of view, the education of the children placed under his care offered to him the prelude of his after life.

He had before long, in spite of his almost childlike looks, gained the esteem and respect of all the inmates of the chateau. He was a thorough master in the art of mingling in his relations with all, a perfect becomingness, delicacy and discretion. His mildness of character was ever the same, and yet did not exclude that firmness necessary for the right guidance of the children under his tutorship. Being naturally good to excess, he was at any one's service, or rather at the mercy of all, and he went so far as even to curtail his hours of rest, already sufficiently diminished, in order to find time to instruct the servants of the chateau. The poor, too, soon knew his charity.

"My money," he says a short time after his arrival, "begins to slip through my fingers, and already I have given away a considerable sum. It affords such pleasure to the poor people whom I see in misery, hunger and nakedness to receive a trifle, and it is so pleasant for me to bestow it.

"The day before yesterday, I met a farmer's little boy, fourteen years of age, who was off to the fields, skipping and singing down the winding lanes. I drew him near to me, and made him chat with me. Alas! he had lost his father, and said he was very unhappy; he leads a hard life, and regrets above all that beautiful time which he was able to pass at school, thanks to the munificence of the marquis, when for five years he had naught to do but to fulfil the simple tasks of a scholar, and spend the rest of the day free from books and every care, in roaming over the fields with his comrades. Touched to the heart with the confidence he showed me, and moved by his sad tale, I sent him off happy and contented with some money in his hand. Alas! from the noble lady in her chateau, even to this poor orphan, who laughed and sang on the wayside, every one has to bear his sorrows and troubles. Why should I refuse my share? Thus, I seldom returned from any little expeditions without some new happiness, or without having exchanged a few words with these good folks, who in their turn show themselves so well disposed towards me. There are so many acquaintances that I make in the neighborhood of the chateau."

Every one, too, loved Master Paul, respected his happy qualities and admired his talents. The Marchioness du Dresnay, who was able to enter into closer relations with him, and could thus better appreciate his worth, looked upon the presence " of this angel" in her house as a blessing from heaven, and she had always, besides the tenderness of a mother, a true veneration for one whom she delighted in calling "our little Saint Aloysius Gonzaya."*

Nevertheless, the best side of this chosen soul lay hid, beneath the veil of humility, from the scrutiny of men. But God, who penetrates into the inmost recesses of the heart, saw the virtue of the youth, like the seed fallen upon good ground, take root and increase in silence, fertilized by good works, and strengthened by daily trials.

* In this portion of our work we make use of the interesting notes furnished by the Marchioness of Dresnay to M. L'Abbe Seigneret, Paul's uncle, concerning the stay of the young tutor at Dréneuc. They give us to understand what a favorable impression he left behind him in that house.

And, indeed, in spite of the affection with which he saw himself surrounded, and to which he was very sensible, it was not long before he felt the burden of the cross.

He already found it a considerable trial to live away from his family. " My heart asks you back," he wrote in his first letter from Dréneuc, " and in the morning I awake saying to myself, that not a single one of those dear to me is near, to whom I might address my first words of welcome and affection."

But his new kind of life was, above all, highly opposed to his turn of mind, and the demands of his heart. His studies which were so dear to him abandoned, his interior solitude in which he delighted, invaded and disturbed, his days altogether taken up with duties whose very continuity made them tedious, all this at times caused him bitter sadness. But when he learnt for certain that his trial was to last two years, he could not help thus expressing his sorrow :—

" I can scarcely bear to think of throwing two whole years to the winds, of depriving my mind so long of its nourishment, and of passing uselessly this precious part of my youth, when I would have wished to dedicate its best days to God."

But grace taught him to bear with love, as coming from the hand of God, that against which nature revolted. We see also, at this moment of his life, that love of the cross, which was lately so remarkable in the student of the Lycée, still increasing within him, and already we perceive that craving after sacrifice which later on will prompt him to cry out at the sight of martyrdom in these striking terms, worthy of a Saint Francis of Sales:

"A hard and heavy cross has been sent me. and God has laid it upon my shoulders, because it is necessary that I should crucify my desires, my inclinations and my will. Let us thank Him who imposes it! And, my God, what does it signify of what wood this cross be made? Is it not rather desirable that the wood be as heavy and hard as possible, and all covered with thorns, so that every part of my being might have its pang? Oh! would I were judged worthy to bear a still heavier one! O, good cross! I embrace thee with love, because armed with thee, I shall be able, pure and worthy, to arrive at the term of all my desires. *O mi bone Jesu, Jesu dulcissime!* What ought not we to suffer when you have suffered so much for us! It is this thought that makes me desire to accept all the bitterness of the cross you send me."

And these were not merely vain words, the offspring of an over-heated imagination, or an excited sensibility, but were realized in those every-day actions which are the best proof of genuine virtue, and, for the most part, have God alone for witness. The young tutor led without any affectation a very sanctified life, and Madame du Dresnay, who knew his fervor, saw with admiration the effects which it produced. "He is like one of those hidden and sweet smelling violets," she writes to M. l'Abbé Seigneret, "that one meets on his path but rarely." "This gentle youth will be one day the

glory of your family, as he is already its blessing."
" His is truly a nature fashioned for heaven."

One day, however, she thought it her duty to make known the excessive austerity of the " little anchorite." He delighted in reading the lives of the saints ; he had just read the life of the Curé of Ars, and spurred on by such an heroic example he imposed upon himself privations severe enough to injure his health. Aware that his uncle had been informed of this, he wrote to him in the following amiable and jesting tone.

" I see from here a dark storm of admonitions, and mild reproaches gathering at Angiers, and ready to break over me. My dear uncle, I beg of you to leave alone such trifles, and may God forgive me for serving Him so unworthily and so wretchedly ! Really it is showing too much solicitude for Mister Gaster ; it is a vile beast that must be despised and broken in. When we have gained the mastery, we shall be able then to soar the higher and love the more purely. Besides, I am doing nothing worthy either of attention or blame. So think no more about it."

He continued his daily mortifications as much as he was able without attracting attention ; he practised the greatest sobriety at meals, and drank as a rule only water, and knew how to deprive himself cleverly of the most dainty morsels. Doubtless very many of these little sacrifices have remained the secret of God.

Although very sensible to the cold, and notwithstanding the rigor of winter, which, according to his own expression, " froze his soul as well as his body," he scarcely ever had a fire, in order, as he used to say, "to become the more hardy for after years, and to prepare my body as well as my mind for the life to which I am called, and in which I shall have to undergo so much labor and fatigue."

In a letter, bearing the date of Oct. 20th, 1865, where he speaks of this subject, we meet with these generous words: "For the last fortnight a terrible wind from the sea brings up storm after storm, and torrents of rain. Farewell then to fine weather! An enemy now rises before me, whom I am determined to grapple with and overcome; winter's hard, rough hand makes me not only suffer, but at times succeeds in plunging me into a state of melancholy that renders me dull and torpid. I thank God for having made me so sensible to the cold, and this year I wish to strive against it not merely with resignation, but with pleasure and love. I am beginning full of joyful ardor; may the end find me the same, and may I continue so all my life long!"

His love of suffering urged him on to practices still more extraordinary. The servant who arranged his room found one morning on his bed something which was altogether new to him. He did not take the liberty to touch it, but ran to tell Madame du Dresnay, who soon recognized in it the young penitent's hair shirt. She bid the servant say nothing about the matter, and, that the young man might have no reason to suspect any thing, she gave orders that his room should not be touched before his return. The youth's modesty was spared, thanks to this delicate attention, and he never knew that the secret of his penance had been discovered.

It was this same hair shirt which drew from him one of the finest letters he has written. In it we can best see all that unbounded confidence which induced him to disclose to his father that which he hid from every one else besides. The pious youth, after using all kinds of delicate precautions, asks for the hair shirt that he had inadvertently left at Epinal, and which he could not at that time easily replace.

"My very dear father," he writes on 5th November, 1865, "after having been for a long time tormented with regret, and being now encouraged by the tender affection that you show me in your last letter, I have resolved to ask of you a favor which I have often been upon the point of requesting. But allow me first of all to tell you a story I read when a child, and which at that time made a great impression upon me.

"There was once a prince who, in the first years of his life, was full of faults and malice, and committed all sorts of wickedness that it was possible for a child to commit: in one word, he was a little demon. Nevertheless, he began to reflect, and with reflection came a strong desire to correct himself, and an earnest wish to atone for all the pain he had caused his parents, by affording them now as much consolation as he had till then given them sorrow. In these happy dispositions he went to ask the advice of his fairy governess. She gave him a ring which pricked his finger every time he was about to do a wicked action, or a bad thought crossed his mind, and these continual warnings, were of such effect that the prince, formerly so wicked, came at length to be called by all the amiable prince.

"Though I am not a prince, I have yet been very wicked, and what am I even now? How often when a child have I longed for this enchanted ring to help me to correct myself! Being now a young man, a bright thought has struck me ; no doubt it was suggested to me by my good angel, and it fully realizes the story of the prince with the enchanted ring.

"I have hesitated for a long time, my dear father, about laying open to you this secret of my heart ; but your last letter has cleared away every obstacle. . . Besides, when once I have confided this secret to your fatherly heart, can I fear that you will ever make it known, when I now ask you to promise never to speak of it to any one?

"There are people in the world who, at the bare mention of what I am going to say, would cry out as if at a thing that had long ago served its time, and was fit only for penitents of the middle ages, or they would be struck all at once with admiration. And yet it is so simple. You, my dear father, who have an impartial and clear judgment, you will understand me, and I am sure I can speak of it to you.

"Last year, at my earnest entreaty, my confessor procured for me a little instrument which scarcely ever sees the light now, except in monasteries,—a hair shirt. It was my companion and

. my monitor when by any wicked action, any word, or thought, I offended the Master of my heart. It was one of my best friends, and perhaps my only one. Alas! I put it off during the vacation on account of the heat. I had concealed it carefully, but the many things that engross one's thoughts at departure drove it completely out of my head. But as we were flying off to Paris in a beautiful moonlight night, the thought of my unfortunate friend crossed my mind, and brought along with it much uneasiness and regret. What was I to do? Soon, however, I began to think of you; I saw you quietly asleep in your corner, and the happiness I felt at having been with you these last few days soon made me forget my regrets. They came back again, nevertheless, with all their former force. If you only knew how much I feel the want of my hair shirt! It was such a happiness to have this little companion continually warning me that it was necessary to keep the thought of God in my heart. It recalled to me at every moment that I had given myself up entirely to Him, that, miserable as I am, I desired to be for ever at His service; it strengthened me against all the encroachments of the world, by reminding me that I belonged to the most gentle of Masters. At class it checked the slightest impatience; in my conversation it reproached me with the least deviation from the rules of modesty or chastity:—in one word, my dear father, every day I lament its absence. The things that you have to send me made me think of asking it from you. I have hesitated a long time through fear of making the request, and it is only after many struggles that I confide all to you.

"Oh! I am sure that you at any rate will understand that there is nothing unpleasant in keeping this little instrument near me, and that it is rather a happiness, though others may christen it folly. Yes, you know that, far from doing me any harm, it will make me the happiest of mortals, since it will shut me up in that interior life, where alone we can find true happiness. Yes, you will understand, too, that it is not a foolish presumption which urges me on to ape the saints. If I make use of it, it is because I am a miserable wretch, and subject to a thousand faults and failings which I strive to overcome as best I can.

"Oh! how happy you will make me then, if you can send me this precious monitor, whose absence I so much bemoan.

"And now, my dear father, let me tell you once more what a happiness I feel in having a father like you, to whom I can speak openly, and with an entire confidence about the most secret things. It is a fresh favor which I must mark down in the book of gratitude, that I keep at the bottom of my heart. . . ."

But bodily mortifications were accounted little by the fervent and saintly young man. His soul lived continually in too elevated a sphere to trouble itself much about its prison of flesh. And it was for this reason that he offered up to God, as a better and more worthy sacrifice, the privation of pleasures to which his heart was much more closely attached. His every-day life and the time of probation that had to elapse before he was able to follow his desires furnished him an ever ready occasion for such mortification.

But the demands of duty and his practices of penance in no way cooled the fervor of his soul.

It is a mistake of the world to imagine that an application to details in the acquirement of virtue, and particularly in the practice of Christian mortification, narrows our views, deadens our feelings, and to use the expression, cruelly imprisons the soul in a cell where it is stifled. The life of Paul Seigneret shows clearly the injustice of this prejudice. If we are mortified, as he so well observes, " we only soar the higher, and love more purely."

And every day he proved the truth of this by his own example. His love for God visibly increased and betrayed itself by those acts which grace has invariably inspired the saints to perform; but the tenderness and warmth of his earthly affections were in no way changed; his soul remained wide open to all that was beautiful, all that was worthy of love; nothing could be less exclusive than his enthusiasm.

His correspondence, during these two years, is a remarkable proof of this. One cannot see and not be struck with that richness of sentiment, those touching effusions of the heart, that inexhaustible flow of poetry, which he spreads over everything which he touches.

The letters in which he pours forth the love that he felt for his family are above all remarkable for their expression of tenderness. Some of them yet bear the marks of the tears that would sometimes drop from his eyes, while he wrote the lines in which filial affection and the love of God were so beautifully blended.

On the last day of the year 1865, he sends his New Year greetings to his parents in the following terms :—

"With a heart more than ever overflowing with affection, I offer you my good wishes for the New Year. I present them to you, my dear father, and to you my dearest mother ; they are the riches of my heart, and, if efficacious, they would bring you endless blessings. There is no sacrifice that I would not make with pleasure for your happiness ; but, since there is nothing that I can do for you, my desires burst forth with greater force, and turn into prayers so fervent that I hope they will not fail to reach and touch Him who dispenses at pleasure happiness and sorrow."

One day that he had received a little souvenir of maternal affection, he thus expresses his gratitude :—" First of all, my dearest mother, I thank you for the agreeable surprise you prepared for me. In putting. my things in order, I found among them a little book with gilt edges, *Le Bonheur a la Sainte Table.* I opened it and read the words which your dear hand had written there. I can only thank you by telling you that each day I look at these lines with new pleasure, I kiss the page which seems still to bear the impression of your hand. Ah ! God's blessing cannot be wanting, when you demand it for me. May He shower down upon you, my dear mother, health and happiness in return for all your kindness to me."

Another day, it is the portrait of his father that calls forth from him these words of tender affection :—" As I looked upon your likeness, tears of joy filled my eyes. I fancied I saw your dear self again, and a whole crowd of reminiscences, that to me appeared realities, carried me back to Epinal and you, whom I seemed to have quitted ages ago. Gazing upon your calm and resolute face, all the years of my existence passed again rapidly before me,—sweet scenes of home. Peaceful pleasures, all your gentle exhortations, your reprimands at Angiers, the little happiness I have brought you since, all came crowding into my mind, now filling me with joy and now with sorrow. O my dear father ! never upon earth shall I be able to love you enough, or repay all the affection and care you have lavished upon me. All the pleasures of childhood, the sweet happiness of home,—we shall find all this again when united in the bosom of our Heavenly Father, with this difference, however, that whilst these things here below are fleeting, rife with troubles, and, as it were, only a few tiny drops of happiness, in heaven they will be without end, without a pang, and flowing in torrents inexhaustible as the plenitude of God Himself.

" You seem to remark with sorrow the furrows of age upon your face. But then, dear father, how is it that each time I go back to see you, I secretly rejoice to find you always with a fresher and healthier look ? It is the portrait that has

cast a shadow over you, as it does over every one.
And if you did notice the traces of age upon
your face, even then, dear father, what sadness
can you feel? Ought you not rather to see old
age drawing near, with the peaceful calm of a
tired laborer, who, at the close of the day, rests
awhile to cast a glance at the lengthened shadows,
as they herald the approaching hour of repose?
When I look back at your life, I find it so beautiful! The work you have been called to do, the
steadiness with which you have done it, and above
all the manner in which Divine Providence leading you, as it were, by the hand, has placed you
in posts of greater and greater importance, till at
last it has put you in that which you now fill,
where honor and esteem surround you. In the
midst of all your labors and troubles, your whole
desire and only occupation has always been the
good of those over whom you have been placed,
and especially that of your children. Now, therefore, my dear father, after the long and happy
days of old age that I wish you, I can only repeat
with gladness that nothing more is wanting to
you, than to receive the magnificent reward that
God has in store for His servants.

"One of my first thoughts upon receiving
your letter was, that without doubt you were not
the only one to have your portrait taken, and that
that of another one equally dear will follow.
When shall I have that of my dear mother?"

A few days before the first Communion of his
sister, he thus speaks of the part he would take
in the joy of his family, and the happy remembrances it would call up before him :—

"What sweet moments are there awaiting your paternal heart! You will soon see your youngest child receive her God with all her innocence and simple love. May He take her for ever to Himself. Though all will take place far from me, I shall be present there in spirit ; I shall pass the whole of that happy day with you, and in the evening I will be one of the happy circle around your table.

"Among the most precious souvenirs of affection that I hold from you, are the words you addressed to me on the morning of my first Communion. On that occasion you called me from the study-room, and borrowing from the circumstances a more serious tone than usual, you spoke to me of things so tender, so touching, that the memory of them remains engraved for ever in my heart. Besides these sweet reminiscences, how many more are there which your affection has scattered here and there over my existence."

In fine, a last example will help to show to what a degree these home affections existed in the heart of the pious youth, and how they were ever elevated and sanctified by the truly Christian sentiments that dominated them. He offers to his father thoughts founded on faith, in order to console him when disappointed in certain hopes which had vanished at the very moment they ought to have been realized.

"The day is then past," he writes, "without bringing the least change, the day which, notwithstanding all our submission to the designs of Divine Providence, I saw approach amid the charms of hope! Allow me to bid a passing adieu to this illusion, which has now disappeared, adieu very short indeed, for disappointment soon gives place to contentment and joy. Ah, my dear father! you are too good, and too well loved by God, it seems, to be surrounded by the unearned and pangless joys of this life. Work and anxiety are your portion, and such struggles as we have seen you go through with a calm and courage at once so touching and worthy of admiration. Let me tell you, then, my dear father, I am happy with a happiness which gladdens my heart and buoys it up with hope ; I am happy at seeing your lot cast amid such struggles, because one cannot fail to recognize in you one of God's blest and chosen ones, and hope that one day you will give back your life into His hands, only to receive it again with glory, after having gone through so many trials, and gained so much merit. May you then, dear father, never feel the least regret for the miserable goods of this world, which leave us so soon, without even, for the most part, having given us the scanty happiness we expected from them. . . ."

Is it astonishing that the father of this noble youth, though accustomed to like expressions of tenderness, was surprised at the extraordinary outbursts of his affectionate heart. Accordingly he thus comments upon them in the following letter :

" I find in Paul's letters a warmth habitual, it is true, with him, yet greater than usual. There is an innocence throughout, adorned with thoughts and sentiments, which seem to mark him for the cloister. With his manner of living and feeling, he would do well, I think, to shut himself up in a monastery—everything would clash with him in the world, which gives a rude shock to all with whom it comes in contact."

The foregoing words show us that the tenderness of Paul Seigneret had undergone a serious modification, and it was, in fact, these new aspirations which occupied his mind, and animated him during the two years he passed at Dréneuc.

The world of which he now had a nearer view, held out no greater enticements to him, and one can remark that he feels a secret happiness in affirming on every occasion, now in jest, now in a more serious tone, yet always with a certain force, that he is not made for its life of material preoccupations and necessary distractions.

It happened from time to time that the solitude of the Chateau was animated by the presence of numerous and distinguished guests, and the young tutor had thus occasion to take part in those reunions which constitute the charm of life in the world, amongst people of good society. Without despising this advantage, and admiring, more than any one, a great name when it was borne well, he strongly felt that he was called to live in a society which was better still.

"For some time lately," he wrote one day in a tone full of gaiety, "we have had visitors at the Chateau, and I have performed a most awkward part, which I am going to describe, in order that you may laugh a little at my expense. As we were passing into the drawing-room after dinner, Madame de . . . . was without a partner, and M. du Dresnay invited me, though altogether unprepared for such an invitation, to give her my arm. It was to no purpose that I stammered out some excuse about my small size; I was unfortunately as tall as the lady, and I saw it was necessary to yield. Your worthy son must have been taken that evening for a greenhorn. Blushing to the ears, I did not know how to perform my part and I was trembling with fear lest, in my embarrassment, I should tread upon the lady's toes, or strike against her shoulder. We reached the drawing-room at last and my torture was over, but I did not dare to whisper a word till I had escaped from them all. That is all my success in the world! But it happened because I was taken altogether unawares, having never imagined that I should have to offer my arm to a lady, unless, perhaps, to my dear little sister. But happily my awkwardness has passed unnoticed.

"That very evening, I was questioned about my prospects for the future, and, whilst I answered the questions with my lips, my heart sang within me songs of gratitude and love. I am accustomed to keep these delightful thoughts locked up in the secret of my heart, and it is for this reason that, when others speak to me of these things I am struck with astonishment and filled with thankfulness to God, who has given me so grand a vocation, and marked me out for so happy a state."

And truly, God drew this choice heart towards

Himself with an irresistible attraction. The first aspirations of the young Paul to the ecclesiastical state had by degrees taken a form more definite, and more in harmony with the desires of sacrifice, which were the moving principles of his life. It was no longer now the seminary, but the cloister, which appeared to him "that pure and shining height," whither he would go to fix his dwelling nearer heaven.

A letter written in February, 1865, discovers to us the first appearance of these new desires, and the motives which suggested them.

"For a long time," he says," my small size, and odd appearance made me think, that perhaps it would be a mistake to consecrate myself to the active ministry, where the good I could do would be spoiled by the ridicule of my person. And yet, God is pleased to allow me to consecrate myself entirely and for ever to His service. What then can I do, but cut myself off from the world, which inspires me with nothing but disgust, and shut myself up in one of those happy retreats where our whole life is passed in pleasing God by mortification and prayers."

His generous soul was roused by the noble aim that he had in view, and his desires suddenly took a character of extraordinary intensity. He repeated and committed with exultation of heart that verse of the Psalm : "*Quem ad modum desiderat cervus ad fontes aquarum, ità desiderat anima mea ad te, Deus.*" "As the heart panteth after the fountains of water, so my soul panteth after Thee, O God" (Ps. xli. 1.). He made a vow to go on a pilgrimage to the Champ des Martyrs, near Angiers,* in order that he might receive light to know his vocation and grace to follow it.

A few days of vacation, which he passed at Angiers at this time, gave him an opportunity of fulfilling his vow. Every morning at break of day, he set out with a heart burning with fervor and love from the College of Mongazon, and accomplished the distance which separates that establishment from the Champ des Martyrs. He describes, with all that poetry which is natural to him, these morning walks, when every step brought back some pleasant reminiscence of childhood. "Ah! recall to mind that charming view of the city of Angiers, as it is seen from the heights of the Champ des Martyrs, at the moment when the rising sun wraps in golden mist the cathedral spires which raise themselves up so gracefully out of the compact mass of the town. The bells of all the churches ring for the morning Masses, and send their pious and soothing peals with every gust of wind. When we enter the town, we meet again that pleasant animation, and those strange cries which are peculiar to our own dear Angiers. There would be nothing more wanting, if you were only here, my very dear parents.

---

* The Champ des Martyrs, or " Field of Martyrs," which is a mile and a quarter distant from Angiers, is now a much frequented pilgrimage. There, under the Reign of Terror, took place awful scenes of death by which the representatives of the people thought to drown in blood the " fanaticism " of la Vendee. A chapel has since been raised on the spot where the executions took place, and in it are the countless ex votos which bear witness to the graces that have there been received.

" It seems to me that I see you again walking along the road to the Champ des Martyrs, which we have trodden so often. Nothing is changed, either in the road or the chapel, whose silence is so great a help to recollection and prayer. The chairs are still there and the stone on which my mother used to kneel, and there I seem yet to see her as formerly. My fervor is increased by the thought, and tears of joy roll down my cheeks, and I console myself by saying that, if at that time I was a wicked son, I am at least a little better now, and that my only wish is to become altogether good."

At the end of this novena, he felt his attraction for the monastic life grow stronger, and the advice which he received confirmed him in the belief that he would honor God more and serve his neighbor better under the shadow of the cloister, than in the ministry upon which his miserable appearance seemed to forbid him to enter. La Trappe, with its austerities and sacrifices, was the place on which his generous heart first fixed its desires. He was, however, convinced by others that the weakness of his constitution did not allow him to think of it. The Abbey of Solesmes was next suggested to him, where the beautiful offices of the choir, the serious studies of a Benedictine, and the charms of religious fraternity, seemed best to answer the demands and aspirations of his soul. A short visit to the Abbey, where he spent a day, made him fall in love with this beautiful retreat, and he came back rejoicing at the thought, that there too he could satisfy the yearnings of his heart, though it were in a manner different from that of which he had first dreamed. From that moment Solesmes appears to be, as he himself says in his own beautiful language : "the harbor in which my bark will go to cast anchor after its short voyage in the world, the field in which my soul will take root and open out its flowers to God." "My heart leaps with joy," he says on another occasion, "at the thought that my future would be henceforward fixed in God, and I should like to know all the Psalms, in which the psalmist cries out, " *Exaltate, jubilate,*" in order the better to express my happiness."

He felt, however, that so prompt a decision would raise doubts in the mind of others as to its maturity, and that they would not, without some appearance of reason, "find his flame for Solesmes very quickly lighted." His suspicions were realized, and it was not without pain that his family learned his sudden change of thought. His father was too good a Christian to oppose a real vocation, but he wished to be assured that something more than an overwrought imagination or a passing enthusiasm was moving the heart of his son. It was for this reason that he determined to lengthen the trial, and the young Paul was obliged to content himself with seeing only at a distance that which was for him the land of promise.

He had, besides, too great a respect for the decisions of his parents, and too much love for them, not to yield with simplicity in this matter to what they required of him. "I see then," he wrote to them, "that I have occasioned the loving resistance, or, to speak more correctly, the serious and well-grounded doubt about my vocation, which I foresaw and feared. How shall I be able to clear· it away? . . . I can only put all in the hands of God, who, after having called me, will, if such is His pleasure, remove all difficulties, and above all, will give me that perfect confidence with regard to my vocation, which I will beg every day from His bounty. . . . I accept your decision with sorrow, and yet at the same time with a certain bitter satisfaction, as seeing that thus a longer time is given me to prepare myself for that of which I am so unworthy. I hope that the desires of my heart will reach and touch the heart of God, and that the tears which I shed in secret may be turned into pearls that will enrich my poor stock of merit. Let the matter then rest there : it was not the will of God ! He was at liberty to call his unworthy servant either sooner or later. I thank you with a deep and lively emotion for your kindness in following after me in this new path in which I walk, and at the same time, for the prudence with which you have acted. You have put a restraint on my desires which no doubt were too presumptuous. Is this not another new reason for me to be grateful to you ?"

From this moment, the looking forward to the day on which he should consecrate himself to God occupied his thoughts and upheld his courage. One sees this idea always uppermost in his mind ; everything recalls it to him, and he loves to repeat it under the thousand forms which his rich imagination presented to him. On the occasion of his twentieth birthday, in December, 1865, he writes as follows to his uncle :

"Do not forget to ask God to bless this new year, which He adds to the rest that have already passed over my head, which, after I have gone through the bitter sorrows of parting, I shall see die out serene and happy in the holy house where I have fixed my abode. Oh! how happy is your poor nephew, whose lot it is to turn aside from the high road, to leave its dust and bustle, and to follow the little pathway, silent and apart, blest by God, and loved by those who tread it! A thousand flowers of virtue and happiness spread their charms on the way. Happy, oh! too happy, indeed, those whom God calls to follow it!

"When assisting at the magnificent offices of the Church, as during the hours of tranquil adoration in the hallowed silence of my cell, or amid the tasks of my daily life, how my thoughts will love to revert to you all, and gather you together again in my prayers for your prosperity and happiness. Owing to my size and weak voice, which would agree but ill with the full voices of my brethren, I shall, no doubt, be often chosen to serve at the Altar, and then what fervent prayers will I pour forth to God in the Blessed Sacrament, sending them up to Him along with the wreaths of incense from my thurible, or mingling them with the thrilling harmony of the organ! And to think that all this happiness is in store for your poor nephew, and is to be mine in a few months! Away, then, idle sorrow, silly fears, you importune God's goodness which has no reserve for me."

Another day he writes from the Chateau where he was staying, in Poitou :

"A few months more in the world, and then I shall be freed from its vain distractions, which rob God always of a portion of our love. Here they have given me a splendid room—marble and mahogany, velvet and silk, on all sides. All this luxury is too much for me, and makes me sick at heart. In a few months I shall no longer sit at the table of the rich, or sleep in a couch whose very magnificence oppresses me. With what pleasure I shall greet my cell with its humble bed, my frugal meal, my old books and papers, my crucifix, at the foot of which, my whole life long I will give myself up to prayers and tears, and the chapel where I shall mingle my voice with those of my brethren, in singing the praises of my God. There, there will be no distractions : none of that well-meaning, but troublesome, attention of which I am here the object. Alone with God ! God at every moment, and in every place ! He alone occupies my heart. Oh ! when will that time come, and when will this dream be realized ?"

If at any time a cloud of sadness passed over his soul, if some temptation to discouragement assailed him, it was towards this longed-for harbor that he turned his glance, hoping thus to regain his peace of heart. "Courage," he would say, after a few days of interior trouble, "sail gently on, my bark, whilst I slumber in peace, and take my rest in God, until the shock upon the shore awakes me and puts me in joyful possesion of my long-wished for home."

He prepared himself for his high vocation by an angelic piety. Nothing is more admirable than his fervor at this moment. The feasts of the Church were to him a source of joy so great that his heart was unable to contain itself:

"What joys await me at the beginning of each week! On Sunday I take leave of the Chateau and my little pupils, in order to fly to my dear Church of Fégréac. Just as the Knights of old kept their night-watch over their arms, so I hope henceforth to pass my Christmas night in offering up in the silent and solitary church my loving prayers to God, up to the hour when the good religious Bretons come in crowds to fill the illuminated aisles, and to celebrate this touching feast of love, which for eighteen hundred years has brought joy to so many Christian generations."

"It was a happy night, indeed," he wrote a few days after this same solemnity. "Choirs of children joined their voices to those of the men in singing Christmas carols, whose sweet and simple harmony seemed to mingle with the wreaths of incense, and together with the thousand lights of the Altar, conspired to fill me with delight. So great are the crowds of these good and pious people that the church is scarce large enough to contain them as they stream on, silent and recollected to the Holy Table, where the heavenly banquet awaits them. Every heart beats with emotion. Their very looks seem to say: "Yes, we are all children of the same God, all,—peasants, nobles, rich and poor, we are all brothers, all bound by mutual charity in order the better to love our common Father, all on the same journey towards a common fatherland."

" This happiness lasted from eleven o'clock till three, and I said to myself on leaving, are these happy moments then already fled, for which I had been waiting so long? Thus it is that our hours of joy fly by ; like grains of dust that flutter in the sunbeams, they glitter a moment and are gone. But with me, in my heart, I carried off the source of all happiness and joy."

When it was impossible for him during the week to assist at Mass in the Chateau, he set out on Sunday at early morn, for the Church of Fégréac, where he received Communion and spent long hours in sweet converse with Jesus Christ. On these days his happiness and strength were both renewed. He calls them in one of his letters, "Jewels fallen from heaven, which are thrown in to break the monotony of each chain of days, and to shed a sweet lustre about them."

" O, delightful Sundays !" he exclaims one day, " ye come from time to time to bring new warmth to my heart, and fill my soul again with fervor. O, sweet reflection of the light of heaven ! O, days of love, which God offers to His poor creature, whom they always find covered with stains and misery. For I know no expression capable of conveying to you the happiness I then enjoy, and when at evening I look back upon these beautiful days, only one regret remains, that of seeing them so quickly past, as also only one hope, and one consolation lingers with me, that of seeing the time approach when they will end no more. Then my ears will be greeted only by the harmony of sacred songs, my tongue will only tell God's praises, my body only move to serve Him, and my heart only beat with His love."

"Scarcely," he continues, still speaking of his weekly Communions, " scarcely has the time of thanksgiving for the last Communion elapsed, when another arrives, and life is thus one long chain of happy moments, which are linked together by God Himself, and unite the soul to Him."

Sometimes during the fine weather, he was able to go as far as the town, where the ceremonies which he so much loved were performed with greater solemnity.

" On Sunday mornings," he says, " I set out, between four and five o'clock, alone and on foot, from Dréneuc for Redon, with a heart full of peaceful gladness, and overflowing with that joy which one feels at the dawn of a day which is to be one of unclouded happiness. How short those two leagues appear! During these happy moments I offer to God, the Father of ineffable bounties, the first and most tender expressions of my gratitude and love, and I thank Him for the happiness which seems to penetrate through every pore, and to come to me along with the sweet scent from the flowers and the wings of the birds. The source of all this happiness is the thought that I am going to meet my God. . . .Thus occupied, I reach my destination about six o'clock. . . . In the church I have reserved for me a corner near the choir, from which I am only separated by a railing, so that, without being disturbed, I can follow the pomp of the ceremonies, and contemplate at ease the tabernacle from which issues forth the rays of Divine love from the God who resides within. . . . Oh! what happiness you shower down upon me, my God! Henceforth you shall be my life, and in eternity my strength, my light, my beauty, and my glory! What mean, then, those worldlings who pretend that our happiness is only imaginary and incomplete, when really it so fills one's heart that, were a simple rose-leaf added, it would make the vessel overflow ?"

After having described most vividly the beauties of the offices of the Church, he ends thus :

"I return to Dréneuc on foot, after Vespers, by a delightful path where I behold all the beauties of summer, and can hear the loud voice of the wind, which comes sweeping along the earth, and seems to drown in its low hollow song every other sound.

"There are people who will say that this is passing the day like some simple and innocent person : and more than once have I seen a smile upon the face of strangers greet me at my return. Yet men will remain whole days before the beauties of nature and art,—before a painting,—is it not, then, proper that we should remain lost in admiration, not a day only, but years, and throughout eternity, before the beauty and goodness of God ?"

During the stay which he made along with the

Dresnay family in Poitou, at the Chateau de la Faille, which was within a short distance of Nioet, he used to go into the town on Saturday evening, in order to pass the Sunday there. As he was quite unknown, he was able without hindrance to satisfy his devotion. His apartment was near the Church of Notre Dame, the spire of which was visible from his window. It has been ascertained that on those nights he did not go to bed, and at daybreak, when they came to open the church-door, they found him on his knees upon the threshold. One of his letters, too, bearing the date of the 29th June, 1865, describes in burning language, how he then spent his time.

"I have here, too, days of real happiness. I have passed the last three or four Sundays at Nioet, leaving on Saturday evening, and returning on Sunday for dinner. But as they are unwilling that I should go any more on foot, I can no longer enjoy those happy days, since I cannot permit that they should send the carriage simply for me.

"On the afternoon, then, of Saturday the carriage drove off with me to Nioet, and set me down at the large unfrequented hotel in the Rue Notre Dame. Saturday free! Sunday free! Nothing else to do than to be occupied with God! This thought makes me so happy that the day appears to me brighter and more festival-like, and the night more lovely and charming. Sleep is chased away by so much happiness, and all night long, through the open window, I hear the wind sighing in the deserted streets, and the cry of the night-birds that sit perched on the steeple of Notre Dame, which rises in black outline against the sky, and seems lost in the clouds. Each toll of the bells sends a thrill through me, for it brings nearer and nearer the longed-for hour of Sunday morning. In fine, those are nights during which, whilst our own hearts are palpitating from emot'on, we ask ourselves how any one is able not to love this God of infinite charity, who reveals Himself so clearly everywhere; —in nature, by its scenes so varied and so beautiful,—in His religion, by the last magnificent and divine memorial of His love, which overwhelms all thoughts of doubt,—by His mysteries, those abysses of goodness and charity, which the deepest contemplation cannot fathom;—in a word, in all that touches our senses, and awakens our intelligence, and which cries out at every moment and in every place; God! God! God!

"Yet it is during these moments that I feel all my dreadful unworthiness! O Lord, my God, when will it be given me to love Thee, as Thou deservest to be loved? Thou who lovest me with an infinite love, make me love Thee. Thou who thinkest always of me, make me ever mindful of Thee. Possess my heart and my mind; possess me wholly and entirely, O Jesus, who deignest to desire that I should wholly possess Thee.

"At three o'clock, the early dawn lit up the sky, and invited me to enjoy in silence the charming sight of the breaking of day. O lovely golden clouds! O fiery orb, that riseth forth so majestic from the ruddy vapors of the horizon, how well thou tellest the glory of Him who has created thee in all this magnificence? Why not tell you all in one word, dear Father ! My day was all for God, and my heart was full of Him.

"The towns people, on their side, wearing their best festival looks, were busy adorning the way which the blessed Sacrament was to follow. The streets were hung with carpets and drapery, ornamented with flowers, and were decked with crowns and garlands. The perfume of the flowers strewn upon the way, the harmony of the bells, the dazzling splendor of the day,—all seemed combined to touch the heart and render one happy. I saw the beautiful procession pass by : recollection was on every face ; young maidens robed in white, sung hymns to the Queen of Virgins ; children bore a thousand little standards floating in the breeze, whilst the crosses and banners bent down to pass through the arches of foliage. At last came slowly along the God of majesty and love. At each of the various altars, which the inhabitants had raised in the streets, the Lanciers' Band played some of those warlike strains that so well beseem the majesty of the God of armies, while the silent and prostrate crowd received the Benediction.

"O Jesus ! When You were on earth, a blind man hearing that You were passing by, cried out : Jesus, Son of David, have mercy on me ! In the same way, ten lepers asked to be cured of their disease, and they were healed. Another day, when drawing nigh to Jericho, You saw Zacheus, the publican, who had climbed up into a tree ; You made him come down, that You might abide in his house. O Jesus ! there are so many blind, leprous and covetous amongst us. Cure these miserable blind, who though they touch You, and hear You everywhere, yet do not see You, or wish to love You. Cure these publicans, who seem to have but one desire, and one end in life;—to become wealthy, and to procure for themselves the material enjoyment of the senses. Cure these poor lepers, eaten away by the leprosy of vice, and who without Your aid are about to perish. In fine, O God, who lovest us all, cure each of us, in order that we may have but one common end,—Your glory; one only desire,—Your love, and the eternal beatific vision!"

But a slight cloud suddenly arises to darken the horizon which had till then been so clear, and to cast a gloom over these happy days.

"My happiness," he writes some weeks later, " from the time of my arrival until I had returned, was such as I have told you if I except one little incident which gave me great annoyance. At half-past eight, seeing the night was setting in, I turned aside into a quiet avenue to eat my dinner, thinking that I should be seen by no one. On these beautiful festive days hunger and sleep seemed to take flight. A small roll eaten in the open air, in the public garden or anywhere else, is quite enough to satisfy me. But on the occasion of which I speak, I had scarcely begun to take something, when I saw M. de M——, a frlend of the du Dresnay family coming to meet me. In my embarrassment I blushed up to the ears, and was not able to hide my half-penny roll. M. de M—— is an old soldier. He fell into a passion at me because I did not go to take my meals at his house, and made me promise that I would do so in future. I thanked him certainly very much for his kindness ; but these days will now lose their charm for me, since I shall no longer be entirely alone and occupied with God. Henceforward I shall not be as free as formerly, and this is a great misfortune."

It will be easily imagined that worldly feasts had little effect on the heart of one who was thus wrapt up in God. He showed only indifference and contempt for them, and when he was obliged to take part in them, he returned with all possible speed to that in which alone he found true joy. "Whilst our good town of Epinal is pursuing its usual quiet course of life, this one seems carried off by the follies of the feasting. There is talk of nothing else. Exhibitions, district competitions, the Godard balloon, band competitions, lotteries, fire-works,—all have their turn, and came to disturb the tranquility of Nioet and its environs. For my part, I saw the exhibition, and was present at the band competition, from which I expected to derive great pleasure. But the music was without soul, and I have learnt once more that in all this there is nothing but vanity. Everywhere in the crowd, amongst the high as well as amongst the low, there is nothing but vain frivolity or tedious coarseness, which both alike bring sorrow and weariness of heart, and force you to lift your eyes up to that beautiful starry vault, where you can find Him, who alone is Beauty and Truth. It was evening, in the open air, and over head, above all those ridiculous lamp illuminations, the moon showered down her soft light.

"Happily we can oppose to the diversions of the world the feasts of the Church, those feasts of the heart which fill it with happiness and love. On two successive Sundays there have been First Communions at Notre Dame and St. Andrew's; and what a touching, pure and holy sight it is to see the dear little children shining with purity and supernatural beauty on the day when they first receive our Lord. Then his Lordship, the Bishop of Poitiers, blessed the three fine bells which the gentry of Nioet had presented to the Church of St. Andrew. It was there that I heard a magnificent sermon. Ah! there are times when one feels the need of a zeal that would consume him, and make him wish to have a thousand lives that he might give them all, one after another."

But in the midst of all these joys which God made him experience in His service, the pious young man felt the want of a more special direction, and one more suited to the end at which he aimed. His inexperience was great in all that concerned the conduct of the soul. The instincts of his heart guided him; but he perceived that on many points his ideas were vague and insufficient. He spoke one day on this subject, with a simplicity which beautifully set forth the admirable dispositions that divine grace had implanted in his heart. He had just read a book that is well known to all young aspirants to the priesthood: *Nepotian, or the Student of the Sanctuary.*

"This book," he says on the 31st March, 1865, "has touched me in many different ways, as I am going to tell you. The first condition I have read, that is required for a true vocation, is that we should be called, not that we should call ourselves; that we should be called notwithstanding our resistance, our repugnance, our dread, even, at the thought of the awful holiness of the priesthood. And how have I been called? When I was only fifteen years old, I felt the love of our good God, together with a strong desire to belong entirely to Him, increase within me, and take possession of my soul. I yielded gladly, as· was natural, to these holy inspirations, but I was not pushed on to this by my confessor, as it would seem was necessary. If I have deeply felt my unworthiness, I have never been much terrified at the thought of it, remembering the goodness of God. But is this not the work of a vain presumption, of a guilty pride? I perceive, too, from reading this book, that Lamartine-like I have had a rather too vague and poetical idea of the priesthood. But from its very vagueness my esteem of it has been all the higher. . . . Oh! how beautiful, how holy, how dreadful, and yet, at the same time, how enviable, is the model of a priest which this book sets before me. He is always in conflict with himself and the world, always devoted to the service of God and his neighbor."

It was natural that the future novice should turn towards Solesmes, for which he felt so strong an attraction, to seek enlightenment with regard to his vocation. He therefore resolved to go and take a few days of retreat there in Holy Week, of the year 1866. He was already known and expected at the monastery, and the letters he had sent there had enriched all with the greatest admiration for him on account of the graces with which God had enriched his generous soul. He prepared himself for his retreat as for the greatest event of his life : he proposed to make a general confession, and "to hand over at last that heart, which tires itself out in pursuing without result its own unguided reflections." During the three months that preceded his departure for Solesmes, the examination of his past life was that which most occupied his mind, and kept him in sentiments of the deepest humility.

"Have pity then upon me, you who know me," he said to his uncle, "and do not lay upon me the load of your good opinion. I could never have gained your esteem unless by hypocrisy. I am nothing but filth, misery, weakness, and I am just asking myself if really they will be kind enough to receive me at Solesmes."

He accused himself bitterly of the slightest fallings off of fervor and courage. And feeling the weariness of those days of labor oppressing him the more, in proportion as he thought oftener of the peace and liberty of life in the cloister, he accused himself of this, calling it weakness and cowardice.

"What strange inconsistency there is in my poor soul, which promises to make the greatest sacrifices and yet find hard the most ordinary mortifications of every day ! alas, I am consumed

with desires for the future, and I don't know how
to take advantage of the present, and whilst others
think me good, I must confess to you, with tears
in my eyes, what my conscience cries out to me,
and my conduct every moment betrays, that there
is naught in me but cowardice, and the lowest
miseries."

Under the influence of these thoughts he even
abstained for two weeks from communion on
Sunday, thus depriving himself of his greatest
happiness on account of his unworthiness.

Nevertheless, there was still hope and joy at
the bottom of his heart, as we see clearly from
the following letter, one of the last he wrote before
he had began the journey on which he was so
impatient to set out. It was addressed to his
uncle, and followed the former after an interval of
three or four days:

"You will say that I am growing talkative,
but after drawing such a lucky number yesterday
at the conscription, how can I be silent? 132.
Truly I was born under a happy star, and this
thought often comes to my mind in a more serious
form, when I think of the inestimable happiness
of my destiny. For, O my God, what a thing is
the religious life! It is a few years passed in
enjoying the only true happiness that there can
be in this world, in loving You, and waiting
patiently for that happy moment, when His divine
mercy shall have brought us to our end, when we
shall have reached the term of our deliverance,
that beautiful summer evening, when the hand of
the divine Gardener will pull us as a fruit ripe for

eternity. Is it possible that for a true religious the slightest cloud can rise to dim the brightness of those days which God has given him for life? Obedience! But is not this his severity, his peace? Mortification! But is it not a necessity for him to deprive himself of sleep in order to lengthen the day, and thus hasten his maturity for heaven, to deny himself everything in which there is the least sensuality, in order to wing more easily his flight towards the God of love? The company of the other religious! But are they not our brethren and loved as such? . . . I see nothing, then, in the religious life, but peace and happiness, I might say, supreme felicity, if this sort of life was not passed like the rest, upon an earth full of mercy, and if the exile did not carry with him everywhere in his heart a sincere and deep regret that he was free from his native land. Glory, thanksgiving and love, then, now and for all eternity, be to the Father who has traced out so beautiful a life for me, and who, since I am unable to fly to Him, brings to me His love, as the bird bears food to its young. . . .

"Another thing which makes me so gracious is that I am writing in my room this morning with the window open, for the first time since winter. Everything is so fresh, so tender, so beautiful, so peaceful and harmonious, that, with every gust of wind, that comes sifting through the pine trees, my heart begins to sing songs of happiness and love. Ah! if men were wise, if they did not let their hearts be engrossed by a thousand foolish occupations, if they did not run after their pleasures which enslave them, what happiness would they not find in living peacefully in union with God, what gladness would they not feel in their hearts, what pleasures would their senses afford them, what joy the thought of all the wonders of God, both visible and invisible, would bring them! If they would but follow their true destiny, what would the earth become but a temple, in which every human heart would render a tribute of love and gratitude, that would mount towards God as the smoke from a censer of incense! Fair dream, beautiful illusion, which comes to us on this prostitute earth, but will only be realized in the heavenly Jerusalem!

"But, alas, why does my heart sing so joyfully? This is the first Sunday, for a long time, that comes to find me sorrowful and desolate, and leaves me without the hope of enjoying my usual happiness. No, in order to draw near to the awful majesty of God, before I can dare to receive Him into my heart, it is necessary first to throw off this burden, which weighs so heavily upon me. . . .

"But let us look to the future. In a fortnight Easter will be here; Easter which will dawn upon me, and be for me like a new resurrection, the bright morn of a new life; Easter to which nothing will be wanting. I shall experience the joys of divine love, the happiness of being in the blessed place where I have so much longed to be, and I shall have the pleasure of throwing myself into your arms, my very dear uncle! . . .

"It is only a sun-beam of spring that has

reached us.   My hands, red and swollen with the cold, warn me that it is time to shut the window, so I bid you adieu, and send you my love on the wings of the wind."

The days that he so ardently longed for came at last, and Paul was able to go and assist at the solemnities of Holy week and Easter in the Abbey of Solesmes.   He was received there with a charity which charmed him, and inspired him with a filial confidence in those who were soon to be his fathers in religion.*   And these first impressions never afterwards wore away, for when he had left Solesmes he always spoke with feeling and deep gratitude of the affection which he had met with, and of the good which he had experienced in that holy house.

After his retreat, Paul Seigneret returned to Drenéuc, beaming with happiness, and fully confirmed in his resolution to give himself to God without reserve.   He had seen, he said, the adorable hand of providence directing his life to one only end, and conducting him unawares to himself, even in the midst of his forgetfulness and weakness, or at other times dragging him on, all on fire with love and fervor.

"When I thus think of the unspeakable goodness with which God has treated me, I would like to have a hundred lives that I might conse-

---

* It is to the kindness of the Rev. Father Dom Conturier, Prior of the Abbey of Solesmes, and friend and spiritual father of the young Paul whilst he was there, that we are indebted for the extracts from letters, and the valuable notes of which we will make ample use to honour the cherished memory of him who belongs to Solesmes, as well as to Saint Sulpice.

crate them one after another to His service upon earth, before daring to envy the happiness of those who love Him in heaven."

As the term of his trial drew nigh, his soul was filled with delight, and his heart sought relief for its feelings in more frequent expressions of joy. There is not one of his letters, which does not derive some new beauty from these thoughts.

"In six months, O my God, I will belong to you alone. Oh, how rapidly do I feel that I am rushing on to the fulfilment of my hopes, notwithstanding the apparent slowness of time ! Beautiful life ! Some compare it to a lovely day ; it seems to me like one of those beautiful nights in summer,—for where is there day or any splendour away from God ?—a night of tempests for me at first, but God will now change it into one of those clear nights that are lighted up by the soft and gentle light which falls down from above and makes us think of heaven."

" How often," he says in another letter, "during this beautiful weather, whilst the sun sheds on us its light, and the heaven its joys, do I think of the abode that awaits us on high. The nearer I approach, the more constantly this thought accompanies me. Pentecost already ! A few months more, and I will have done with this cold distracted life of the world !"

These last lines were written from Epinal, whither he had been suddenly called in the month of May by matters of some importance. When he had returned, after this short appearance in the midst of his family, he gives vent in the following terms to his love for his relations, which became every day more tender, without his love for God suffering thereby :

"It is after having drunk in happiness that one feels most of all his heart broken by a new separation, that he recalls more tenderly, or rather more cruelly, to mind all the touching kindnesses received from each one of his relations, and all the affection they bear him : it is then that he remembers the marks of attachment that were shown to him both by word and look, that he measures the charms of their love, and feels his own rooted in the very bottom of his heart. O, my dear father and mother, how loving, how kind you are to me ! It is the thought of this, and of your absence that throws a cloud of deep, melancholy sadness around me. And you, in particular, my dear little sister, my dear angel, who clung to me during these days with so much love, and a confidence that had no bounds. Alas ! all are far from me ! And yet, my dear parents, I feel that, when the first pangs of sorrow are over, far from deserting or forgetting you, I will never love you with so strong, so pure, so constant a love as that which will be strengthened by absence, and which God will rekindle in my heart under the shadow of the cloister."

Before leaving the du Dresnay family, he made with them, in July, 1866, a tour through Brittany, which afforded him the greatest satisfaction. During his stay at Dréneuc he was able to consider and admire the simple manners of the inhabitants of the country, but he was delighted above all to see in them still the ancient faith, "firm as the oaks," rooted in the soil. The · beautiful verses, in which the poet Briseux sings in loving strains the praises of Brittany, caused his heart to thrill, for he naturally sympathised with all that was noble and generous. He liked that " land of the brave," that classic land of fidelity and honour.

He relates how, one day, he went along with a crowd of Breton peasants, on a pilgrimage, which was made yearly on the feast of the guardian Angels, to a little chapel in the neighbourhood of Dréneuc.

" The Chapel is small and wretched, but makes a deep impression upon one. It is formed of four white-washed walls with a roof in which the beams can be seen as in a barn, and which has only known the luxury of slates during the last few years. But there is a history of greatness and generosity connected with this chapel. It was built under the Reign of Terror: and whilst the Blues were masters of Fégréac, at the time when nobles and peasants were shot upon the square before it, which I cross so often, a priest named Orain, whose family is yet held in great veneration in the district, risked all in order to come to the help of his parishoners, and by his indefatigable activity and an often evident protection of God, found means of evading, during the whole period of the Revolution, every research, and of giving to the inhabitants all the benefits of his ministry. It was he who, with the help of the faithful, built this chapel, which was only distinguished from the cottages around by the cross cut in the granite above the door.

"I assisted, then, at Mass in this sanctuary. It was a living picture, an exact representation of a scene of some seventy years ago. On one side were the women telling their beads, on the other the men in dark attire bent down toward the earth, in a posture of the deepest recollection. We were all on our knees on the bare ground, and not another sound was heard but the voice of the priest and the ringing of the bell, which gave warning that God was coming down again into this chapel, to visit the children of those good people of old who were so full of faith and generous self-sacrifice, and who now, I hope, are receiving in heaven their reward for the troubles they went through in life.

"One saw there the same dress, the same manly stern figures, the same faith, thank God ; the only difference was that seventy years had gone by. We all prayed together for the fore-fathers of those who were present, and also that the assistants themselves might never lose the spirit of faith and religion, which had already urged on their fathers to such heroic sacri-fices. The ceremony ended by the benediction of the seed which was to be entrusted to the earth.

"How could the Bretons, with scenes so simple and so grand as these before them, and whilst cherishing the remembrances of such things, stoop to defile themselves like the rest of their nation.

" No ! as Briseux says :

> **Of** Bretons we **are not the last,**
> **Nor have** thy former generations **passed,**
> **Without** transmitting through **our fathers' veins**
> **The** blood, which in **us,** oak-graced **granite land,** remains.

" Or, again, those stirring words :

> O God ! who in creating bid us wield
> The sword of war, or when the strife was o'er
> Take up the poets lyre, or to the field
> Conduct our flocks, or living on the shore,
> Seek from the sea whate'er our life requires,
> To sordid gain ne'er let a Breton turn ;
> But may we be what were of old our sires,
> And from our race the name of merchant spurn."

With such a love as this for Brittany, we can easily imagine how much pleasure Paul Seigneret derived from a tour which enabled him to penetrate more deeply into the heart of this celebrated country, and gain a better knowledge of it. In the letters that he wrote at this time, and which were real newspapers in length,

> Nous ne sommes pas les derniers des Bretons.
> Le vieux sang de tes fils coule encore dans ter veinés,
> O terre de granit, recouverte de chenés.
>
> O Dieu ! qui nous créas ou guerriers ou poëtés,
> Sur la côte marins, et patres dans les champs,
> Sous les vils intérêts ne courbe pas nos têlés,
> Ne fais pas des Brétons un peuple de marchands !

he describes the impressions that were made upon him by the stern and solemn aspect of the country, by the peculiar character of its monuments, and by the many other various records of the past which are found there. His lively imagination was roused by things of the very smallest importance, and they often inspired him to write descriptions which are sometimes very striking.

He stopped for a few days in the Chateau Tromeur, near the village of Plouvorn, in the Department of Finisterre, and he draws the following picture of the landscape he had there before him.

"In getting free of all the noise and bustle of Saint-Brienc, which is, nevertheless, a very unpretending town, I was struck by the lonely meditative air that this part of the country wears. Here there is no splendor ; the sun has lost its brilliancy, and grudges its fostering warmth ; one no longer hears the warbling of the birds, and nature no more displays abroad the grandeur of its riches. The atmosphere is always fresh, or rather cold and foggy, even when the sun reigns alone in the heavens, for he only sheds down his rays through a transparent veil of mist. And then, there is that boisterous wind which, ever blowing, stifles and drowns with its loud, hoarse voice all those thousand sweet harmonies, which are the life of the country everywhere else.

"I am not astonished that a Breton has a sad and pensive look, and that a laugh but rarely comes to relax for a moment the austerity of his countenance ; that the view of nature which, though stern, is solemn and grand, should raise his mind to the thought of the infinite Majesty of God, who seems to reflect Himself on this land, and speak through the all-powerful voice of that wind from the sea, that dreadful breath of the ocean.

"We have here, however, around us a most charming spot of verdure for our path, and a variety of beautiful trees that have stood for ages, through which walks of delicious shade, lined with shrubs and lovely flowers, wind and lose themselves. There at least one is sheltered from the wind, which can do nothing more than toss the tops of the trees, sport with the last leaves of the season, and whistle over all on his one unchanging note. There one can speak to the flowers that seem to look up at you, and there one can forget the harshness of the rest of the country. I go there in the morning to offer up to God every happy day, which brings me nearer to Him and you, and to breathe a prayer for you all, my very dear parents. Sometimes the setting sun darts his rays through the clouds and seems to send forth a shower of golden dust, that makes one think on the happiness of other places more blessed with his favors, and, at the same time, inspires us with greater wonder at that orb of life and beauty."

"I assisted," he writes in another letter from the same place, "on the eve of the feast of Saint Ann, at the most picturesque and touching scene that I have witnessed since I came to Brittany. At night-fall we were warned by the church-bell to assemble on a sort of esplanade, where it is the custom to light every year, on that evening, an immense bon-fire.

"About a hundred peasants, standing upright with their arms crossed, in that solemn haughty attitude which is natural to an Armorican, assisted at these simple rejoicings in profound silence, whilst their faces were lit up by the bright streams of light from the fire. At last, when the crackling of the flames had ceased and the fallen pile only scattered around dying glimmers of light, a young man advanced out of the circle of spectators, and with a strong voice began, in a slow and melancholy tone, a Breton lament. Whilst he was singing, the fire died out, and the moon, rising like a queen on the horizon, came to shed down her light on the solemn scene. As for me, I thought I perceived in the song that spirit of sadness and melancholy thought of the noble Brittany of old,—a sadness which betrays our longings for the regions above. An unbroken stillness reigned all around, as we stood there motionless. A feeling of melancholy gradually took possession of us, and the tears soon came to our eyes. O God! it is thus that we all languish and sigh : we wait in expectation, in that solemn mysterious expectation, which this song expressed so well."

On his return from this tour, Paul Seigneret passed a few more days at the Chateau du Dréneuc, from whence he was to depart for Poitou, in passing by Angiers, and soon after leave for Solesmes.

It was not without emotion that he left the manor of Dréneuc, where he had passed a life at once "so busy and so peaceful, so wearisome, and yet so full of joys;" his dear church of Fégréac, where he had so frequently tasted the sweets of heaven, and his little shady walks, where he so often saw the children with ruddy faces, stretching their heads over the thick hedges to say to him in a silvery tone: "Good day, Master Paul!"

The account of his journey from Angiers to Nioet shows us how close a resemblance he bore to a young martyr,[*] who is now encircled with a halo of glory, and whose name recalls to our mind that freshness of sentiment, that ardent love, that joy in death which charm us in Paul Seigneret.

From Airvault, a little town in Poitou, where the incidents of his journey had brought him, he went on a pilgrimage to the birthplace of Theophanüs Venard. Would not one be inclined to say that the following lines were written for him who traced them?

"One day, following the course of the Thouet, we came by beautiful shady paths to Saint-Loup, that lovely village of cherished memory, whose name makes one's heart beat quick. There was born a young and amiable martyr, whose imagination, catching its charms from the loveliness of these parts, scattered happiness and joy around him wherever he went. It was here that he passed his early youth, and hither his looks and affections were continually directed. He died in 1860. Everywhere round about Saint-Loup, one perceives the perfume of his holy life; and you might say that the wild flowers of the valley send

* Theophanus Venard, priest of the Congregation of Foreign Missions, who died for the faith in China, in 1860, and whose beautiful life has been written.

you with their scent the sweet odor of his virtues,
and the breeze, which makes the leaf tremble on
the tree, seems to toss before your eyes the transparent form of him we so much regret. I have
read his life before now. I have never met
another so poetically beautiful, so touching and
so edifying. When in his twenty-eighth year, he
saw that he was on the point of reaching the
glory of martyrdom, he wrote a letter to his
parents. This letter, which was placarded on a
pillar of the church, reminds us of that simple .
heroic language with which Polyeuctes was inspired.

"Alas! everything has an end, and that so
soon!" adds the youth, pursuing the interesting
account of his journey. "Every happiness passes,
even before we can enjoy it as we wish! It was
necessary to depart..... Another night in the
coach made me pass through a dreadful storm,
and assist at its different stages of fury. The
battalions of black threatening clouds rolled on,
rent asunder ever and anon by bright sheets of
lightning; one could follow their march, which
was silent and rapid, though not a breath of wind
was blowing. The coach was full of women, who
but lately were entertaining a coarse conversation
with the driver; but every one was silent now;
we could only hear the weary trot of the horses,
and at every moment dreadful flashes of lightning made the harness shine with a pale glimmer-
ing light. What a grand sight! We were alone,
—alone in the stillness and darkness of the night,
in the presence of the power or the anger of God,

which was rolling over us. The uneasiness increased with every flash of lightning, at every crash of the approaching thunder, or as the rain poured down more heavily; the signs of the cross became every minute more frequent amongst the women; and the driver, who but a moment ago was so coarse and brave, did not dare now to whisper, or if he did open his mouth, it was only to speak of the danger we were running. At last, we could perceive in the distance a miserable inn, and before long we were all shut up with doors and shutters closed, in a room full of smoke, where the air was nearly insupportable, impregnated with the foul vapors arising from the drinking revels of the preceding evening. It was there, I will not say that we saw, but that we heard, or felt by the dreadful crashes which made the house shake to its very foundations, that army of thunder pass. How grand a storm like that is, and how well fitted, O my God, to fill the hearts of men with that fear, tempered with love, which we ought to have for You Who appear so powerful, and before Whom we have not words to utter our weakness!

"Nothing could be more lovely than the morning which followed that furious storm. The rising sun pierced the last clouds with his golden darts, and made a thousand diamonds glitter on the dew-covered grass.

"At last, another coach conveyed me over the last stage from Parthenay to Saint-Maixent, by a road running through the woods, which was green and fresh like the avenue of a park, and soon the train drew me with unslacking speed over the distance between this town and Nioet ; Nioet ! whose white spires I hailed with emotion. How often, last year, did I listen to their bells, breaking with their harmonious voices the religious silence of the night !

"But all those innocent pleasures have long ago gone by, and they will only serve to awake in me the remembrance of joys that now exist no more."

When Paul Seigneret wrote this letter, only a few days separated him from the moment he was to leave the world for God.

But here occurs, in the history of his vocation, a strange incident, which gives us to understand, better than words, the ardor of the flame that devoured his soul. We have seen the joy which the thought of his approaching entry at Solesmes caused him, and how each day that glided by, made his joy sink deeper into his heart. All at once our young friend was seized with the thought that he would be too happy at Solesmes, and that God required from him even the sacrifice of his happiness. He remembered how his first tendencies were towards a most austere life. It seemed to him that he had turned aside from his path, through motives at once too human and too selfish. And as he never hesitated about making a sacrifice, he resolved on the spot to ask admission, at least upon trial, at La Trappe de Bellefontaine, in Anjou. But there still remained the task of disclosing his project, and obtaining the required consent. This was a subject of deep anxiety to him. He first made known his intentions to his uncle, and thus expresses himself towards the end of his letter :—

"Committing the care of this difficult affair to that God of love for Whom I wish to sacrifice, in as profitable a manner as possible, a life otherwise so wretched and so short."

The thought of the sorrow he was about to cause his beloved parents tormented him. Would he have the courage to inflict this blow upon them himself, or would he be unfaithful for the first time to that pious· habit he had formed of telling all without reserve to his parents ? At last he fixed upon the idea of not making known his project, until after a trial of a few days, which it was possible would not succeed, and then he would disclose it by word of mouth rather than by writing.

"If our good God brings to an end this interior trouble, which the thought of communicating every thing to my father brings upon me, I will let him know all. But it would be easier for me to pour out all into his heart by word of mouth, when I should be aided by that emotion and that warmth of affection which his presence inspires, and before which all timidity and embarrassment disappears."

He had also to give an account of his new desires to the Rev. Father Dom Couturier, to whom he had laid bare his whole interior during his retreat at Solesmes, and had often since confided his ardent aspirations after the life of the children of Saint Benedict. He wrote him on the 3d of

April, 1866, the following letter, which resumes the history of his vocation, and states the question in an admirable manner, exactly as he himself understood it.

"The last time I wrote to you was at the moment when, filled with the sweet joys and bright hopes of spring, my heart dreamt naught but happiness. What has then come over me during this interval? Ah! Rev. Father, is it astonishing that I should thus have delayed so long to write to you, when even to-day I only do so in great trouble, and panting under the weight of the burden I have to lay down before you? I beg of you to have pity upon me as you have already done before.

"In the midst of all this turmoil of life, one dominating thought has been continually in my mind, a longing after the religious life, and this it is that has rendered all other kind of life unbearable; all but this seems to me such cruel bitterness, such sickening vanity! Distaste for the world has increased in me more than I can tell you, and contact with it has caused me a sadness that would have overwhelmed me, had it not been continually counteracted and soothed by the joys of the heart, and those magnificent Sunday festivals at which I have been delighted to assist in some of our grand cathedrals. In fine, Rev. Father, I confess with all frankness and humility, the longer I live, the more I love God with an irresistible love, it seems to me, ready to burst all bonds.

"I beg of you, Rev. Father, to think how my

vocation to the religious state first discovered itself, and to consider its gradual development. You will remember how, feeling myself dissuaded from the ecclesiastical state, with one bound my thoughts carried me towards the enticing austerities of a trappist's life. I made known my tendency to my uncle, who told me that an idea of the kind was folly, and speak to me of you, thus gaining for me the happiness of your acquaintance. The visits I made to Solesmes dazzled me, and in the overflow of joy and emotion, banished from my mind all other desires.

"But now behold this first desire returns both strong and urgent, and I spoke of it again to you, pressed by imperious necessity, forced by circumstances, and with the firm resolution of following it, after having first duly referred it to your judgment.

"No one, besides my uncle, knows a word of this sudden change in my ideas. They would look upon it as folly and to trouble them would prove to no purpose. I will not mention it even to my parents, until I have made a rigorous trial, for a week or a fortnight, of the life of La Trappe, in order that I may be able myself to judge of my strength.

"And first of all, should they reproach me with inconstancy, with levity of character and changeableness in my desires and opinions, you, dear Rev. Father, are more competent to judge than others in matters of this kind. Knowing me as you do, do you not see here the finishing-off and crowning of the work which in His mercy

God has been pleased to accomplish in me. He it is who has drawn me from the abyss into which I was plunged, who has breathed into me the holy inspirations, and who, most certainly, requires of me a life of suffering, and of complete sacrifice. Suffering! It is my only dream, that of which I most stand in need, since He has shown me how beautiful it is, how good, and infinitely loving, and how sweet it is to love Him!

"Yet how attractive was that life of a Benedictine, such as I saw and loved it whilst in the midst of you! But now it appears clear to me, that I am not worthy to partake of your joys, or have the happiness of living in your society, as I have so much desired. There is a voice within me which calls for expiation and suffering; a trappist's life would answer all my desires. Oh! too happy should I be could I make an entire sacrifice of this miserable life; indeed, I should like to have a thousand lives in order to pass them all in suffering for God! I consider the trappist as truly dead to the world, and all those family joys, to which my heart is so sensible in that unbroken silence, he reflects without ceasing upon the God of infinite bounty, of whose sufferings we have been the cause; he tries to find some of His purgatories here on earth, he buries himself alive as in a tomb. By manual labour the body is taught to undergo fatigue, as the soul is taught to repent.

"In a word" dear Rev. Father, "this is just the life for which I have felt an attraction, ever since my thoughts first turned towards the religious state. Here I find the life I seek,—complete sacrifice, even of the pleasures of the intelligence. Every one will cry folly, I know, when my health is taken into account, but then I feel better to sustain all this than any one would imagine. And besides, it is a proved fact, that vigorous natures with great wants do not bear against austereties, so well as weak ones who can be content with little. And if, after all, our good God refuses me the necessary strength, at least I shall only yield when I have done all I could to chastise myself, in order to love Him less unworthily, who has loved me so much.

" For a last proof of my vocation, I confess to you all my anguish of heart and deep regret at the thought of sacrificing the smiling life of Solesmes, whose long dreamt of charms I shall never know, since I have decided upon living for ever separated from you all, though the peace and serenity that reign in the Abbey had such great attraction for me."

One can well imagine that this impassioned pleading was insufficient to induce everyone to adopt the views of the fervent youth.

His health presented too great an obstacle.

He avows himself that the doctors found his chest weak, and, what is more, already perceived symptoms of a serious heart disease.

" Here," said he to his uncle, " I put you in possession of what no one else knows, because I am sure you love me for my soul's sake alone."

On the other hand, they replied to him from Solesmes that his excessive ardor was deceiving him, and that, what he imagined to be a means of perfection, would be for him, with the constitution which God had given him, a terrible trial, and a real danger. All this threw him into the greatest perplexity.

Nevertheless he brought much resolution and energy into the struggle. In spite of his docility which was most sincere, he had that tenacity which is peculiar to men of highly susceptible characters, who cannot easily do away with impressions they have once received. He could not help again and again drawing the parallel of the two lives which were before him : " the one in which I should be as happy as a bird of paradise, and the other in which it would be given me really to tread, in sorrow and sacrifice, the royal way of the Cross, which Jesus trod for me,—for me in particular." And his heart thrilled with emotion at the thought of all this sacrifice.

A compromise had to be set on foot between his impatient fervor, which took no obstacle into account, and the indulgent wisdom of his spiritual guides. He received with pleasure the assurance that they were willing to allow him to make the desired trial, and that if, as they foresaw, it did not succeed, he would find once more at Solesmes that paternal tenderness unchanged which welcomed him on his first visit to the Abbey.

At the beginning of October, then, Paul Seigneret set out for La Trappe Bellefontaine, carrying with him the esteem, the affection and the regret of the family with which he had lived, and which he had edified during the space of two years. Madame du Dresnay gives us this simple and touching testimony :

" He passed amongst us like an angel of good ; each of his steps was a good action, and every word of his had in view our good or our pleasure. " And she graciously added : " I think that the dear youth has committed no other sin than that of leaving us."

He, also, on his part, bid an affectionate adieu to "this abode where he had met with such kind hospitality," and set out "overwhelmed with favors, and laden with gratitude." "O my parents," he writes with his usual neatness of expression, "if you only knew how very kind every one is here; this morning they offered me a magnificent souvenir, little dreaming that they were thus laying upon my heart a load of gratitude. It was a beautiful time-piece, ornamented with the greatest taste. . . . As soon as I saw it, my first thought was of the joy I should have in giving it to you. But I was told it was a young gentleman's time-piece, and this suggested to me at once another idea. Allow me, then, to make a present of it to a young gentleman, to my dear brother Charles. I hope he will accept it as a pledge of my tender affection. Its soft sound will recall to his mind all the charms of our childish love, and bring back the remembrance of a brother who is ever anxious for his welfare. Only he must let me make one condition ; it is that he will take the same care of this precious souvenir as I should have done myself, not on my account, but out of respect for those who gave it to me. To leave it in a neglected state would be, in my opinion, a profanation of the affection which they have always so tenderly lavished upon me."

When the young tutor presented himself at la Trappe, they had considerable difficulty in granting him admittance, even upon trial, so incapable did he appear of supporting so severe a test. Three weeks, in fact, had scarcely elapsed before his feeble body was worn out, and he had to resign himself to a confession of his weakness, and acknowledge he had deceived himself.

He was obliged to go and spend some time in the bosom of his family at Epinal, in order to regain his strength. On his way, he passed by Solesmes, where, he says, " they consent to forget my freak. They told me I was a spoilt child, whom God is drawing towards Himself by all the charms of His love. But they foretold to me that, later on, I should be deprived of these sensible joys and undergo great móral trials, in which doubtless I should find again a hidden but heavier cross than that which I was seeking for amid bodily austerities." God, indeed, was waiting to try him by the painful incertitude to which we shall once more see him fall a prey with regard to the path he was to follow.

CHAPTER III.

THE ABBEY OF SOLESMES.

On his return home, in the month of November, 1866, Paul Seigneret prolonged his stay until Easter of the following year. His desires would have carried him sooner to Solesmes if, after his trial at la Trappe, his health had not required the greatest attention; this was still more urgently demanded as his physical development, after a long stand-still, now began afresh. His family did not think it prudent to allow him to face the winter and Lenten season in the novitiate. And those at Solesmes willingly agreed to this delay, nor were they sorry to see his fervor calm, for though it was sincere, and suggested by pure motives, it did not fail to raise some apprehensions in their minds. The studious youth put this forced leisure to profit, and took up again with his usual activity the historical and literary pursuits which he had been compelled with so much regret to discontinue during the two preceding years.

In the month of January he had devoured the twenty volumes of " the History to the Consulate and the Empire," by M. Thiers, and, for the three months he had still to pass at Epinal, he drew up a programme of work, which comprised, besides his Latin authors, the perusal of Homer, of several of the tragedies of Sophocles and Eschyles, a Review of the Principles of Philosophy, which he had studied at the Lycée, and " all that in order to arrive less unprepared at Solemes. "

At the same time he opened out his soul freely to the joys of family affections, and welcomed, as a favor from God, the happiness that came to embellish his last days in the world.

" I think upon the time past," he says to his uncle, "when I mourned my absence from home, and upon the years to come which will be spent far away from it. This thought keeps me at present close to my dear parents. Their many occupations and cares make it a pleasant duty for me to keep them company when they are free, and render them a thousand little services agreeable alike to them and me. And when the hour of meeting comes round, and we find ourselves all assembled together, our happiness redoubles ! God who has set such great desires in my heart, and yet has never fully satisfied them, now offers me all the joys that life at home affords. It moves me deeply to see the incessant activity of my mother, the generosity she displays in sacrificing herself in presence of her duty, her tenderness for us all who are the object of so much solicitude, of so many prayers, and of those tears of a mother, which ought to have such influence on the heart of God. Thus it is that my admiration and love vie with each other. Our dear good father also shows an affection for us, which is now stamped with that happy calm and extreme tenderness with which age adorns parental affections . . . ."

Loving as he was, our young friend was not ignorant of what a separation without return would cost him ; and the thought of a speedy departure sent many a pang of sorrow to his heart. But he looked calmly upon the sacrifice demanded from him, and marched on with confidence towards the end he had in view.

"You know me too well, my dear uncle," he wrote at parting, "to fear that I take my way to the cloister with hesitation or reluctance. The happiness which I have here enjoyed has nowise changed my desires, and after these days so quickly flown, my convictions still remain the same. The reason of this is, that I could never find in the life of the world anything to equal the pleasures of study, the privilege of singing God's praises and being one of His constant adorers, in fine, anything to be compared with the inestimable favor that Divine Providence has granted to me in calling me to the religious state. Besides, that which I seek there above all things is the fulfilment of God's designs upon me ; happiness will come afterwards by way of interest."

For an instant, he had reason to believe that he was about to be violently drawn aside from his path, His heart, which always sought with passion after self-sacrifice, was now spurred on by a sudden and unexpected event. In April, 1867, a thrill of patriotic enthusiasm ran through the whole of France. Rumors of war, forerunners of the events we have witnessed, which stirred up the public mind. In the eastern provinces,where interests were more at stake, and where there existed a clearer foresight of the danger, possible eventualities were discussed, and all did not cast aside with the same reckless levity the thought of the disasters which were impending. The imagination of Paul Seigneret was awakened. Already he beheld France invaded, his native soil tramped under the foot of the stranger, and his family in danger. His duty in such circumstances appeared to him as clear as it was imperious ; he ought to remain waiting and, if the land was invaded, mingle "as an obscure soldier amid the throng of its defenders"

"Let them call mea boaster and accuse me of because with my feeble arm and womanish looks, I dream of imposing upon myself the hard life of a soldier. But I hold that there is a noble and most sacred duty binding every one, be he weak or strong, to fly to the frontiers as soon as they are threatened, and employ at least the small share of strength he has received from God in protesting, by his presence, and if need be, by his blood, against the odious violation of our country's rights."

It was to the Rev. Father Prior of Solesmes that these lines were addressed.

"I am well aware of all this, added the youth in his ardour when finishing his letter," "and yet I am upon the point of starting. My father bids me take care lest I expose myself, upon fears so slightly founded, to put a hindrance in the way of my admission at Solesmes. Besides, dear Rev.

Father, I shall there find your counsels and those of the Rev. Father Abbot, and as long as religious ties do not bind me to the monastery, if France, overcome in the struggle, has need of the assistance of her weakest children, or if I can prove of use to my parents, would you refuse me the exercise of my duties as a citizen and a son ?"

This warlike manner of entering the noviciate made those smile, no doubt, to whom he had addressed himself with so much simple confidence. But at the same time, it allowed them to conjecture what might be expected later on, from a soul to whom it cost so little to forget self, in order to sacrifice all to the claims of virtue and duty.

It was on the 16th April, 1867, that Paul Seigneret at length crossed the threshold of that retreat where he hoped to find forever his place of rest. As he had expected, his parting adieu to his family rent his heart, but did not shake his resolution.

" I pass over in silence," he writes a few days after his arrival, "all the sadness that has come over my heart. It is in vain that we prepare ourselves a long time before hand to make the sacrifice, we can never form an idea of the pangs that are to accompany it. God knows how dear to me were those joys I have renounced. Yet I beg of Him to keep ever fresh in my mind the bitterness of this separation. I have longed for the monastic life precisely because, through the sacrifices it demanded, I thought I would be more agreeable to Him in it than anywhere else. The sacrifice of my life, I know not why, would have been so small a thing for me, that it could have merited nothing. In the life of a parish-priest—that long dreamt-of idyll—in which I imagined myself distributing my time, my cares, my means amongst all, I should have been too happy to have deserved any reward. It is therefore in the act of leaving home, and giving up my joy in the world, together with all the affections which I might have formed, that I have found my greatest sacrifice.

After some days passed in the guest's house, according to the custom, he was admitted to take part in the exercise of the community, and his first taste of the religious life carried him out of himself with joy. On the 4th of May, he writes :

" Now I see what the religious life is, and curious enough, the reality surpasses all my imaginings. It is indeed a life of continual prayer :——the choir offices and the many other religious exercises, scattered throughout the day, make us bear on continually towards God. I learn thus to love Him as the Father of our country, and in falling back on Him at each moment, I find the same happiness as that of which I never grew tired when near my very dear parents. Those who are not men of faith ask themselves, what good comes of singing psalms and saying so many prayers : but others understand that, to be led back to God, for whom we have quitted all, is our only joy and the increasing demand of our heart. In him we find again all the affections we have sacrificed, our first fervor, our happiness ; and to Him our soul turns with a gratitude always new.

We are truly on earth only to sing God's praises, we form His court, we never cease to tell Him of our love, or try to repair His injured honor outraged by the wickedness and unbelief of men. Yet, at the close of the day, how we regret all the graces we have lost by levity and our inexperience of so sublime a life.

On the 9th of May, he was admitted amongst the postulants of the Abbey and received the habit.

" Nothing * could equal the joy that he felt on that great day. The following night he could not sleep. He had laid out in his cell his cassock, girdle, and scapular, so that he could see them from his bed, and the sight of them brought tears of joy to his eyes. He rose from his bed, reverently kissed those insignias of the monastic life, and, in a childlike yet serious manner, addressing to each one of them outbursts of poetry and love, he hailed the morning hour when he would put them on. Thus he began in the midst of us that life of prayer and study, in which he was a bright model for all his brethren."

He himself, too, in a letter to his parents, gives an account of the emotions that were produced in him by this ceremony, at which his uncle and his brother were present, in order to represent his family : " I will not try to tell you of that joyful day, since my uncle or Charles will no doubt have told you all already. Yet, would that I could describe it ! It was like a dream,

---

* Notes of Dom Conturier

during which my soul was filled with delight : I saw draw nearer and nearer every moment the hour when I was to give myself wholly to God, whilst my heart burnt with an intense love for Him and a boundless affection for you and all the rest. During the whole ceremony, and after it was over, God and yourselves seemed to form but one in my mind.

" This festive day was not followed, as the rejoicings of the world, with regrets on the morrow. It was but the introduction to this life so long desired which now each day appears to me more beautiful and more holy, and ever calls forth fresh gratitude from my heart. I talk to you freely, dear parents, of joys and festive days without fearing that you will doubt for one moment of my ever increasing affection for you. Besides, regret was not altogether wanting in the midst of that day's happiness, especially at the moment when I met and embraced Charles as the representative of you all !

" From that day dates for me the beginning of the religious life in earnest, would that I could tell you, too, my astonishment, and the gratitude I experience in seeing myself clad in this black costume, which appears to me so strange and yet so beautiful, the respect I have for myself in seeing that I am consecrated by this uniform of combat and glory to the service of God, the touching and salutary thoughts this keeps bringing to my mind —then you might form some idea of my happiness ! And to be able to say that henceforward my life will be employed in loving and glorifying

God, in perfecting myself even more and more, and in loving you, my dear parents, and everyone with an affection which will make me very anxious for your welfare! . . . This is too great and glorious a mission for one so unworthy as I am! You can scarcely believe how much resolution and attention is required, that we may be able to follow out this holy rule in every point, and how dissatisfied we are with ourselves at evening, when we find that, through our own fault, we have been robbed of so many good works which might have made us more pleasing to God. There lies the monk's great struggle. But since God heaps so many graces upon me, and since my coming here has cost you such anguish, how much more strictly is all this demanded of me, and how guilty should I be if I only served God with tepidity and negligence, and if I had saddened your heart only to turn out a bad religious.

"How can I thank you too, for that touching attention which prompted you to send at this solemn moment all that I have asked of you—your full approbation and your blessing. I have read over and over again that letter which I guard with so much care ; it will lie henceforward, with all your other letters, at the foot of the crucifix you gave me, and will be ever there to inspire me with good counsel for my guidance, and fresh affection for you, my beloved parents. Is this then a real separation, which cannot prevent us from reuniting ourselves at will by mutual love and a never ceasing rememberance?"

The yonng novice brought to the practice of

the religious life a truly wonderful zeal. The perfect observance of the rules seemed nothing to his fervor.

" The more difficult he found obedience,* the more ready he was to submit, and he performed all with such a look of satisfaction and willingness as gave joy to his superiors and brethren. He always turned by preference to the most unpleasant offices, and loved to take upon himself the burdens of others. Though always forgetful of self, he was ever attentive to the wants of all ; no one acted towards his brethren with more delicacy, loved them with greater tenderness, or with an affection freer from all self-love and interest."

But the cloister only developed and brought to bear upon particular observances the virtues which we have already seen adorning each day the life of this youth. If, however, there was nothing wanting to his preparation of heart, his mind had yet to become familiar with ecclesiastical studies, and it was in this respect that Paul Seigneret felt most the happy influence of the noviciate of Solesmes. His mind, though highly cultivated and well-stocked with profane knowledge, was nevertheless, altogether unacquainted with those sciences which should be the food for the mind and the heart of a religious and a priest. It was on account of this that, hearing others discuss questions of Holy Scripture, liturgy, or church history, " I confess," he said, " I am frightened at all I see and hear with regard to studies ;

* Notes of Dom Couturier.

they form a world so entirely new to me, and I am so ignorant in all these matters!"

He soon perceived, too, that, in certain religious questions, his ideas, acquired at exclusively university sources, were not always in perfect harmony with those held by all those around him. He had drawn from the atmosphere in which his intellect had been trained, many appreciations of men and things, both past and present, which a more complete course of studies showed him to be not altogether free from prejudice. As the smell of the first liquor remains in the vessel which contained it, so the traces of his first education could not easily be removed ; and at times certain unlooked-for estimates of things, certain sympathies, or unusual opinions, betrayed the old scholar of the university, though hid under the cassock of the monk, or, later on, under the *soutane* of the seminarist. He learnt, whilst at Solesmes, to distrust these preconceived ideas, and he rectified them with a perfect uprightness as soon as he had recognised his error.

One can imagine with what ardor he dived into those beautiful ecclesiastical studies, so well suited to please his lofty mind, and give food to his heart, which greedily seized upon all that could help to carry him to the love of God. It was, as he himself afterwards said, "one continual jubilee."

"It was already a long time ago,* since the reputation of the Very Rev. Father Abbott had caught hold of the imagination of Paul. And

* Notes of Dom Couturier.

now that he had become his disciple, he tasted all the happiness of being able to follow his lessons. The conferences of Solesmes opened out to the eager gaze of the young novice a new field of ideas, and often, during the divine offices, one could see him trembling under the impressions of truths which had just been revealed to him for the first time. The Holy Gospel, the Epistles of St. Paul and the Psalms became the study of his predilection, and the best stimulant of his piety. He delights to speak of them in all his letters. He felt also a special attraction for history. Whilst hearing the Rev. Father Abbott explain to us the great events in the history of the Church, and teach us how to appreciate them, he felt his prejudices of college giving way little by little ; light shone upon his soul ; he saw that he was in " possession of the truth of history."

Whilst his intellect acquired new riches from studies which he pursued with delight, he experienced the sweetest consolations of heart in daily assisting at the offices of choir, and in taking a a more active part in those beautiful ceremonies of the Church, which had afforded him the deepest joy, when he was yet in the world. He tasted with the gladness of a novice that peaceful happiness expressed by these words of the Psalmist, which he loved to repeat ; *quam dilecta tabernacula tua Domine virtutum :* How lovely are thy tabernacles, O Lord of hosts.

He was soon chosen to fill the office of acolythe at the altar, and referring to this in one of his letters, he says :—" **You know** my timidity ;

I am somewhat frightened at the thought of it. But then, what a joy to be thus employed in the service of God, to be there under His very eyes, so near to Him on the altar !" And soon after: —"It is some weeks already since I have begun to be employed in the ceremonies ; and now that I have got rid of the uneasiness which I at first experienced, I find in these offices joys which I have not words to express." *

It was thus that he passed his time happily at Solesmes, whilst his soul, ever in the presence of God, was gradually advancing further and further in the path of virtue. A letter, bearing date of the 31st July, 1867, and addressed to his uncle, who was then in vacation, lets us catch a glimpse of all his happiness.

"You know," he says in excuse for writing so seldom, "you know what a life of unceasing and ever new occupation we lead here. I can say that since I have become a monk, every day has been passed in struggling with time, that I might be able to do all that my rule requires ; and I have never succeeded in doing so yet.

"Having then made my excuses, I can now participate more fully in the joy which I hope now fills your heart. Though you have grown old in the office of professor, it seems to me that years can never have deadened in you those feel-

* A magistrate of some distinction, who had a great love for Paul Seigneret, on seeing him at Solesmes fulfilling his office in levite's dress, with a piety and recollection which was altogether heavenly, said, "He is an angel, there is nothing wanting but the wings."

ings of pleasure, which one experiences at every moment, during the first days of vacation. Whether one be master or scholar, with what delight he looks on those two good months of full and perfect liberty, of travelling, of open sun, of unmixed happiness. What are your feelings this year then, my very dear uncle, now that you are about to see all again, as in the meeting that took place five years ago, of which we cherish so carefully the remembrance! . . . A good journey to you ; I wish you happiness and joys of all sorts.

"You will say that I am excited, that I lose myself at the very mention of vacation, journeys and meetings. You see that I anticipate your thoughts. But you cannot expect that I should not feel a certain sadness in leaving all these things which till now have brought me so much happiness. Yet, if you knew how all these pleasures of the world, how the free enjoyment of nature, how the joys of home, thoughts still dear, seem little in comparison with the advantages and the beauty of the religious life, you would, without fear, allow me to speak freely to you of those sweet thoughts and affections which I have sacrificed. Where could I live elsewhere as I do here, in a focus from which charity scatters her rays. And then, besides feeling beforehand the happiness of a day that is to be given to God, I think every morning with delight of all the beautiful things which we will see in Conference. How I loved Greek poetry! how I love it yet! But nothing can be compared with the Psalter, the Prophets, the Gospels, when explained by men so

deeply penetrated with the things of God, so
awake to the beautiful and true. Every day un-
rolls before my eyes a part of that magnificent
sight, in which, I confess, I scarcely perceived
anything at first, but grand, though rather vague
poetry. How unfortunate one is in the world to
know nothing of the things of God, to be preserved and kept in His love only by a more or
less misty idea of His infinite goodness and
supreme beauty, without seeing that living God,
that God who is magnificent, good to excess, terrible in His justice, such as Sacred Scripture
paints Him to us on every page. It is this picture
that we study every day, so that we only live by
God and are only happy through Him."

But a sudden storm burst out in the midst of
this peace. Towards the end of September,
Paul Seigneret received from his family news
which filled him with alarm. He persuaded himself that filial duty required, that he should sacrifice all in order to devote himself entirely to the
service of his family. His love would brook no
delay. "You understand," he wrote immediately
to his uncle, "that, in these circumstances, I cannot think of remaining any longer here. . . I am
not able to do much, but I have courage and a
strong desire to succeed. You know yourself that
if you were in my place, the very earth would be
burning under your feet."

It was with the greatest difficulty that his excitement could be calmed, and that he could be
persuaded to write at least to his father, and
await an answer. This answer, joined to the

prudent advice that he received, made him see things in another light, and showed him that the movements of his heart had made him too hasty, and had led him astray. He accused himself of his mistake in addressing to his parents the following touching lines :—

"Yes, I fully confess that, in doing this, I committed a great fault ; giddiness, self-sufficiency, obstinacy, all were urging me on. I acknowledge and confess all. But bear in mind the anguish I have felt, and how violently I was pushed on to sacrifice all for you ; it was that which made me go wrong. If my conduct has led you to suppose that I seized on the first opportunity to get clear of a path on which I am beginning to regret that I have entered, think of my likings, think of the desires which I have so long and so constantly manifested, think of the happiness I experienced only fifteen days ago, of all the ties that bind me to Solesmes, of my unchangeable conviction that as far as my personal happiness is concerned, I would never find anything better suited to my wishes than the religious life. God grant, that amongst all your other trials, any anxiety about me may not weigh upon your minds ! "

"Come," he wrote at the same time to his uncle, " you will bring back the sunshine after the storm."

The storm had, indeed, passed over, but not without leaving some slight clouds on the minds of the directors of the young novice, which made them doubt about his true vocation. It was evident to all that God had reserved for Himself a soul on which He had lavished such excellent gifts. Even his illusions and his hasty resolutions gave proof of his unbounded generosity and complete forgetfulness of self. But is it in the cloister that God will at last fix this youth, whose will is ever as steady in its desire to pursue what is best, as his mind is changeable in conceiving what really is so. "So inflammable a little head," wrote the Rev. Dom Couturier at that time, "does not leave us without anxiety."

Nevertheless, when the crisis was over, the young Paul, without being troubled with any apprehensions about the future, turned to enjoy with all his heart the happiness that the noviciate afforded him. We can easily perceive a feeling of satisfaction running through his letters during several months which follow this period. On the 25th of February, 1868, he writes : "I pursue my course as best I can. The days roll on here with incredible rapidity, now fair, now cloudy, now golden, as one finds them everywhere in life. *In loco pascuæ ibi me collocavit.* The field is open before me, the horizon is boundless and sparkles with a thousand incomparable splendors. May God be pleased to bless my youthful ardor, and make something good of me for His own glory and for the benefit of the world which I have left, but to which I am nevertheless attached by so many ties of sympathy and affection."

One may perceive that he returns in these lines, as if unconsciously, to his longings for that life more active and more directly consecrated to the service of souls, which had at first attracted his heart.

At the end of the month of March, however, Paul bound himself to Solesmes by closer ties. Until then merely postulant, he now became novice, and received the cowl. He made this step with joy; it gave him new fervor and already he looked forward to that moment when, after another year of probation, he could at last make his religious profession.

"I do not wish," he wrote at that time, whilst inviting a person, who took a great interest in him, to that ceremony,—"I do not wish to take this important step without being sure that you will help me with your prayers. Pray to God for me, I beg of you, this ceremony may not, like so many others, be fruitless for me. Besides, I hope you will, without fear, see me advance another step towards that solemn profession whose promises will bind me for life. I feel that God has conducted me here. Before I fully understood what the religious life was I looked upon it as a sacrifice of our existence to God, and, considering it a burden, I was not generous enough not to feel the weight of it, nor feel that I might one day seek to throw it off. But now I can appreciate things better. I have really felt how sweet and light is the yoke of the Lord: I have seen a broad horizon open itself out before my eyes, and, with so bright and so grand a future in view, I have learnt, that far from giving something to God, it is He who heaps His infinite favors upon me; it is He, the Almighty Benefactor, who watches over me, as He watches over the whole creation, and comes to me in my miserable existence to shower down His blessings upon me; and now I can say that I follow the course which is marked out for me, without any regret, or rather with the greatest pleasure, and I might say, without having to make any sacrifice; for I find all the affections that I have relinquished present and more perfect in God."

He advanced, therefore, in peace, persuaded that he was following the path traced out for him by Providence.

But soon the thoughts, which for some time had now and again stealthily crossed his mind, acquired greater persistency. He began to doubt if the cloister were really the place where God wished him to be. He still felt the greatest delight in being able to adore God and sing His praises, and in being able to fill his mind, through study, with truth. But the more he knew and loved this divine truth, the more he felt increase his desire of becoming its apostle. To be the servant of all, and especially of the lowly and poor; to bring light and consolation to his brethren; to lead them to God by his tenderness and devotedness: this had been his first idea of the duties of the priest. It was only with regret that he had turned away his thoughts from the sacred ministry incurred in this light, and merely because he judged that his despicable appearance rendered him incapable of performing the good that he desired. But that obstacle now no longer existed: his exterior had been changed by a rapid growth. His first aspirations returned with redoubled force, and he felt that the monastic life only answered imperfectly the longings of his soul. The persistency of these desires of self-sacrifice, which we will henceforward see betraying themselves in nearly every letter, make it sufficiently clear that, in this new phase of his vocation, he was yielding to a deep and irresistible attraction.

There was another thing which helped to turn him from the religious life. His character was not naturally of that kind which can easily adapt itself to a state of life that requires a great conformity of ideas and feelings; which not only demands that all should be of one heart, but that they should be of one mind also, and where these qualities are wanting community-life loses a great part of its advantages and all its charms. Paul Seigneret both by nature and by choice, was somewhat inclined to solitude. He had his own way of viewing things ; he had above all his own manner of feeling, which was extremely keen and delicate, and in a community must needs have often caused him pain. He discovered this at Solesmes ; he experienced it afterwards in the Seminary ; he would have suffered from it in any society in which he lived in contact with those whose ideas were different from his own, and who would often not have shared and sometimes not have understood the keenness of his sentiments.

It was after many painful struggles and with great anguish of heart that Paul Seigneret took the resolution to leave a place in which he had tasted the sweetest joys, and separate himself from a religious family that had inspired him with the deepest affection and a most profound respect. But it was evident that his **decision would this time be irrevocable.** During the two **months and more** that his **trial** lasted, he observed towards his **uncle** an altogether unwonted **silence.** He broke it at **last by the** following letter, which **he wrote on the 25th of** May, 1868.:

"It sometimes **happens** that we **have to pass through** trials so **painful that we cannot speak of them with calmness and moderation.** It is then **better to remain** silent ; when **the** storm is **over, when the decision is** taken, it **is time** to break **the silence.** I **remember** how **often** you and my **parents** impressed **upon me the** necessity of making good profit **of my novitiate,** in order to discover **my vocation, and how** you always bade me **leave if I felt that I was not** called. Since **I** have been **here, I have often** thought of **Issy, of** Saint **Sulpice, where my father** had **at first intend-ed to send me.** The time to take the cowl has **now come,** charmed **by the love of all around me, and enticed by the brilliant field of study which lay stretched out before me.** I advanced **without very much reflection.** God has permitted that, **before** going further, **I should know** my real **senti-ments.** It is impossible **for me to** make **the pro-fession,** whatever may **be** the pre-eminence **and utility of the** religious life. I **feel** that it **could never satisfy** my **most ardent aspirations.** Being **now strengthened in body and, as I hope, likewise in soul, I desire to devote myself to the active** ministry.

"The **pain** of detaching myself **from** this place **has been of long** duration, and hard to bear. But my superiors, after doing all in their power to gain light on the subject, are at last convinced that I am not made for the religious life : they charge me to come to some decision, and tell me I ought to take the measures necessary for entering Saint Sulpice, after having arranged the matter with my parents.

"You see, now, my dear uncle, the great news. This will no doubt cause you grief, but I hope that the thoughts of my good intentions will suffice to console you. God is my witness that I only act under the inspiration of His love, and that I am only guided by my ever-increasing desire of serving Him by doing all the good I can. . . . People will not fail to put strange interpretations upon my conduct. I have happily in my favor the testimony of all those who have known me."

He spoke truly, and every one at Solesmes was eager to remove any anxieties to which his conduct might have given rise. "The piety of this youth," wrote Dom Couturier, "and his love for ecclesiastical studies, inspired us with the hope that he had a vocation for the monastic life. If our hopes have fled, you must not suppose that this dear brother has lost his first fervor. He has remained good and pious, as he was when confided to us. The practices of the religious life have developed in a wonderful degree his love for holy things, and in particular, his love for Holy Scripture. He leaves the abbey, then, in the best disposition, and carries with him the regret of his fathers and brethren in religion."

Resolved upon quitting Solesmes, Paul Seigneret had turned his looks to the seminary of St. Sulpice. A secret attraction drew him towards Paris, where he saw there was so much good to be done, and an ample field open to his zeal for the salvation of souls, which could there deploy itself more according to the wishes of his heart. He repulsed vigorously the thought which some suggested to him, of making another stay in the world, and wished, if possible, to enter immediately the seminary of philosophy of Saint Sulpice at Issy.

"I need," he said, "at this moment a life of hard and serious study, and I shall find it at the seminary. I shall have need, later on, of an active life—it awaits me when once my arms are given to me, come what may. I shall always have the present in my hands, and there will be always a sure future in view, to which I shall look forward, and which, I trust, will inspire me, unceasingly with new ardor for study and greater love for God and man. . . . May God's grace come to aid and strengthen my good-will! It is He who determines vocations, and not our own desires. May He take me, then, beneath His holy protection, and deign to call me to the ranks of His humblest servants. As for myself, all the ardor, all the good resolutions, all the love of which man's heart is capable—all this I feel within me, in presence of the incomparable happiness of living solely for His service."

It was in such dispositions that he left Solesmes on the 30th of June, 1868. He had desired to celebrate again in this place, so dear to his heart, the feast of SS. Peter and Paul, the latter of

whom, his patron, he had learnt, he said, to know
and love so well.

Though his superiors at the abbey had yielded to his longings after an active life, they did
not then see so clearly as afterwards, the designs of
God upon him ; and they were astonished at the
energy with which he pursued that which he had
now in view.

" Nothing* could keep him back, neither
the tears of his fellow-religious, whom he loved
as another family, and who came on the
feast of St. Paul to give him the most touching testimonies of their affection, nor the paternal tenderness of the Rev. Father Abbot.   He
surmounted every obstacle, though shedding floods
of tears, and left us astonished at so much resolution, the secret of which we could not penetrate.
Scarcely had he arrived at Paris, and reached the
term of his desires, when he was himself surprised
at what he had dared to do, and asked himself
what hand could have been able to snatch him
thus from a place he loved so dearly ? "

" The thought of God," he wrote, " dazzled me
at the moment of departure ; for unless it had been
so, how could I have torn myself away from
you ? "

But does he wish to give an explanation or
excuse, he still speaks of the powerful attraction
that drew him towards Paris, and which we then
had so much trouble to understand.

" My sole consolation," he continues, " is to

* From the notes of Dom Couturier.

think on God, and to cast a glance upon Paris which I love so ardently. I already perceive there the modest post where, in self-sacrifice and humility, I hope to prove myself worthy of you."

On another occasion he wrote thus to one of his fellow novices. " I am ignorant of what form the good I long to do will take. But Providence will know best how to determine it for me. Besides, it ought to be easy at Paris, providing one has a little fellow-feeling, to dry up many a tear and lighten many a misfortune, and to bring back the hope of better things to many souls who are being carried off by the cold indifference of the world."

In fine, wishing to account for his happiness at the seminary of Issy, he will write again : . . . " And then my heart begins to beat. We have recreation in the cool of the evening until nine o'clock. Seated upon the grass at the highest point of the park, Paris, with its garlands of light, appears to us in the distance like a great furnace. O how many souls are there to be drawn away from evil ! how much good to be done ! This is for me one of the best and most pleasant moments of the day."

These lines bear the date of his first days at the seminary of Issy. He had presented himself there, after his departure from Solesmes, still clad in the monastic habit. Most of the seminarists were at that moment leaving for the vacation. But solitude did not frighten the young Benedictine. He proposed, therefore, to remain at Issy during the whole vacation, and there to work in recollection and peace, to prepare himself for the coming year. At the end of a few weeks, however, a fever came on, which obliged him to go and seek rest at Epinal, where he awaited in the bosom of his family the re-opening of studies in the month of October, 1868.

CHAPTER IV.

THE SEMINARY OF ST. SULPICE.

THE Seminary of Issy was, on his departure from Solesmes, the place best suited and most likely to soften quickly the bitterness of his regrets. This venerable abode, with its unpretending little rooms, its pious oratories, and its beautiful shady walks knits us to it by some unknown charm that has been felt by all those who have passed there the first years of their preparation for the priesthood. Everything is embalmed with such a fervent piety and true brotherly love as immediately draws the heart towards God! Many generations of saintly priests have grown up in silence, peace and happiness, near that venerated sanctuary of Loretto, which was lately destroyed by the vandal fury of the Communists, but with the help of the children of Saint Sulpice has again risen from the midst of its ruins and desolation.

The tender and generous heart of Paul Seigneret was found to enjoy the quiet of this pious place, and to derive benefit from the blessing with which Heaven seemed to surround it. When he arrived there he was anxious and pre-occupied about the future. Would he now at last find out his way ? The failure of the first attempts which he had made with such perfect good faith had rendered him distrustful, and it was not without anxiety that he viewed this new trial.

" My future," he writes, " forms all the poetry of my life ; to it my longing heart turns whilst I wait till it brings me my merit. I do not pass a day without asking God to remove the dark clouds that hang around me yet.

" Should this attempt fail, too, what will become of me with the irresistible and ever-growing necessity that I feel of giving myself to God and my fellow-men ! I will go to the Foreign Missions and I will then be only too happy. But I do not deny that by doing so I should sacrifice all my dreams. I fear very much that with my nature and my tastes I would find myself altogether out of place amongst the Chinese. And yet it is necessary that my life should belong to God."

Yes, that was the unchangeable and truly sincere desire of his heart, that was the point which remained unmoved whilst he was tossed about by doubts and uncertainties, and this alone would have sufficed to reassure a soul less humble and less inexperienced than his. He desired to be able to say to himself that if he missed his aim he had at least done all in his power to attain it.

" After eight long years of waiting, during which my desires have only been gaining strength, I behold at last before me the field I have so much sighed to see, that on which one can undergo the greatest struggles and can make the best sacrifice of self. Shall it be that all this has captivated me

only to escape from me at last? God sees my
intentions, He knows how firm I am in my resolution to do all in order to serve Him. I hope that
He will not forsake me. You would not believe
how studious I purpose to be, and how determined
I am to throw my heart into everything. One
might make me pass through the eye of a needle.
For I do not aspire after honor or any human happiness; it is for God that I work to prepare myself
for His service in the Divine priesthood."

These apprehensions pursued him for some
time, and it was with difficulty that calm was
brought back to his mind. But after following for
two months the peaceful, laborious and bracing life
of the seminary, he felt confidence return to his
heart. He began to breathe easily in that atmosphere of study and piety ; and those around already
began to perceive in him an excellent heart and
a gifted intelligence. The dispositions of his soul are
made known to us in those letters where, in
answer to the inquiries of his uncle, he tells him
everything with a charming simplicity.

On the 22d November he writes: "I have
thrown all my heart into the work and life of the
seminary, and I have only to congratulate myself
on having done so. I will soon have passed two
months here already, and I feel confidence returning
by degrees. I succeed well in my studies, and
they afford me the greatest pleasure; the encouragement I derive from this only urges me on to
work still harder. When I have done all I can,
God, I hope, will bless my efforts. In the mean
time I feel growing within me the desire of

giving to God a life which, till now, has only been happy in His service. May He bless this wish that He himself has fostered within me for the last eight years."

"I confess," he says a few days after, "I give way to a certain weakness in longing so ardently for the Tonsure. But it will make me belong entirely to God. I will be His possession, and He will be my inheritance. And lastly the Tonsure will satisfy me, and make up for the profession and complete surrender of myself, which I would have made at Solesmes on the 28th of next March. I live on, then, in hope. . . .

"I have been warned not to give way to excessive eagerness in my desires, which, by their continuance and intensity, would seem to force my director and even God Himself into compliance with them. One ought always to offer himself to God with the firm persuasion that he has no right whatever to claim acceptance at His hands. I wish, therefore, to submit and detach myself from my own will, although it seems true that to snatch from me what I long for would be worse than to snatch away from me my life. Yes, I hope, I hope! *God's goodness to me and my love for Him are too great to allow our union ever to be broken.* . . .

You ask me how I stand with regard to my fellow-seminarists. I could not be on better terms with them, thank God. I have to reproach myself, however, for wearing a pre-occupied look of sadness which others notice in me, I will throw this off; I desire to be gay everywhere and kind to all.

11

Health? Excellent. I think I am still growing—
My wants? I have many on one side and none
on the other. I am in want of the indulgence you
have shown me till now, that you may still be able
to love me as you do. I require that you should
always love me in the same way. I am in need
of your prayers, my dear uncle; offer me to God
that I may be consecrated to Him, and one day
entirely devoted to His service, ever full of love
for Him, ever pure in His sight. As for the rest *I
live in clover.* You are all occupied about me ;
you lavish on me kindness and affection ; of what
should I be in need? Impressions produced?
Peace, satisfaction, consolation, heartfelt gratitude.

" I pursue my course with joy of heart drawn on
by the beauty of the end I have in view. Every
one is satisfied with my work and my conduct. My
fears, then, on that score are vanishing. But
the fewer exterior faults I find to fight against, the
more I desire to concentrate the struggle upon
myself, to fight, to fight unceasingly ; for it is impossible to be too generous with the Master whom
we serve."

When he reached the month of March all his
pre-occupation had at last completely disappeared,
a perfect success had crowned his efforts, and he
now gave himself up to the pursuits of those noble
thoughts which arose in his mind, and to the enjoyment of the gladness that filled his heart, when
he reflected that his future was, from this time forward, assured.

" I have important news to communicate to
you," he writes to a person who took a friendly in-

terest in him, "that of my recent admission into the diocese of Paris. It is not without a certain dread of heart that I announce this to you, because I feel now more than ever the weight of the engagements I contract, and how little I am qualified to undertake what I purpose. I hope, however, that God, Who during the last eight years has been continually drawing me closer to Himself, will allow me to employ myself usefully in His service, and labor to the best of my power for the salvation of men. I know all that a priest ought to do, above all in these times, in order to represent God worthily; and I feel how much knowledge, holiness, kind-heartedness and resolution he should in consequence strive to acquire. These are just so many qualities that are wanting in me. May God bless my fervent promise to do all in my power to acquire them."

"I cannot tell you," he wrote at the same time to his uncle, "in what excellent relations I stand towards every one here, and how happy I feel in every way. You can imagine with what ardor I have put myself to work again. I was eager for it when I was only a bird upon the bush. What then should be my zeal now that I have a nest here, and my future is certain! I assure you, again and again, that I do not know how to thank God sufficiently for having made my trial so easy, and for having so soon restored to me peace and happiness. Nature is bringing round to us its sunny days again, but I find them already in my soul. Good-by, my dear uncle, I am going to plunge myself into the torrent. Do not fear that I will drown my heart in it.

The remembrance of the past and the thoughts of the future are there to keep it up and give it new life and warmth."

It is thus that his heart overflowed with delight in tasting the joys of the present, and was buoyed up by the hope of a future which every day made more certain. The better one knew the young Seminarist the more visibly he could see shining in him with wonderful lustre those marks which leave no doubt of a vocation to the priesthood. The attraction which drew him to the service of God and of souls, was so strong and irresistible that it might have given reason to suppose that he was laboring under some illusion or was carried off by an excessive attachment to his own opinions, if the motives which he proposed to himself had been less lofty or the attraction itself less constant, or if in fine the uprightness and simplicity of the youth could have been called in question. But it was evident to all, that there burned within him that holy flame of zeal, which is the mark of excellence of a priest.

The life and studies of the Seminary brought likewise out into relief those qualities which fitted him so well for the priestly state, and which now gave promise to the church of a minister as distinguished as he would be virtuous. That true virtue which sets duty and the will of God before everything else had already become an old habit in Paul Seigneret. No other Seminarist was more faithful in observing the minutest details of the rules, and no one thought less of boasting of his fidelity. He did not consider it anything extraordinary to employ, with a rigid exactitude, all the means that would conduct him most surely to the end for which he so ardently longed. He was one of those whom it is necessary to watch closely in a community, in order to moderate their zeal and hinder them from attempting what is beyond their strength. How often, when his health, which was speedily impaired, demanded unceasing attention, was it not necessary to insist, before he would consent to take the needful precautions! He yielded with simplicity to a wish or an order that was clearly expressed; but he hastened to return to the common rule, as soon as he thought he had sufficiently fulfilled the injunction he had received. Being less known on his entry into the Seminary, and likewise less betrayed by his strength, he managed, without drawing too much attention, to pass the winter without fire, and fast every day of Lent.

One can easily imagine that the tender piety, which had been the beauty and the charm of his earlier years, did not wear away at the Seminary of Issy. It became more calm without losing anything of its fervor or force.

A happy change of a similar character took place in his intelligence. The study of Philosophy, to which he gave himself up with an ever growing interest, moderated without extinguishing that enthusiasm which would have injured the correctness of his judgment. It was this study that gave reason the ascendant over his excessive sensibility, and one could already affirm without fear, that he would be possessed of a clear under-

standing which would be rendered more valuable
by having at its service a rich imagination and a
warm heart.   That love for ecclesiastical studies,
which he had acquired at Solesmes, continued
still to animate him at the Seminary.   He felt
keenly that, now more than ever, there lies upon
the priest the obligation of sustaining the honor
of his office by means of solid knowledge and a
high mental culture.

"A priest who lives on study," he then wrote,
"and who is at the same time consumed with the
sacred flame of zeal, is alone in a condition to fulfil his office, especially here."

It was these sentiments that urged him on to
work, and made him lay out with jealous care every
moment of his time to the best advantage ; and
he rejoiced to think that thus he was already com-
mencing the life of a priest, "a life essentially
spent in work, like that of the laborer who knows
no rest."   The papers to which he committed the
result of his studies are written and arranged with
a neatness we do not often meet, and bear testimony
to a wonderful precision of mind, and tell of indefatigable labor.   His fellow-students had often
recourse to them, in order to find some forgotten
explanation, or complete what had not been sufficiently comprehended.

In fine, the good understanding which his
tender charity to all constantly maintained between him and his fellow-seminarists, showed
what might be expected for the good of souls from
a heart which could love with so much disinter-
estedness and force.

There reigns in the Seminary of Issy a spirit of concord and true brotherly affection, which has been handed down and maintained through many successive generations. Those who have dwelt in this place, under the protection of Mary, its queen, know the peculiar charm there is in experiencing here how good and sweet it is to live together like brothers in unity.

Paul Seigneret had no difficulty in entering fully into this spirit which harmonized so well with his own feelings. He was always kind, delicate in his attention to others, ever ready to oblige them, happy when he could perform some service, and overflowing with gratitude for the slightest favor received. But a few only of his companions were able to know and appreciate the exquisite tenderness of his heart and the ardor of his holy desires. His best qualities remained unknown to many. It was not easy to *take the pitch* of his noble soul, and when he perceived that others did not share his views, or could not account for his enthusiasm, he closed instinctively like certain flowers, when an ungentle hand has touched them. He then sunk out of sight, spoke little, and by his conduct led others sometimes to suppose that he was guided by haughtiness or disdain, when he was only filled with timidity, embarrassment, and an excessive fear of giving annoyance to any of his companions.

When youths of this nature aspire to the priesthood, they become the joy of those who are called to direct them, and no cloud ever comes to throw a shadow of doubt on the designs that God has upon them.   Paul Seigneret was, therefore, called to prepare himself for the Tonsure, and his heart beat quick with emotion in announcing this fact in his letters.

" I am called to receive the Tonsure, and on Saturday, the 22d of May, I shall be clerk, and then all the incomparable grandeurs which the Church reserves for her ministers will be in store for me.   I cannot express the emotion and deep joy I feel, when I think that those cherished hopes which I have entertained so long are now at length being realized, in a manner that can no longer leave any doubt upon my mind.   And all this fills me with such courage and gratitude and urges me on to form such fervent promises for the future, as it is impossible for me to describe.   May God help me to accomplish them ! "

The speedy arrival of that happy day, when he was at last to consecrate himself to God, inspires him again with the following beautiful thoughts on the vocation of the priesthood :

" I think I have already told you, that I shall have the happiness of being Tonsured at Trinity. Yes ; and when I did so, you sent me in return your best wishes.   I thank you, my dear uncle : it gives me pleasure to think that I am thus supported by your love and prayers.   I have never known better than now how desirable it is, that he whom God marks out for such incomprehensible things, should be free from every reproach, and be able to say in his heart that he has ever done all in his power to correspond to so many graces.

" It is now no longer a mere surrender of self,

which every one might make ; nor is it a prize proposed to generous souls, such as is the religious life. It is the choice made by God of those who are to continue the mission of Jesus Christ and be His representatives on earth, who will have daily intercourse with Almighty God Himself, and who should possess an overflowing abundance of peace, heavenly joy and charity, in order to be able to impart them to all those who are deprived of them ; it is a choice, in fine, of those who have to fulfil an office of incomparable grandeur, which they have long sighed after, but which, when it is about to be conferred on them, makes them ask by what title they dare to seek it. I will advance, however, because those who have more experience bid me do so without fear, and also, because, *being penetrated with the unspeakable beauty of the designs of God upon me, if I tried to turn away, I could not ; so strongly do I feel that my life is bound up with them !* The cry of my soul to God is —the future, those few years that will be given me, and which I promise so firmly to consecrate to Him along with all my powers of mind and heart. . . . when I come to think that only three times more this dream of a year must pass, and then I shall be a priest, with nothing more to desire upon earth!"

From this moment he felt sure of his vocation, and no doubt ever again crossed his mind with regard to it, during the two years that formed, in the designs of God, that future for which his generous heart so ardently longed ; and he now only thought of leading a life which would correspond to the high end he had in view.

He received the Tonsure with joy. How was
it possible that he should not be happy when the
moment at last came for which he had looked so
long and prepared himself with so much care? He
afterwards called to mind with delight the beautiful hymn that was sung in the choir at Issy on
the evening of that happy day, beneath the trembling leaves of the trees :

> Receive this crown, O Virgin Mother,
> Before thy throne a pledge to lie,
> A happy earnest of that other,
> Which you reserve for us on high.*

We find, however, only in the first letter that
he wrote after his ordination, a sentence which
betrays the impression produced on him by this
great action of his life, but here it is a cry of joy
that escapes him : " How happy I am in belonging entirely to God !"

We may account for his silence with regard to
his joy on this occasion, by remembering the reason that prompted the letter of which we have
just spoken. It conveyed the intelligence that
the doctors had ordered him to leave the Seminary
without delay. His hard work and deep emotions
had told seriously upon his frame ; he continued,
however, to study as usual, till his strength was
exhausted ; but his frequent fainting-fits betrayed
him at last, and forced him to seek some relief.

> * Vierge, recois cette couronne ;
> Fais qu'elle soit le gage heureux
> De celle qu'auprès de ton trone
> Tu nous reserves dans les cieux.

He had, therefore, to leave, though he only consented to do so with a sad and heavy heart.

"They have had enough of me, here," he writes, "and now wish to drive me away. I must yield. . . . Strength fails me, and I find myself obliged to sacrifice an examination for which I am prepared, and which is just about to begin : I am forced, in a word, like a cowardly soldier, to forsake the standard before my time is expired. . . . Yet it must be so ! . . . ."

His state of health, however, caused him little anxiety, for he thought his indisposition would soon pass, and he quitted the seminary forming projects for study, which, if realized, would have made him spend a very useful and serious vacation.

"I should be unworthy of my clerical crown," he said, "if I passed three months and a half in laziness."

After a few days of repose he found himself in condition to continue again his preparation for the future. In his eagerness to advance, he would not believe that it was a heart disease with which he was affected.

"All that was necessary," he wrote full of joy, "was to break the course of that exciting life of the seminary, which was continually acting upon me and consuming me. How much I would regret to be forced to adopt such measures against this malady as would hinder me from pursuing that which my vocation demands of me. I see with unspeakable happiness that every day my fears are growing more groundless. I shall be able to employ my vocation as I so much desire to do.

"I should like to be able to tell you what attention and kindness I meet with on all sides here. I think often of the affections I have sacrificed, and compare them with those I find again : these thoughts bring with them both sadness and joy, and lead me to the love of God who appears so beautiful in the reflection of His goodness. It is my consolation and happiness to think that I too will soon have to pour out in my turn upon others all that kindness which I receive from those with whom providence puts me in contact. As I have often told you, my heart is naturally full of gratitude. The more I see of men, and the better I know what life is, the better, too, I understand what an inestimable blessing God has bestowed upon me by calling me to His service. If it had been otherwise, I feel that life would have been a dreadful sea of sadness, whilst now all is beautiful and perfect. . . . The infinite God Himself has given Himself to me, that I might give Him to others. Who will ever be able to understand this."

He studied during the vacation unceasingly. And when his doctor had made some observations about his too great ardor for work, he sent him the following lines in reply :

" If I sin by excess in the matter of which you speak again at such length in your letter, it will certainly not be for want of being warned. . . And yet I imagine that I put my trust purely and simply in Divine Providence, who can second my efforts and make me such as I should be, in order to represent the priesthood worthily. This is all my ambition. I do not desire to be learned or anything of that kind. But I remember that it is said of the priest : ‘Vos estes lux mundi.’ One must possess the light himself before he can enlighten others, and besides that charity which comes from God the priest ought to seek to possess the truth which convinces by its clearness and force. These thoughts, and the remembrance that I have sometimes seen the priestly character lowered by a visible ignorance and a want of largeness of mind is what pushes me on to study."

The time flew by too quickly, if we consider the task which he had imposed upon himself. "I would require," he wrote, " six months yet before entering upon theology." He read the ancient Philosphers and above all Plato, for whom he felt particular attraction ; " Plato, who fills me at once with delight and despair," he writes, "for I shall never have the time to get to the end of him."

He spent whole hours every day in the study of Holy Scripture, which he loved far above all the books of men.

The following is the account of his life and study during this vacation, which was the first after he had been in the Seminary.

" . . . . I love to call to mind every day of this year that I spent so happily at Issy. After these thoughts I always find some new reason for blessing God, who has made us all to love each other like brothers, and draw from union a force and fervor that I hope we will feel throughout our whole lives. . .

"I can lead a regular, calm, and collected life here. In the morning I go to hear Holy Mass and make my meditation in the church. I pass delicious hours there before Our Lord with the Soliloquies of St. Augustine near me, and a thousand thoughts of absent friends come floating into my head from all quarters ; that is as much as to say that I think much of Issy and in particular of you, who were my spiritual father there, and so kind and patient with me. I easily get through my other exercises during the day, and in the evening, from five to six o'clock, I go to renew again near Our Saviour the joys of the morning. Alas ! it is needless to tell you that on this picture, which I paint as so beautiful, many weaknesses cast their shadows, to say nothing of my many distractions, coldnesses and all that selfish part of our nature, which is always tending downwards, when it should be mounting on high.

"I can only excuse my delay in writing to you by allaying the greediness with which my mind seeks to satisfy its cravings. I found in the library the beautiful translation of Plato by Cousin, and I am devouring it, and have always to be dragged by the ears away from it. I find in it so true and deep a philosophy, and beauties so majestic in their antiquity that, wishing to take notes, I should go on copying all if I did not put a restraint upon myself. I pursue, too, with ever increasing pleasure my study of Holy Scripture. I have already analyzed up to the Books of

Wisdom, classifying all the texts which may serve for after use, and gathering together all the allusions, figures, and predictions which foretell Our Saviour Jesus Christ."

From this period also, of his life, dates the beginning of an undertaking which displays in forcible manner the activity and tenderness of his mind. He had been presented with a set of large ledgers in two volumes, to serve as a repertory, in which, under titles chosen and arranged by himself, he could gather the most striking and useful passages he met with in the course of his readings. I have enough here for my whole life, he said. His life, alas! was to be very short, and the books were very large. Yet he almost finished the whole of them, and a third volume had already been added to them, too.

We have these books before us, in which the studious youth amassed his treasures. One asks himself with astonishment how, with his usual studies, which were never neglected, he could ever have been able to do so much in less than two years. Everything is there arranged in order, and written in a hand steady and clear as his soul itself : an index, which remains unfinished, would have allowed him easy access to so rich a store. From the extracts, it is not hard to tell his favorite authors. His capacious mind seizes the true and beautiful wherever it meets it. Yet he evidently has his likings, and they are remarkable, for his rich intelligence knew how to draw from the right fountain-heads. **Plato, Saint** Augustine and Bossuet, are the names **we** meet most frequently. But the Bible is the book which he loved and meditated most : its texts fill the greatest part of the long columns of his repertory, and one sees how he forsook more and more the books of men for the Book of God. His whole soul is at times in the thoughts that suddenly strike him, and which he immediately notes down. We could not read, without being deeply moved, that sentence written in one of the last pages of his collection : " To be enamored of death,"—St. Ignatius, Martyr.

He generally contented himself with gathering the texts from which he hoped later on to draw some profit. At times, however, the words he had just written went home to his breast, and caused to burst forth some sparks of that fire which always burned within. Thus the word *Eucharist*, which he set as title at the head of a page, recalled the joys which the Holy Communion brought him, in these touching lines :

" O God! who made St. John the Baptist leap for joy whilst yet in his mother's womb : *Exultavit in gaudio infans in utero matris sua*, come come not only near me, but into me.

" *Et unde hoc mihi, veniat mater Domini mei ad me!* exclaims St. Elizabeth. And it is not only the mother that comes to us, but the Son of God whom she bore! . . .

" Zachary, at the birth of the Precursor, exclaimed : *Benedictus Dominus quia visitavit.* . .

" And I behold accomplished that which he only saw before.

" Mary sang her glory in bringing forth the Word of God : *Magnificat.* . . And I also carry you in my bosom: and my soul doth magnify You, as You, my God, do exalt it.

"The holy old man Simeon, upon receiving You into his arms, cried out in a transport of joy ; *Nunc dimittis. . .* And I my God, I receive You into my heart. Ah! I could die :—or rather no, let me live in order to merit so many favors."

The month of October witnessed Paul Seigneret's return to the seminary of Saint Sulpice at Paris. His malady, which the vacation had partially cured, had left behind it a dead pain at the heart, which was continually menacing him. He was determined, however, not to lose courage. "I feel confident about the future," he writes, "because without it my life would be absurd and without meaning."

Nevertheless, we cannot help noticing from this time forth a presentiment which carries sadness always with it, but which he soon overcomes by an act of pure submission to the will of God.

"I return to Saint Sulpice full of joy, and I might say penetrated with respect for the theological studies upon which I am about to enter. I am determined to throw myself heart and soul into the work before me. May God bring me to see the time when I may be useful to others, and . then, either everything is cruel illusion, and our nature knows no stability, or else I will devote my time, heart and life to God's service, as I have so often promised during the last eight or nine years. . . . There lies my brightest ambition, and it seems to me, the sole reason of my existence. Life, in fact, only appears to me beautiful and worthy of envy inasmuch as it is lit up by the idea of duty, and of the good that must be done before quitting the scene of our labors.   From the day of my priesthood a new life will begin for me, one of expansion, far different from that of these years of slow and difficult formation.   May I then employ each moment of the time accorded me, be it long or short, in showing abundantly those good actions which St. Bernard calls the seeds of eternity *"semina eternitatis !"* . . . The name of your old friend, written upon the book you sent me, reminds me too that our most lawful expectation must be relinquished, when there is question of the will of God, and that we must above all things make good use of the present, and nowise count upon the future, which is at best uncertain, unless it be at times to rouse our fervor.   My motto is the famous saying : *'Fais ce que dois, adrienne que pourra,' 'Do your duty, and come what may.'*   And should God refuse me those oft-wished for days, we know that we are but useless instruments in His hands, and cannot put forth the slighest claim to use.   Above all, purity of heart and a holy and ever growing love of God ; such are the dispositions in which I resume my broken studies."

At the Seminary of Paris, as at that of Issy, he spread around him the sweet perfume of his unpretending and amiable virtues.   We meet here the same regularity, the same strong and tender piety, the same charity towards his fellows, the same contempt of self, the same zeal for work ; or rather, all these virtues were gaining new strength and he was advancing day by day in the love of Jesus Christ and His Church, and ever growing more eager in his desire to devote himself to the work of the salvation of souls. To serve the Church, to save souls, to love God without measure and to forget self, such were the noble aspirations that filled the heart of the young seminarist and stirred up his fervor.

"God," he says "will without doubt make His Church triumph over modern society, by the Divine beauty of its doctrines and the zeal of its ministers. I feed myself on these hopes, and, in order to do all I can for their accomplishment, I renew every day before God my desire to forget myself and to love souls as He has loved them. And after all, in this life which passes quickly by under a sky so often clouded, there is nothing so beautiful or so desirable as to do good, and it is the hopes of accomplishing the good I propose, that even now brightens every one of my days, and lights up my whole future. This, too, is a hope of which I cannot be cheated, if in the midst of all the deceptions of the world I keep God on my side, and preserve the love of souls and contempt of self in my heart."

These thoughts were ever present to his mind and gave his virtue a character of the greatest simplicity. They were sufficient to spur him on to everything. They were the ordinary food of his piety and the subjects on which he loved most to meditate. With them the hour of morning meditation at Saint Sulpice seemed neither long nor weary.

During meditation he did not pursue long

trains of thought. He ordinarily put himself by a simple word in the presence of one of those thoughts which were the life of his soul,—the love of the Father who is in heaven, the charity of Jesus Christ, the beauty of devoting one's self to the salvation of others, the excellence of self-sacrifice. One of these subjects was sufficient to occupy his mind to great advantage, to fill him with the greatest joy, and leave him at the end of the meditation full of ardor, and ready to do all that God required of him.

He never felt the need or the inclination to draw out for himself one of these rules of life, which many souls aiming at perfection find it necessary to trace for themselves, and in which they mark out with precision the failings they must overcome, the virtues they must strive to gain, the means they will employ to reach these ends, and the special practice of piety they will adopt. Paul Seigneret left behind him nothing of this kind. But it was not because he neglected details, without which all perfection is impossible. No; he eagerly embraced on the contrary all the practices that are followed at the Seminary; he loved all the devotions which are there held in esteem. He would have received and observed the rules with the same readiness and fidelity, if they had seemed to him as hard as in reality they appeared easy. But he did all this without requiring to think of it, so to speak, and without drawing out any definite resolution, with regard to it. Everything was implied in these meaning words which we have already quoted : " God, the love of souls, contempt of self."

It was these lofty thoughts that roused and sanctified his ardor for the studies of the Seminary, whose necessity he so well understood: "I have already got some knowledge," he says after a few months, "of what grand and important questions we meet in the study of theology. In them I truly find one of the joys of my life, and a deep-felt pleasure which inspires me with gratitude towards God who has thus brought me to live on truth."

"Our Seminary life," he writes again, "is the time in which we must lay up our treasures. One would like to have giant arms and time at pleasure, in order to seize everything for the sake of those souls whom he already embraces at a distance, and to whom he would fain hold out, in order to gain them, all that is most beautiful, most winning and convincing."

His studies, which were always serious and pursued out of love for truth alone, soon began to correct the little inexactitudes still found in some of his ideas in consequence of his secular education, and they made him likewise foresee the mistakes into which the generosity of his heart and his burning desire to do good might otherwise have drawn him.

But though all these studies seemed to him full of beauty and afforded him delight, God inspired him with a special love for the Holy Word contained in the sacred books. It is in the following terms that he expresses his gratitude to the professor who had directed him in his studies of Holy Scripture.

"It is above all when absent, and living consequently mostly upon remembrances, that I feel it my duty to recall to mind all I owe you for the joys you have procured us, and the good which you have done to us. I acknowledge, for my part, that it is to you I am indebted for having my soul filled with those enrapturing beauties of Holy Scripture, which it can never more forget. I ask God to make me worthy of always enjoying this treasure which we should receive with tears of gratitude in our eyes, adoring Him who gave it. I often think of the gentleness and force we would require for the work of the sacred ministry if we did all in our power to correspond with the action produced on the intelligence, the will and the heart by the divine words which penetrate and move us like the rays of the infinite Beauty and Goodness."

It was in the Gospel above all that he found his delight. He worked assiduously at a concordance of the four Gospels, which he was making for his own use, and which he finished and drew out with wonderful care. Later on, during the long and weary days, when the war and sickness kept him powerless at home, he found his greatest consolation in pushing forward a long work which he had undertaken on the New Testament. In it he viewed Jesus Christ under the various aspects in which he is represented to us in these holy books, and classed under each of the titles applied to our Divine Lord, the most remarkable passages in which

they are contained.   This work afforded him endless pleasure.

"Our Saviour," he wrote to a friend who
shared his tastes, and took part in his work,—"our
Saviour has invited us both to the same feast.   I
cannot tell you how much joy I find in this work.
I have often to upbraid myself with a want of
regularity in my studies: I sometimes remain
four or five hours ruminating on the divine
words of which my mind is full.   Jesus Christ,
the everlasting Comforter; Jesus Christ, the
joy of the world: Jesus Christ, the Physician of
souls.   What beautiful things these words disclose to us."

But those who penetrated further into his
heart were happy to see him advancing with so
firm and resolute a step towards that at which he
now felt assured it was God's will that he should
aim.   They saw clearly that his enthusiasm and
the burning words which sometimes escaped from
his heart were only the simple and natural result
of true, deep-rooted sentiments, which would
stand the trial of real life; and they thought
with happiness of the good this young apostle
would be able to do, if God granted him a little
of that future for which he so much longed.
How well he would have been able, for instance,
guided by his broad and lofty mind, and with
the help of those delicate, poetical figures, in
which he loved to clothe his thoughts, to have
gone straight to the hearts of the young men
of his own age, and have made that religion,
with which he himself was ravished, appear beau-

tiful and lovely to them.   How easily he would
have gained them with that heart of love, which
made him one day cry out in transports of gratitude :

"It is so beautiful to be kind ; how ungrateful
I would be, if I did not one day give myself en·
tirely to others, since every one has been so kind
to me."

Kindness, benevolence, gentleness, nothing.
charmed him more than these amiable qualities,
and, in his artlessness and generosity, he imagined that nothing could draw more powerfully
to the truth those who had the misfortune of
being deprived of it, than the beauty of these
three virtues.   He was grieved whenever he saw
amongst men, in their intercourse with each
other, anything which was opposed to the spirit of
charity and gentleness, and he set before himself, as his rule of conduct, those beautiful words
which were addressed by the Sovereign Pon-
tiff to the Abbé Henri Perreyve : "*Strike the
errors boldly, but have a mother's heart for the
men.*"

We have met often in the papers of Paul Seigneret the name of Henri Perreyve. A kindred
sympathy of feeling united their two hearts
together, and a comparison between them has at
once presented itself to the minds of those who
knew both well.   The humble seminarist of Saint
Sulpice had of course scarcely begun life, and it
is but imperfectly that we can compare the flower
in bloom with the bud which only gives us promises.   But in the great family of priests, both

belonged to that chosen band, whose mission seems to be to surround the priesthood, in the eyes of the world, with a halo of beauty and honor. It was the same flame that burnt within their hearts and consumed the earthly shroud that covered them. The one as well as the other found in his vocation to the priesthood "the joy of joys," the only reason of his life.* When we read those beautiful pages on the "*Love of men*," which have come forth from the heart of Henri Perreyve, we, who have had a near view of him whose life we write, can recognize his soul in every line; in mind and heart and in the noble ambition of doing good, Paul Seigneret appears to us the brother of Henri Perreyve.

The weeks and months rolled quickly by in the seminary where he loved so well to live, and where he employed his time to such advantage. But the young Seminarist began to feel earlier than in the preceding year, in the beginning of May, the dreaded presence of that disease which had got root in his heart, and now made itself known by its violent attacks. He struggled on as long as he could, but had at last once more to yield, and depart with sorrow at heart and tears in his eyes. "It is just as I expected; all is settled; I must be off. It is an order that rends my heart— and yet I must resign myself. . . It is needless to tell you how much interest every one takes in me. It would seem to be my lot to be over-

* *Henri Perreyve*, by the Pere Gratry, page 174.

whelmed with kindness, and be able to make no return. . . Remember me in your prayers. It will be so hard in every way to make anything good of me." He left for Lons-le-Saunier, whither his father had been called to occupy the post of Inspector of the Academy de Jura, and where he had fixed his residence. The doctors, who were seriously alarmed, declared that a whole year of rest at home would be necessary. But the young seminarist could not yet pursuade himself that the future was altogether shut against him. He saw no doubt that the horizon was narrowing, but this did not frighten him, and he hoped that God would still reserve for him the joy of a few days devoted to His service.

"I look at the future without anxiety," he wrote when leaving; "I see that God is always there, that He smiles at me and draws me on towards Him. Besides, I do not ask that my bones should grow old; I only wish to have the time to do a little good and pour out upon those around me all the kindness and love that I have received from God and men, and which seems to have been shown to me only on condition that I should transmit it to others again. Give me but one short year in which I can serve God, and I will die content."

That was the hope to which he now fondly clung, and upon it he built the plans he drew out for himself, which were far different from those proposed to him by others. In the month of June he thus makes known his situation and the line of conduct which it leads him to adopt. "Every one, doctors, directors, parents, all want me to interrupt my studies for the next year. I do not know if it will please God to make me escape the dangers of this conspiracy, which is formed by those who love me. As for me, I take a very simple view of the matter. One must be blind not to see how few years, in all human probability, I have before me. A late overgrowth has exhausted my strength : I am now five feet ten inches in height. The more I think of all this, the more I would like to have this year which our good God may yet give me, that I may be able to do the good which I so much long to accomplish. It is a short and precious period which I must not let slip past. I have only two more years at the Seminary. Could I not reach the end and then give myself with my whole heart for a short time to the service of those whom God has loved so well! This is my constant desire and my greatest ambition. I leave all certainly to the will of God, but at the same time I ask Him to let me do a little to satisfy my longings. I have always said that the saving of one soul would be a greater recompense than I deserve for all the efforts of my life ; to die after that, would it not be to fall asleep in peace ? "

He did all he could to obtain a decision in accordance with his wishes. He besought his uncle to come to his aid, and with this view wrote the following letter :

" I cannot look without trembling at the prospect of this year which the doctors at Paris as well as the doctor here, condemn me to pass out of the Seminary. I think that, if Providence does not intervene, this remedy will prove more baneful than the active life of preparation for the future—for that future after which I long above all things . . . I am already seriously affected with aneurism of the heart, which ruins my chest by the blood it makes me lose. . . The doctor at Paris, who thought he could tell me the truth, when he would perhaps have hidden it from others, gave me clearly enough to understand that I would not hold out very long : all that can be done is to prolong my life for a few useless years, by keeping far from me all exertion or fatigue. But, my dear uncle, put yourself in my place, in the place of any man of spirit, who found himself in such circumstances. Is it not a hundred times better to march on, and die upon the beach, than to drag out my life listlessly, a burden to myself and every one else ? I hate an unprofitable life.

"I put such confidence in the generosity of your heart, my dear uncle, that though I know your tender love would rather perhaps incline you to do for me what seems better in the eyes of the world, I trust you will support me in doing that which appears to me most profitable and best. And do not be at all grieved at the thought of what has happened to me. You know that nothing charmed me in this world but the love of God and the thought of working a little for His glory, and the good of men, If I cannot labor as I desire, to love is ever in my power, and this is more than sufficient to fill my heart. I will have to thank God without ceasing, who, by even smiling at me in the midst of my sorrows, has brightened my life, and been the strength and joy of my youth. I had certainly fondly hoped to make you, who have loved me so well, rejoice at seeing the zeal with which I did all the good in my power. But if God refuses me this happiness, He who is the source of all good, who inspires and rewards all true affection, can recompense you better than I could have done."

But, notwithstanding his resistance, it was settled that he should take for a year that rest which was absolutely necessary for him ; and obedience made him accept the remedy which was for him a sacrifice. He announced to one of his companions of St. Sulpice, on the 12th July, 1870, in the following terms, the determination at which his parents had arrived :

"Next year, the year of my Subdeaconship, you will all come back I hope to begin that Seminary life, whose unspeakable charm we can never better understand than when we are absent. As for me, I regret that I shall not be able to be with you. I thank God that I can tell you this with the calmness and resignation I now feel in doing so. Only eight days ago I turned away from this thought with loathing, as from a cup too bitter for me to drink, and the very idea of such a trial made me cry like a child, and more than once it was impossible for me to hide the tears that flowed from my eyes. Now all is decided, and I am resigned.... Since the matter has been thus settled, I have drawn out for myself my line of conduct:—to think no more of the future, for longing after it consumes me and it now seems distant and uncertain : to keep close to Our Lord, the Comforter and Strength of souls, and by loving Him, more to seek compensation for the Sacrifice which I shall have to make, if I am not able to draw others to love Him ; lastly, to lead a life resembling that of a religious in the cloister, thanking God for the favors I have already received in too great abundance, and waiting patiently for the accomplishment of his designs upon me."

Every sentence that the pious youth wrote, during the first months that followed his departure from the Seminary derives from the circumstances in which he was placed, a tinge of gentleness and sadness, something at once simple and solemn, that makes a deep impression upon us, and charms us with its beauty. Everything in this world appeared to him in the light of which the great thoughts of death and eternity throw upon human life ; and he looked upon all with the calm and serenity of a child of God, who would no doubt have wished to make his heavenly Father known and loved here below, but who after all will be happy to go and see him soon. In some of the pages that he wrote under the influence of these thoughts, there are beauties which we cannot pass over unnoticed.

In the diary in which he had proposed to write down day by day his thoughts, we read these lines. bearing the date of 23d May, 1870:

"God only knows if I shall read these lines again ; He alone can say if they will be continued and come in after years like a far-off echo, to awaken once more the thoughts of the past, or if death will make me leave them unfinished, by bursting the heart that prompts them. I put all with most loving submission at the disposal of the will of God ; I wish nothing, I long for nothing in the world, but the full accomplishment of His divine decrees concerning me. I desired as much as man could desire, a future sufficient to let me do some good. There are two things to be done here below ; to love God and bring men to love Him. If God does not let me perform the second, I have still only to bless Him always for having brought me to taste the sweetness of the first. Perhaps He has designed to take me off in the purity of my desires, and to give me for my only title to reward that name which was the glory of Daniel : *Vir desideriorum.* At the thought I am tempted to cry out ; O happy, happy lot ! and yet I feel in my heart a weight of sadness that *I carry with* me everywhere. Grant, O my God, that I may relinquish all my own wishes more completely. I feel joyful, and yet full of sadness. There is something in my heart which tells me that there is no future for me.

"Tuesday, 31st May. To-day ends the month of May which I hailed with so much joy, and began in utter ignorance of all that was to happen to me. I only thought of turning to greater profit the graces and the life of the Seminary. God has ordered it otherwise. Such is life. One day, however fair it may be, gives us no assurance for the mor-row ; and death often overtakes us after our re-joicings. *Vigilate et orate.* Death, which terrifies our nature, and which is nevertheless so sweet in it-self, *the possession of God for all eternity.* This evening the young maidens sang in clear voices a parting farewell till their meeting next year at Mary's feet. How many of them, and how many out of all those spectators, will be wanting when the time of meeting comes ! Perhaps I, my God, will be miss-ing. This thought saddens me at once and fills me with joy. But I submit all without reserve to the divine will, and only allow myself one humble prudent prayer, to die rather than lead a useless life.

"My present state," he writes about the same time, "helps me always to keep eternity in sight ; eternity, the thoughts of which elevates man here below, and is to him a safeguard. Far from sad-dening one's life, it throws upon it a brighter light, and is an inexhaustible source of consolation and strength. Ever to walk with one eye fixed upon heaven, to take no part in things of this world unless it be to make others happy as far as I can without looking for self in anything ; that is my rule and the rule of every Christian. I ob-serve it, alas ! but imperfectly, and yet it ever at-tracts me by its simple, supernatural beauty.

"You remember," he says to his director, "the words in which I used to find an antidote to every evil : *it will pass.* But I confess that I scarcely ever utter them, unless through an in-stinctive need of driving away from me all sadness with regard to what may befall me. In reality I put very little belief in them ; and the longer I live the more I ponder over the great thoughts of life, and the more clearly I think I perceive that the future is shut against me. But I think of that without the slightest sorrow, unless it be that I grieve at the pain I may cause to those who love me, and regret that I shall not be able to do the good I have so much desired to perform. But I ask God for those whom I may afflict by a spirit of faith, by which they will rejoice in whatever befalls me, and then, as regards the good I wished to do, since God seems not to deem me worthy of accomplishing it, how much ought I not to bless His goodness who will gather me to Himself, perhaps before my time, after having made me experience the joys of His divine love, without letting me undergo the trials that He requires we should endure in return. But I am entertaining you with *thoughts of the grave.* Yet how can I hide from you the reflections which are ever uppermost in my mind. I put all, however, with most loving confidence into the hands of our Heavenly Father, without any thoughts of discouragement or surrender, and without ceasing to continue my preparation for the future with the same zeal as if it were in every way certain."

In a touching, though more familiar tone, he addresses the same thoughts, stamped with a like gentle calmness, to his brother Charles, whose lofty soul was able to appreciate this grandeur.

"I am laboring under no illusion ; I still spit blood ; whether that comes from the heart or from

the chest, it is no good sign. My heart sometimes
nearly stifles me. I tell you this because you can
judge of life, and know how wretched and worthless it is. There is no doubt that the future is shut
against me, and it is useless to worry myself with
longings. One thing gives me composure, it is
that, if any misfortune overtakes me, you know my
feelings and my character sufficiently to be able
to say:—He is really happy. Nothing captivated
me so much in life as the thoughts of doing good;
the hope is now vanishing, and I have nothing
left to do but to love you with my whole heart, and
above all God whom I shall have to bless for all
eternity, for having let me taste the delights of
true love. It will, perhaps, seem strange to say this,
but I am too full of such thoughts not to speak
of them to you. I trust that the greatness of your
soul and the loftiness of your ideas, will not allow
all this to sadden you. It is a mere question of
time. One day sooner or later will end all."

" How thankful I am, my dear Charles," he says
again a few days later, " for the ever growing interest you take in my welfare ! I beg of you not to
trouble yourself about me ; my greatest sorrow
would be to make you sad. As for myself, I enjoy
the most perfect tranquillity. The only pangs that I
feel in my heart come from the thought that I
might leave this world without. doing anything
for those who have loved me so well, anything
for God who has been the strength and the joy
of my youth, anything for men towards whom I
have contracted so many debts by the kindness
I have always received from them. There are

my only sad thoughts. Besides, I trust sufficiently in the special Providence of God upon every one of us, to believe that whatever comes to me from Him will be that which is most desirable for me. If the time for doing good is taken from me, it is because I am not worthy of it."

The greatest consolation that he found in his solitude and separation, was to return in spirit to the Seminary ; he found the source of that interior life which his soul required. He wished still to continue his relations with St. Sulpice, and loved to join, though absent, in all that was done there for the great interests he had so deeply at heart. An ordination was to take place shortly after his return to his family. Though he would not have taken part in it, his habit of viewing all things by whatever appeared great and noble in them, inspired him on the occasion of this ceremony with the most sublime thoughts, and urged him to the most earnest prayer. He saw already the great day on which he would be subdeacon, he pictured to himself the emotions of those who had the happiness of giving themselves irrevocably to God, the joys they would that day feel, and how they would be renewed at waking on the morrow, and would accompany them throughout their whole life ; he desired to participate in the fruit of their first prayers as subdeacons, and raising his soul above men who pass, he looked with enraptured gaze at the divine and imperishable work of the Catholic priesthood, which is so necessary to the world, and yet so independent of individuals, and so sure of finding, by the call of God, souls who will make no

account of sacrificing themselves and all they
possess.

"Through longing to take part in this great
work of good in the world, I, poor creature, like the
fly in the fable,* as if all depended upon me, will
soon begin to think it a loss for it—a slight one no
doubt, but still a loss—if I am obliged to relinquish my share in it.   Humility will do away with
all that, I think.   How true it is that we are naught
but useless servants whom God may call away,
and change without losing thereby a tittle of the
good He wishes to realize? Everything here below
passes and disappears like a shadow, the word of
God alone remains, the word of God not neglected
and despised, but always winning to itself souls all
on fire with love, and ready to devote themselves
to the work of bringing others to know it. O divine
consolation! O everlasting priesthood! Its work
does not perish like the men who take part in it ;
and he who dies before his time, worn out with
toil and suffering, passes to others the flame of
divine love, which he was charged to keep burning, breathes out his soul in joy, feeling sure that
God will be glorified, that Jesus Christ will con-
quer, and that many souls will be saved by others
who will crown the work which he labored to complete and continued with so much zeal.

"It is thus that I speak to myself,—in order to
accustom my soul to look at things from a higher
point of view. I desire much less to seek the

* Fables of La Fontaine. The fly, pricking the horses and
making them run, thinks that the drawing of the coach should
be attributed to him. (Translator.)

realization of the little good I might be able to perform, than to see the accomplishment of all the good which I know God wishes to achieve in the world : *Adveniat reguum tuum.* That is the desire before which every other wish and every other thought of self, would disappear. On this depends, not only the order of the world and the harmony that should exist between God and us, but likewise the true happiness of individuals, and the stability of human society. Have you read the account of the International Society, which is growing so powerful and will be so formidable in the future. How much suffering to be soothed, what unhappy ambition to be moderated, what divine light must be scattered there to change these men ! Who can stop them, if not God, who gives morals to man and holds him in awe of His power and draws him to Himself by the expectation of a better life ? He who sees all the evils that surge around us, and the storms that threaten to break over us, can in His kindness enlighten and carry off for his service a still greater army of noble youths who have no attachment to the world, whose hearts burn with love, whose minds are lofty, and who will become the bearers of the Gospel-peace, who will be able to make the name of Jesus Christ adored, though it is now so unjustly despised, and will reconcile to Him so many souls more unhappy than they are guilty. This is one of the thoughts to which I love most to return. There are so many souls around us who would be full of ardor for the things of God if, in consequence of those prejudices, and that ignorance about religious matters, so common now-a-days, Jesus Christ had not to say to them, as He said of old to the woman of Samaria : *Si scires donum Dei.* If you knew who I am, the divine beauty of my religion and the incomprehensible delights of my love, how everything would fade away before your eyes ! How gladly you would fall down at my·feet in the transports of love which would know no end and never count with difficulties ! . . . ."

It was thus that his noble mind and generous heart soared aloft, without effort, to those regions of supernatural thought, in which he loved to dwell, and where all the miseries of this world, even those that afflict us most, viewed in the light of God, led him to admire and bless Him who in His justice, permits them, and Who too, in His goodness, knows how to apply the remedy that will heal them.

It might be thought that this youth, as yet only on the threshold of the sanctuary, had formed beautiful and dazzling illusions about the reality of the priestly life and fruits of zeal, and that his imagination bore a great part in the grandeur of ideas, and the poetry of his sentiments. No doubt long years of experience had not as yet brought him to maturity. But the qualities of the young soldier, who has not yet engaged, are not the same as those of the warrior who has grown old in the battle-fields. The latter takes a cool view of things, and weighs exactly the difficulties or the chances of success. The former is burning with ardor, which, linked with a love and zeal for discipline, makes the chosen soldier, and on the day of battle, the hero.

This control of a rule which is loved and followed with generosity, was never wanting to Paul Seigneret in the midst of all his ardent aspirations. Though full of grand thoughts and noble desires, he knew how to offer up to God those little daily sacrifices which can never be undergone by souls who are merely carried off by enthusiasm, and whose virtue has got no depth. We have seen how he received with simplicity, and unswervingly fulfilled all the observances of community-life. When out of the Seminary, his greatest delight was to follow the exercises that were practised there; and in the midst of his sufferings he traced for himself a life of prayer and study, by means of which he put his time to as great profit as he could have done in his beloved little room at Saint-Sulpice. It is in the following terms that he makes known to his spiritual director how he employed his days of sickness.

"June 13th, 1870.—In the morning.—What will you say when I tell you that I am generally in the church from five till six o'clock? The reason is because, during my best nights, I have only four hours sleep, and the Doctor himself is of opinion that, in this beautiful weather, I suffer less when out of bed, and I must say that I see with so much gratitude the day coming on, that I am forced to go and tell my thankfulness to God in that old church-choir, where all the joys of past generations seem to come into my heart. . . I do not grow tired there, for I am nearly always seated, and I divide my time between Mass and meditation, now thinking with Bossuet, and then leaving him to dive

into those unfathomable thoughts of the designs of
God upon us,—thoughts that make me thrill with
delight far more than all the glories of this world.

"I open my day in this way : I take an hour of
Holy Scripture, and find this a pleasant and re-
freshing occupation ; I read a sermon of Bourda-
loue, where I always meet something to note. I
study Church History, recite the office of the
Blessed Virgin, and run through the newspapers
which I confess I greedily devour. In the evening
I go back to the church from five till six o'clock :
and last of all, before going to bed, I look over my
day's work and then read a chapter of the Imitation.
This last is an old practice and one that has always
afforded me the greatest consolation. After that
I thank God for giving me still, days that are
somewhat full. I do not tire myself. My heart
rises towards God of its own accord. When it
does not, I help it on with a little reading."

By means of the lively correspondence which
he kept up with his directors and fellow-students,
he was able, as he said, to carry the Seminary
about with him :

"There is nothing that gives me so much happiness as letters from Saint-Sulpice. They make
me remember the studies and the great thoughts
which should be uppermost in one's mind at the
Seminary ; they recall to me my engagements, my
wants, my enthusiasms, and a thousand secret wishes
which lie hidden in my heart. Oh ! may I never
lose sight of all these things, may I ever find in
them my delights, and live on them as long as it
will please God to deprive me of that invigorating

life which we find in the Seminary, or wherever else we are working strenuously in the service of our Maker. This is my daily prayer; it is this which I ask in my communions and oftentimes throughout the day because I feel that it gives me strength and new life and keeps me in union with God."

His gratitude towards those whom God made use of to do him good was without bounds. He eagerly seized the occasion of telling them, in the warmest terms, how much he was touched by their kindness; and if he could not have the pleasure of expressing to them his thankfulness, he did so to himself. We find for instance, in the note-book in which he put down for his own benefit his inmost thoughts, the following lines written after he had received a letter from his spiritual director:

" Received from M. N—— the first letter.—A first letter causes so many emotions. In it one meets again all past kindnesses, and experiences an indefinable feeling of joy, on having received this new mark of friendship, mixed with regret that the friend himself is absent. . . . I feel the necessity of writing to M. N—— just as I felt the necessity of writing to my father; the same relations, those between father and son, exist between us. He has become the confidant of the secrets of my soul, and knows them far better than he could know them by our letters, which are always too rare."

So many happy qualities of mind and heart, displayed amongst a number of young men, such as fill a Seminary, could not fail to draw gently towards him, those of his fellow-students who were able to know and understand him best. And we see that, at the end of his first two years, he had already contracted those pure and holy friendships, which we form with others by mutually offering all that is best and noblest in us, those friendships of which God is the firmest link, and which, being based upon our common desires of raising ourselves to Him, and a like view of the means we must employ to attain that end, we double our strength in the difficult undertaking.

Those who have had the happiness of being connected by these closer ties with Paul Seigneret, will no doubt gladly recall this as one of the things in their life of which they will cherish most the remembrance. And from his glorious tomb, or rather from heaven, where he does not cease to love them, this saintly friend will still speak to them : *Defunctus adhuc loquitor.* He will address to them some of those touching words which he knew how to utter, they will hear his persuasive, voice, that so often urged them on to good, and which joined to his example, was for them, as many have often said, the most efficacious preaching.

These truly brotherly connections inspired him with the most beautiful lines that he has perhaps written. He never wrote anything unmeaning or frivolous to his friends, but with them he felt at ease, and his soul would give vent to those tender manly sentiments with which he was filled, to those beautiful thoughts which he knew how to gather every where, and express often in a most charming manner. And all that was, as it were, clothed and impregnated with the love of God. His holy name adorns and sanctifies all that he writes.

"God is so good," he says, "to have made us love each other, and love each other in such a way, that in the midst of our affections His divine charity should always increase in us more and more."

In these few lines he gives us the character of his affections, and at the same time unwittingly explains why every one can admire and feel all that he wrote to his most intimate friends.

A month after he had left the Seminary, he wrote to one of them in these terms :

"I am longing to give you, in my absence, the first mark of that strong and tender affection which you know I bear you, and which God has made use of to raise my soul to Him, and make me love more and more all that is good and noble. I thank Him for these past joys, for your kind sympathy, for our common desire to do good, now that, being left more alone with my heart, I see with gratitude what strength, what life they brought to my soul. Oh! yes, my dear friend, God, who is so beautiful in all His works is above all surpassingly beautiful in the affection he inspires, and in that thirst after what is good, which we have felt in common. That is one of my chief thoughts now that, being separated from so many I loved, I can see how God gives Himself to souls through those in whom He reflects His beauties, and with whom He has deigned always to surround me."

" Thank God," he says again, " friendships such as those of the Seminary, formed as they are under the eyes of God, become too holy, and are too well sustained by our common love for Him, to be but for a day, like so many others. It is a real blessing, for which we must thank God, without, however forgetting to show our gratitude to man likewise, to be thus able to renew our strength in fortifying affections, then above all, when sadness threatens to creep in upon us. Let us bless God then, who is so amiable in the affections He inspires, and who makes us find such joy here below in loving one another :—it is a sweet foretaste of the future happiness which we shall find in the fulness of love."

After the beautiful letter that we have just cited, we offer to the reader one full of playful talk about vacation, redolent at first of poetry and piety, and then becoming little by little, under the pen of the angelic young man, a beautiful meditation, in which he pours out the love and adoration that overflows his heart. It is dated from Lons-le-Saunier, 4th July, 1870.

"My very dear friend, I have put off writing to you until the vacation began, because I thought that your emotions at leaving Saint-Sulpice, and the joy of finding yourself again in the bosom of your family, would make you remember, with greater pleasure, a friend who comes to take part in your happiness. And certainly the beginning of vacation brings with it a succession of delightful days. The impressions they produce upon me do not lesson as years roll on. Our hearts are like to burst and yet we are happy,—happy with a joy which heaven and earth, parents and friends, the past and future seem to take part in producing, and the thought of God is there to crown all. We can appreciate better at a distance the charms of life in the Seminary, though we are nearly unconscious of them when there ; and we bless God who has put us in contact with so many noble souls that grow ripe there in His presence, and who are burning to do good, who encourage us and rouse our zeal. We feel we possess the affection of all those dear to us at home, and this is the sweetest happiness God has given to us on earth. And lastly, quite surprised and full of childlike admiration, we find again that eversmiling nature, with which we were enraptured formerly in youth, and which will charm us again in the decline of our days, if God brings us to old age.

"In thus calling back my own emotions, I am sure I am expressing yours ; it is the same tale for all young loving hearts.

"You have your beautiful Normandy, with the pleasure of finding, no doubt, at every step something that reminds you of the first transport of your heart, whilst admiring the beauty of God in the world. Happy those who never leave the place of their childhood ! . . .

"But I am not badly off either in my quarter of the world. An open field, the sun, and a blue sky would be quite enough to create for me most delightful scenery. I have, however, something superior to that. There is not far off a height that overlooks the town, and I have not been able to resist the temptation of going there four or five times already, walking very slowly, and yet almost out of breath. I was there only yesterday evening as the sun was setting, and, seated on that bare hill-top, I thought of God, of men, of you : of Saint-Sulpice which is now being deserted, of that future which passes quickly and then becomes eternal,—in a word I thought of everything. For our thoughts run free and know no bounds in presence of so much beauty, when we stand under so magnificent an expanse of heaven, whilst the wind is blowing and no other sound is heard. On one side is the Jura, which piles up its shelving rocks upon its rugged basis ; on the other are all the riches of nature, and as far as the eye can reach the fertile plains of Burgundy stretch themselves out like the sea, till they meet the sky on the horizon. At my feet lies Lons, basking in the sun, and, all around, resting on the slopes and nestled in the vineyards are the villages, betraying themselves only by their streaks of smoke and the distant sounds they send us. Five or six old ruins crown the heights, and add a new charm to the beauty and everlasting freshness of nature, and, at the same time, bring to our mind the thoughts of past generations, and make us remember the frailty of everything human. Ah, what peace, my dear friend, what an atmosphere of joy reigns over those plains, which seem to lie wrapt in an ecstasy of gratitude to God ! Ah! yes ; if God had not made us to be happy, He would never have given us this beautiful abode, into which the sorrows without number, that now crush poor human mortals, should never have found their way.

" Formerly I would have stopped at these reflections, and been content to adore the divine beauty whose traces were visible in the world. But now, thank God, this is only the starting-point ; it is impossible not to rise higher. Before such a sight, the thought of the other world immediately presents itself,—of that other world which is infinitely more beautiful, infinitely more full of the sovereign munificence of God. There is another Sun which has shone upon this land, and filled the whole earth with supernatural joy,—Jesus Christ, who was hailed from afar as the light of nations ; Jesus Christ, who can alone explain and take away that perplexing contradiction existing between these appearances of happiness and the miseries of men ; Jesus Christ, who descends into the very furrows of the earth, to bring joy to the least of its laborers ; Jesus Christ, a thousand times more quickening than the sun of this world. Let men not say that our God is a hard God, and that He cannot be reached unless by chosen souls. You, who have suffered so much for the salvation of souls, you have then suffered to no avail ; and will it be that those souls, whom you have loved so well, can gain anything by the price of your blood ! No ; your blood and your grace will sink into the hearts of men, and, thanks to your providential care, will make them fertile, more than the warmth and dew of heaven can fructify the earth ; and this land, which you have made so rich, this atmosphere of happiness which you have spread over it, all that cannot be compared to the work that you have accomplished with your cross, or the unspeakable felicity you hold in store for those who love you.

"O Holy Father! the light and the joy of men, with what reverence we adore you! How we would wish in our love for you to have the everlasting steadfastness of these mountains, that seem to bow down to adore you in your beautiful heaven above! To think that I, a worthless wretch of a weak vacillating heart, to think that I am called to speak of you to men, to bend down their hearts before your unspeakable beauty! You have conquered the world by your love. Yesterday, on the top of that hill I read this in Jesus Christ's farewell to His disciples: *Pater, venit hora; clarifica filium tuum ut filius tuus clarificet te. Et nunc clarifica me tu, Pater, claritate quam habui prius quam mundus esset apud te:* Father the hour is come: let Thy beauty, my bounty, which nails me to the wood of the cross, burst forth in the midst of my sacrifice. I shall be a thousand times more beautiful there dying for men; My infinite goodness will be a thousand times more clearly known than when I created the universe.

"And knowing the heart of man, and foreseeing the future, you have said again: *Cum exaltatus fuero a terro, omnia traham ad meipsum.* Yes, yes, the heart of humanity is irrevocably yours! O holy words of the Gospel, you praise and light up our hearts like the days of eternal beauty! . . .

" How could we stand in the presence of such things, and not be lost in the thought of God, in whom alone we can find an explanation for this world ; of Jesus Christ, who is the perfection of its beauty. I pictured to myself our Saviour with His apostles in the midst of the multitude, seated like myself, on the slopes of the mountain, but in far-off Judæa, and there, with that picturesque and lovely country spread out before Him, inflaming their hearts with love for His Heavenly Father, and rousing the zeal of His disciples for the conversion of the human race, by representing it to them under images borrowed from the scene beneath His eyes : *Videte regiones quia albæ sunt jam ad messem,—messis quidem multa...*—Or again, He is proposing to them the parable of the sower or speaks of the providence of God Who feeds the birds of the air and clothes the lilies of the field with so much beauty that not even Solomon in all his glory was arrayed as one of them, or of a thousand other things which delight, beyond expression, all those who listen to Him.

" O my dear friend, whether we meet with success or adversity, whether we are in good health or ill, what a happiness it is thus to catch a glimpse of the ravishing beauty of God ! How I reproach myself every day for loving Him so little, and yet unhappily my reproaches do not make me better ! Let us pray for each other, for this will be our best consolation."

Whilst the saintly young man, detaching his heart from the things of earth, thus soared aloft in the regions of peace and love, the serious events

that were taking place in the country came to give
a new turn to his thoughts, and to kindle again his
passion for self-sacrifice and make it burst forth
in another form. The disastrous war of 1870
was going on, and the honor of France was fool-
ishly set up to be contended for, and her fate to
be decided by the issue of battle. No name
after that of God and His Church made the heart
of Paul Seigneret beat so quick as the name of
his country. He followed with a feverish anxiety
the account of France's misfortunes which followed each other in rapid succession.

He felt his heart swell with enthusiasm, when,
at the beginning of the struggle, he saw "so many
heroic young men come forward and offer to sacrifice themselves for the common good." And
being unable to imitate them, he consoled himself with the hope that his health would soon permit him to continue again his preparation for a
state of life in which he too could sacrifice himself to interests of a still higher order, to the interests of souls.

"The hidden life of self-sacrifice which the
priest embraces," he writes 26th July, "can alone
keep me from coveting the glorious sacrifice which
the soldier makes of himself. And I thank God with
my whole heart, that I am able with new strength
to follow the call which He has given me, now
that a sacred duty requires that so many of my
fellow-countrymen should devote themselves without reserve, to the service of their country."

At the beginning of the vacation, before
the misfortunes of France had come to fill all hearts

with sadness, he was invited to make a tour which would have given him great pleasure, and would have contributed much, it was hoped, to the complete restoration of his health. After expressing his thankfulness for so kind an offer, and giving the reason which obliged him to decline it, he added : " And after all, even if these obstacles were not in the way, I could never consent to make a tour which would naturally cause me great pleasure, at a time when so many noble youths, whose lot I should share were I able, make the greatest sacrifices in order to maintain the safety and defend the honor of our country ! Heroic youths ! What generosity, what joy they must experience in thus sacrificing themselves ! How many there are who laugh and sing to-day, and who to-morrow will be numbered with the dead. This death will not be known ; they will only have lived to give their life for the public weal. Oh ! how much I envy them their happy lot ! Life is of so little worth that it must be a real happiness to find an opportunity of making a noble and ready sacrifice of it. But I do not forget that God has also required my life of me that I should dedicate it to His service, to be continually employed for the good of souls. Now, more than ever, I am urged on by an imperious necessity to consecrate it, though in a different way, to that common weal which I see calls forth so much noble generosity.

" In a few months, if God wills it, you will be able to change the present that you wished to send me, into another which you have promised —that of my breviary. . . . ."

He betook himself to work—in the hope that by continually keeping his mind entirely employed, he would thus calm a little the ardor of those desires which burned in his heart. He composed about this time a sermon which he intended to present on his entry into the Seminary, if it should please God that he should return there again. The subject he chose, as well as the manner in which he viewed it, shows us what were the ordinary tendencies of his mind, and the thoughts on which he loved to meditate. It was our love for the Church, proposed as the best expression of the love which we ought to have for God and man.

· "In the midst of all the sadness and misery through which we pass," he writes while engaged in this work, "it makes us happy to reflect a little on those grand thoughts of justice, peace and universal love, which have so completely changed the world during the last eighteen hundred years, and which even now make us hope for a better future."

"Another lesson," he says again, on 19th Aug., 1870, speaking of his hopes and consolations, "another lesson that we should draw from what we see happening around us, is how to sacrifice all when duty calls us. We have now before us a thousand noble examples of men who practice this heroic virtue. May I never forget them, or may I never have to blush when I compare what so many men have done for mere earthly interests with what I myself have done in the holiest of causes !

"As the vacation advances I become more

painfully anxious to know what will become of me next year. I can scarcely endure the thought of discontinuing my studies, and losing a year of that life in which I should gain so much merit. I feel really better, and this makes me ask myself if I am obliged to sacrifice any time through fear of accidents which perhaps will never happen. Should not duty rather urge us always to work on as long as we have strength left, without troubling ourselves about the future, of which no one can be sure ! My parents, of course, do not yield to such reasoning. I leave all in the hands of God ; He will determine everything in his own good time. My consolation, in the midst of all these troubles, whether great or small, is to betake myself to God and to my work in which I find a real pleasure. In this way we can live in a higher world and one which makes us forget for a time the miseries of earth : we there find again those ideas of justice, right and universal love, which are so unworthily outraged here below, and by which, nevertheless, this world should be governed. But I am not a pessimist, and I hope that, notwithstanding the making advances towards that reign of justice, which eighteen centuries of Christianity have been drawing on, in spite of a thousand difficulties and reverses."

But soon, when he considered that so many others were wearing themselves out with fatigue and sacrificing even life itself for their country, his own inaction became insupportable to him : and this is why we see him repeatedly make the greatest efforts to obtain permission to join the ambulances that accompanied the army. His brother Charles was then in Paris, and Paul wrote to him the following letter in which we see burst forth with such violence his desire of doing all he could amid the difficulties of the moment.

"My dearest Charles, think seriously of the favor I ask ; it is the greatest service you could do for me. Whether Paris is beseiged or not, there will be an immense number of wounded, above all if, as it is thought, a great battle is to be fought around the walls of the city. Tell me quickly then, I beg of you, if you think I would be of any use. Do not let any family consideration or fears about my health disturb you. Try at once if you could not find me a place in some flying or stationary ambulance, or in a hospital or anywhere else, and write immediately to tell me if you have been successful. If you can get what I desire, do so, and I shall look upon this as the best mark of your kindness to me.

"I will not be the only one there in cassock. Paris is evidently our place, and it is there that I have always hoped to work on till my strength was exhausted.

"Send me an answer to-morrow evening, and then do not trouble yourself any further. There can never be too many attending the wounded or bringing them to the hospital. There are many of my fellow students I am sure who are already performing the work in which I am so anxious to take part. The directors of the Seminary will certainly approve of my project, and here at home they will yield at last to my wishes. Do not delay to answer my letter : what I ask of you is that you make it possible for me to accomplish a duty which is most dear to me.

" It is insupportable to remain inactive at such times as these. And you know that my only happiness is in the thought of being able to do something for others. Do not let any fear about my heart disturb you. . This will do it so much good. I am remarkably well.

"In a word, consider the matter immediately and weigh everything coolly, as you would do in the case of a stranger to whom you were desirous of rendering a very great service, and when you have done this, send me quickly your answer. In two days I could be ready to begin work. I do not write to you about all this, without having spoken to my father and mother about it. They make some objection but they will yield. We must be men of energy in this world, and it is at such moments as these that we should know our resolution. If we were always to take into consideration the health of one, and the situation of another, and so on ; what would become of our zeal ? . . ."

Every one, however, was averse to an act whose folly his generosity alone failed to detect. And he himself was soon compelled to acknowledge his imprudence. Having undertaken a walk of some length, in the hopes of thus proving his strength, he was punished for his temerity with a fever which lasted four weeks and was accompanied with spitting of blood. He had scarcely recovered from this blow when his former dreams came back upon him. Misfortune after misfortune fell quickly upon France, and our young friend thought that the hour was now come when every one was called upon to make a last desperate effort, and that, even if he should drop dead into the first ditch, it was his duty, too, to grasp in his feeble hand a weapon. One consideration alone restrained him.   He loved his vocation to the priesthood with so true, so supreme a love, that he could not do any thing that seemed in any way contrary to it.   Tormented with doubt on this subject and harassed beyond endurance with the struggle that was going on within him, he wrote to his director the following letter :

"November 20th, 1870. When I see that France is ever sinking deeper and deeper into misfortune and in consequence requires now more than ever the services of her sons, I will not tell you how often I have bewailed my weakness, or how often I have been on the point of putting into execution the foolish thought of enrolling myself as a soldier, in order to take part in the struggles of my country, and thus with one act, put an end to all my perplexity. But I always hesitated, and then I would set myself to work again, and by well regulating the day and employing every moment of my time, I was not left without feelings of joy and consolation of heart ; all this, however, was not enough to drive away the thought that I could do something better than remain here inactive. Tell me what you think of the matter. Does not God now require equally of us all that we should struggle against the misfortunes with which Providence is chastising us, and out of which He will only draw us

when we have been regenerated by the blood that
we have shed in the conflict, and shown ourselves
worthy of enjoying better days ? . . . .

"You know well that we have now arrived at
a time which demands resolution ; and you will
understand the vehemence of those desires which
I have felt continually during the last three months;
they have been tested severely enough to prove
that they are sincere. You can imagine what a
happiness it is for one to find, in the course of
his life, an occasion of sacrificing for a noble cause
an existence which at any moment might misera-
bly fade away. . . . It is not that I have not sufficient
determination. All that I want is the assurance
that I should not be acting inconsiderately, or in
a measure unbecoming the vocation which is the joy
of my life, of betraying a want of respect for those
who have authority over me. God knows that I
would willingly die a thousand times to save one
of those victims of war. I need not say, of course,
that it is not that awful fury clamoring for the
blood of an enemy, which pushes me on to become
a soldier. No, but it is the noble ambition of
attesting with my life's blood that I am united
with those who struggle against this invasion, or
who suffer from its effects. It is the desire not
to remain inactive while so many are dying
around me. It is the wish to take part in this
sacrifice of self—a sacrifice easy, indeed, for us,
but hard for so many youths who now offer up
life whilst it yet appears to them full of charms
and presents nothing but seducing appearances.

"In acting as I desire, I will be doing nothing

which is not pleasing to God, for He blesses him who is faithful to accomplish his duty. By doing so—and this is my principal aim—I will even serve the Church better, perhaps, than by consecrating to it a life which gives so little promise of good. Is it not right that, as the priest's heart should vibrate in unison with the hearts of the faithful, so they should see also that he is ready, in public calamities such as these, to shed his blood for the common weal?

" I know that some will look upon my proposals as ridiculous pretensions ; but, if I am not strong, I am at least willing, and my good-will will supply for a time the force that is wanting. Besides, if we were always to calculate precisely what seemed possible for us to perform, we should never succeed in anything in this world. We must attempt even that which appears impossible. I am better now. I have gained some strength—quite enough to give a good cuffing. Every one ought generously to come forward now and offer his services, even if he were sure of falling into the first ditch.

It would be idle to object that my arm could not change the destiny of France. With such reasoning as this, every one would count upon his neighbors and remain at home. On such occasions as these every one should take the initiative himself, without thinking what other people will do. . . .

" Weigh well my motives and my desires. God grant that I may have the happiness of sacrificing, once for all, a life which seems to me to be without merit, and to promise little good hereafter!

" I am writing to you in the silence of the night on the eve of the Presentation, and the thought of this feast is filling my mind with sweet reminiscences of the Seminary.* Will God grant me this year the grace of offering up my life in sacrifice to Him ? We die for God when we are struck down by that Hand of Justice which weighs so heavily upon France. But it is too much for me to believe that so much happiness is in store for me. And yet it is within my reach ; give but your consent and I shall be the happiest of men. . ."

A letter written at the same time to his father, who was then absent from Lons-le-Saunier, is full of the like entreaties, and reads thus :

" In fine, my dear father, you would do well to consider seriously before God a project which many will treat as extravagant and pretentious, but which becomes comprehensible and merits approval when viewed in the light of those duties to which our life is to be devoted. Am I to be thought incapable of doing that for which alone life is worth living ?

" You see that, notwithstanding my eagerness, I have been unwilling to leave the beaten track, without the advice of those who have authority over me. Allow me then, in return, to count upon an appreciation, free from all inferior considerations. Here am I, fully decided on the step! Nothing will be an obstacle to me but a formal

---

* This feast is kept with great solemnity at the Seminary of Saint-Sulpice ; it is on this day that the ecclesiastics renew the promises made to God and the Church, on the day of their tonsure.

opposition from you and from my director of Saint-Sulpice."

It cannot be too often repeated that these sentiments, however enthusiastic they may appear, were in him perfectly sincere. His soul was naturally heroic. There is not the least doubt that "to lay down his life in a noble cause" was his dream, his ambition, and that it would have afforded him a real joy to have done so. This will easily be seen by his bearing in face of a death suffered also in a noble cause, but accompanied with as much cruelty as is the soldier's death with glory.

It would have been unreasonable to have acceded to such ardent longings, for a quarter of an hour's forced marching would have been enough to exhaust his bodily forces, so ill-proportioned were they to the energies of his noble soul. His virtue had to be taxed, rather than his reason, in order to bring him to renounce with a willing heart, so easy and ready an occasion of doing." that for which life alone is worth living."

" I console myself," he says, after witnessing the failure of his project, " in my sad situation as spectator of the ruins of my country, by the thought that our turn will come, and prove quite as meritorious as would be the easy duty of laying down one's life for France in her agony. Then each of us, according to the measure of his capacity, will have to do his share in forming a truly Christian generation, capable of repairing our public calamities, and of arresting the interior evils of our country, or in any case, of attaining that eternal happiness compared with which all the happiness of this world is nothing. O yes! that which consoles me in the midst of these overwhelming disasters is the sight of the Cross of Jesus Christ, which still stands firm, eternally beautiful, and triumphant, inflaming all hearts with love, and which alone here below can afford happiness and strength to society, and be the pledge of a better world to come. The sight of the duties it reserves for me hereafter, drowns my regrets in the unspeakable gratitude I experience at feeling within me a life which will be wholly devoted to the glory of God and the good of souls."

But then his life itself was in such a wavering condition that he durst not count upon it. He only trembled lest he should see it wasted in that powerlessness and inactivity which he dreaded above all things.

"If I had only to present myself, as I might do at present, in order to fall for certain as a victim, not a shadow of disquietude would cross my mind; but I have a state of weakness to fear, which, though letting me live, would condemn me to a painful life of inaction."

"God," he writes again upon this subject, December 30, 1870, "sends me at times hours of interior darkness, during which everything tells me that little of the future remains to me, and that this priestly life, which has been the dream of my youth, is kept without doubt, for purer and better souls than mine. . . At times, too, I ask myself seriously what they could make of me. Indeed, what do you think I am good for? No voice, no breath, no real strength. My only hope is, that those whose place it is to examine these things will sufficiently understand my physical capacities to demand for me some humble post in the ministry, such as it is not difficult, I should think, to find at Paris, where I might have the poor and sick for my portion. My ambition is to carry some relief to those that suffer and whose only consolation in the midst of the gay world around them is in the divine promises which at once explain and soften down the bitter inequalities of fortune. At all events I am in the hands of God, who can take or leave me, make use of me or set me aside, as He wills. *Yet I hope indeed to find the means of dying usefully, if I cannot live with profit.*"

In a letter written about the same time to his director, in which he communicates to him his anxiety on this point, he insists at length upon this means of dying usefully, which he reserves as a last resource. He assures him that if, when there was question of the subdeaconship, they should deem him unfit for service, he would go and present himself anew at La Trappe, where he had realized his first aspirations after the religious life. It is true they had been unwilling to admit him there to live, but they would not refuse to receive him there to die in the practice of penance, and in a last cordial reception of the cross ; and he adds : "You would not have the heart to raise an obstacle to such a plan."

Then foreseeing sufficiently the impression produced by such a disclosure, he seeks to calm it down in the following terms: "You think, no doubt, that I have begun to talk extravagantly of late. . .   Yet I deserve to be pardoned if, having inspired myself after the example of our Lord, with the sovereign desire of undertaking noble enterprises for the glory of God and the good of souls, my imagination teems with hopeless projects as some compensation for all the dreams which have made all the happiness of my life ! and often I am not sad.   I simply look upon life as a whole, with its many and various chances, ever ready to fly whither God may call me."

Only a few months were to elapse and God was Himself to resolve the difficulty, by choosing him as a victim of expiation for his justice.

What a thrill would have gone through his soul had it been possible for him then to foresee that this means of dying usefully, which so pre-occupied his thoughts, was to be martyrdom !

He had the consolation, during the last weeks of that cruel war, of devoting himself to the care of the wounded in the ambulances established at Lons.   It is not difficult to imagine the difficulty he experienced, and the tender charity he brought into play in assisting the poor sufferers whom he had occasion to attend.

"It has been a great source of happiness to me," he says, " to see that beneath an exterior disorderly and coarse, these young men still preserve within them honest and Christian sentiments.   I have seen some deaths that have brought tears to my eyes : I shall never forget them, and should esteem myself happy to die in like manner :—deaths of youths, whose moustaches were barely visible,

and who quitted this life with hearts full of peace,
love, contentment and gratitude. Oh! with what
affection one clasps their hands when dying! how
we would like to lay down a thousand lives in order to prolong their existence, who are so worthy to
live! I there contracted friendships which, though
they were not to be of long duration will nevertheless, I hope, have left their impressions on the heart.
I observed the greatest discretion in my relations
with the soldiers and officers, endeavoring to be
affable, simple and full of attention, in order to
leave a favorable feeling behind me, which might
help to do away with the calumnies and prejudices
that exist with regard to us and the divine religion
of Jesus Christ."

For a moment he thought he had attained the
object he pursued with so much ardor, and was
about to see at length his day of sacrifice. In a
letter in which he tells how he had been cheated
of his hopes, he speaks of the war, and of the utter
exhaustion of his country, in terms too patriotic
and too Christianlike to allow us to pass them over
in silence.

"30th January, 1871.—I have always been told
that all my endeavors to take advantage of
present events were not destined to come to
anything. To-day, fifteen thousand men were to
engage at two leagues distance from here. Yesterday I had offered my services for the care of the
wounded. Already I was beginning to experience
the joys and emotions of what I thought would
be my first appearance on the field. I have certainly promised not to spare myself. Would God

really deign to make use of me ? *O gaudium super omne gaudium !* . . . .

" I was even addressing to you thoughts of gratitude and affection, which might have been the last, when at 8 o'clock in the evening there came, as it were, the knell of our poor country, the sad news of· the armistice, which proclaimed at once the drain of its resources, and was the prelude of a ruinous peace. Yes, in spite of all the horror for bloodshed and fratricidal struggles which the religion of peace inspires, so much injustice left unavenged, and so many rights odiously violated cannot but allow us to deplore this barren result of heroic efforts. . .

Ah ! let us hope, at least, that all these misfortunes may help to strengthen our love for our unhappy country, drive every selfish wish from our hearts, and renew in us the spirit of fraternity and self-sacrifice ; in fine, hasten our return to God, who only chastises men in order to bring them more speedily to Himself. If such be really the case, we shall only have to bless the merciful hand that strikes us, and adore the designs of Divine Providence, which deems such things better than the successes and prosperity of this world, since temporal interests are as nothing in comparison with those of eternity. Before wishing to see France great on earth, we ought to desire to behold her ripe for heaven. But alas ! when we perceive amongst us the redoubled efforts of the evil one, and think of the terrible recriminations and social hatreds which, embittered by misfortune and ill-success, madly seek a wide field of action, have we not reason to be sad indeed ?

" Yet, my God, you have given us to understand sufficiently by word and example that that which you most desire to see here below is good and right, prevailing even in spite of men, and unknown to them, and though it has to be drawn out of evil itself, and that moral beauty reigning with which you had so perfectly embellished the world whilst yet it was such as you had at first willed it, and which you have deigned to restore to it in its fallen state. Perchance, like the leaven in the Gospel, His operations here below consist in the working up and raising of societies which, later on, are ravished to see some unlooked-for good come forth from what was nought but apparent discord."

At length, those days of poignant emotion and gloomy sadness were over, and little by little the old life returned. Our young friend's over-excitement, brought on by the ardor of his longing after self-sacrifice, had given place to a state of despondency and regret. He felt that, after all, his lively entreaties had been unreasonable, and reproached himself with having, by his persistency, grieved his parents, and somewhat troubled the peace of the domestic hearth. It was this that closed the last days he spent in the bosom of his family.

The news of the re-opening of the Seminary of Saint-Sulpice, fixed for the 15th March, 1871, came happily to put an end to the regrets which harassed him. The announcement sent a thrill of joy to his heart. Believing his days to be numbered, he was anxious not to lose any, but on the contrary to hasten onwards towards the goal. He was then passing through one of those periods when his malady allowed him to enjoy a little health. . He therefore left home once more, and on the 15th of March was at Paris. We seem still to see him as he arrived that morning after a tedious journey, a sleepless night, and nearly a whole day passed without eating, pale and worn out with fatigue, but radiant with joy.

Yet it was a happiness for all to meet again, after such a long and trying separation, and to find that dear house of Saint-Sulpice untouched after all the dangers of the Prussian siege. Each assailed the other with questions, or hastened to tell the various adventures through which he had passed during the preceding months. All were eager, too, to see Issy, and Rueel again full of joy and gratitude in the sanctuary of our Lady of Loretto, which the Prussian bombs had spared, but which the Commune was soon to burn to the ground.

In a word, every one rejoiced at the thought of entering again upon that life of labor, and tranquil peace with God, which makes the charm of the Seminary. Alas! all these bright prospects were soon to be dispelled by a storm of fire and blood.

CHAPTER V.

THE PRISON.

ABOUT eighty seminarists, as well from Paris
as from the provinces, came in answer to the call
of their masters. The exercise commenced at
the Seminary by a few days of fervent retreat
which had not quite elapsed before the miserable
and disgraceful communistic insurrection broke
out on the 18th of March, 1871. This event at
first filled all hearts with sadness, it did not however cause very serious apprehensions. The state
of Paris at the beginning of the commune was
abnormal ; the regular government was flying off
in disorder, leaving a fair field open for those sedi-
tious men who were now really masters of affairs.
The feelings of those who loved order might be
expressed in one word, incertitude, coupled with a
vague belief that the *denouement* would come soon
and be less terrible than circumstances might
perhaps have seemed to foretell. Moreover, if
we forget for a moment the bloody tragedy of the
22d March, which was executed on the Place
Vendome, order was yet maintained in the streets.
This was especially true of those parts of the
town which lie on the left bank of the river, and
it is in one of these quarters that the Seminary is

situated. Here people were enjoying perfect tranquility, whilst the storm was howling round Montmartre and Belleville.

In this state of affairs, prudence seemed to suggest that the best course to be followed was to wait until it could be seen how affairs would turn out. This was the line of conduct that the directors of the Seminary adopted, though they left every one at perfect liberty to leave if he desired. Few, however, took advantage of this permission. It was too great a sacrifice to break off, without being obliged, a life which all had just begun with so much happiness.

We see from the letters written by Paul Seigneret during these few weeks that he had no pre-occupations about the dangers of their position, but that his mind was troubled by thoughts that cast a shade of sadness over his last days in the Seminary. He had left home with a certain uneasiness weighing upon his heart. It was caused by the thought of the pain that he had given his family. Those feelings only gained strength in the solitude of the Seminary. His fault no doubt was one which might easily be forgiven, since his patriotism and his passion for self-sacrifice, rendered still more imperious by the misfortunes of France, had alone urged him on to struggle against the wishes and representations of his parents, and yet he accuses himself of his fault with bitterness and in tears which would seem to be excessive, if we did not know how great was his veneration for his parents and how utterly insufferable it was for him to feel that there was any coldness existing between him and them.

"My very dear parents," he writes at the end of the retreat, giving vent to the feelings of his heart, "we have just finished our retreat, and though it has been shortened on account of the state of affairs, it has been quite long enough to make me suffer cruelly. I have been obliged, with sorrow of heart, to recognize all my faults. I have seen all your kindness so utterly disregarded, and all your wise recommendations thrown away. Forgive me—I confess all now. I could not have had better parents, nor could you have loved me more, or directed me more wisely than you have done, or been more indulgent to me in every way. And yet you see what return I have made to you for all your goodness! It is thus that I have lost that year of my life in which I could best have enjoyed your presence and could have afforded you so much pleasure. I know that you have forgiven me all; but this very kindness, which makes you so ready to pardon me, only makes me feel all the more how unworthy I am of you. My only excuse is that I had strangely deceived myself with regard to my duty, as well as with regard to those who had authority over me, and all this now inspires me with such a distrust for myself as I hope I shall never forget . . . . My only consolation is to throw myself entirely into the hands of God. He renews the youth of those who purpose generously to do better in future, and then have recourse to Him. He alone can accord that pardon which calms and sanctifies. He

alone can change remorse into vigorous resolution
of leading a better life in future.

"I must thank you, my dear father," he says
again, coming back to the same subject, "I must
thank you for your kind letter. The tears which
it brought to my eyes tell better than words can
express thē emotions it caused me. Your kindness is inexhaustible. It is you who console me
after my faults ; it is you who stretch out your
hand to raise me when I fall. · One day, my dear
parents, when we can see into souls, and when all
our sins have been expiated, you will see how
much reverence, gratitude and love lie hid under
all my illusions, weaknesses and faults. It will
then, let us hope, be the time of eternal love which
knows no sorrow."

Another thought, that of the future, helped to
maintain in his mind a painful incertitude. He
felt anxious to know how things would turn out
for him, for he could now no longer deceive
himself with regard to the state of his health,
which was growing every day worse and more
precarious. He resigned himself to the will of
Providence, struggling on without stopping, and
always applying himself with ardor to his work.
But he could see no solution to the difficulty, and
he felt keenly that inevitable anxiety which attends
those who are walking onward in the dark. He
speaks of these thoughts with much openness in
his letters to his father, and thus lets us once
more catch a glimpse of his extreme delicacy of
feeling.

The state of his health made him fear that he

would bring to the diocese of Paris, into which he had been so readily received, nothing for the service of souls but the unprofitable desire of devoting himself to a labor which his bodily strength would not permit him to execute. It was necessary to encourage and reassure him on this point, for his fine sense of fairness grew troubled at such a thought, and he asked himself if he ought not rather to depart at once, than go on, seeming to entertain hopes, which it became more evident from day to day he would never be able to realize.

"In a few months," he says, "this question will be decided. I will discuss the matter seriously and fairly with my superiors. And I confess that if it could only be reasonably supposed that I could do no more than half a priest's work, or occupy positions on which nothing depended, I would be the first to wish to discontinue. No, I have not relinquished the advantages of the religious state in order to draw out a languid life, fatal to myself and unprofitable to others. That which I had pictured to myself was the sacred ministry, in all its lowliness no doubt, but also with all its activity and generous zeal. But, if it is thought that I have not strength enough for this, I hope, my dear parents, that you will still nobly bless my determination to finish my life in the cloister. I will thus, by a voluntary renouncement, console myself for not being able to accomplish the good that I so much longed to do, but which God judged me unworthy to perform.

"I confess that I often ask myself if I am not too much worn out, both in body and mind, to pretend to be of service to others. I wonder if I have still left enough of youth and life for that. Besides, when I compare my state of health with that of those around me, I cannot but perceive how much weaker I am than they, what good shall I be able to do? God, I hope, will give us light to judge of all these things wisely. All that I can promise you is, that my own will shall have no part in the decision. I will leave time and circumstances to discover what must be done."

We see the same thoughts troubling him in a letter written to his old friends of Solesmes, but there also we perceive his entire resignation to the will of God.

"The great question for me is still that of my health, which seems to be failing rather than improving. I appear in this respect to be disqualified for what the future would require of me, that the very thought frightens me. I cannot mount to the first story even, without being out of breath for the next five minutes. How can I undertake the sacred ministry in that state? *But God will do with me whatever he pleases.*"

Patience! holy youth, in a few weeks God will remove the disproportion which exists between your aspirations and your strength to follow them. He will know where to find the victim which is pleasing to him. *Deus providebit Tibi victimam, fili mi,* (Gen. xxii, 8).

In the meantime affairs at Paris were hastening to a crisis. When our young friend, however, reverts to the events which were taking place around him, we can see that his mind is pre-occu-

pied with thoughts that concern him more closely
and which cast, as it were, a dark shadow over
him, and he only alludes to the state of things in
order to give reassurance to those he loved, or in
order to express how much sorrow the civil war,
which was threatening, caused to a heart full of
patriotic feelings and true Christian charity.

His short communications, however, give a true
statement of the position in which the Seminary
then was, and of the feelings which filled the
hearts of those who were in it.

In a letter, bearing the date of the 19th of
March, we find, in a postscript, these few simple
words :

" I suppose the troubled state of affairs at
Paris does not cause you any fears about me.
The insurgents have got the mastery : cowardice
rather than sympathy is the reason why no one
wishes to attack them. We have nothing to fear.
What could they do with us ? But what will become of France ? "

" We are in a strange situation here," he writes
a few days later, " for we are lost in our beautiful
studies already, and almost forget that Paris is
the scene of such disorders. We are left altogether
unmolested, and all that we hear of the troubles
without is the noisy bawling of the bands that
pass from time to time, the shouts of the national
guards, as they enter or leave the town, or the
booming of the cannons they fire off at intervals
in sign of independence. O when will men's folly
come to an end. All this can scarcely pass without bloodshed, and another carnage must be added

to so many others. Such things as these make us feel the more the necessity of a better world. This one is too old, too worn to satisfy us."

"And you, my dear mother," he writes again at the end of March, "how much anxiety the thought of all these things must cause you! They are not certainly calculated to give you peace of mind. That which we see impending now is more deplorable than all our other disasters. Some day or other not far distant, the French cannons must inevitably be pointed against French breasts. But this has taken place already, and we have heard the shots. Such sounds rend the heart and fill us with dread and horror beyond all expression. Paris is a mere camp now, and we live from day to day, uncertain of what the morrow will bring us."

The last letter that he wrote, whilst he was yet in the Seminary and at liberty, is addressed to his parents: we see in it the same peaceful confidence with regard to all that concerned himself and an ever-increasing sadness at the thought of all the misfortunes that were coming upon Paris and the whole of France:

"The horizon is growing darker and darker," he says, "and affairs are in such a state that I am afraid the same anxiety will harass you now on my account, as you felt when Charles was here during the siege of Paris. I hope, however, you have no fears about me personally, and that your only pain is to think of that struggle which seems impending, when brother will have to fight against brother. Of what have we to be afraid? An at-

tack upon our persons? No one believes that
this is possible. That we shall be drafted in
amongst the national guards? Every one knows
that, though there is a decree placarded all over
Paris, declaring every citizen capable of bearing
arms a national guard, they are much more anxious
to take away the rifles from those who do not inspire them with confidence than to create new
soldiers. That we shall be driven out of the Seminary? Well, if we are sent away, we shall no
doubt meet again at Issy or Orleans. You see
then that we have every reason to suppose that
no harm will befall us.

"Certain families, however, have begun to fear
for their sons, and in consequence, there are some
twenty of my fellow-students who have left the
Seminary. I have been asking myself if, in order
to remove all your fears, I should not guess what
you would like me to do . . . But there are at
least sixty of us here, and we live quietly with
our directors. I am sure you will not be displeased
at me for remaining with this little community.
. . . But do not suppose that my mind is filled
again with those extravagant ideas about self-
sacrifice and devotion, to which I was so long a
prey. No! I only remain here because I am
here, and because I do not see any real danger to
which we are exposed.

"Good-bye, my dear parents. I regret that I
must leave you in the midst of all these cruel
sorrows which press so heavily now on the heart
of every one that loves his country. The storm
is gathering fast and threatens to burst out over

our heads with awful fury. We can easily judge from what we see and hear around us that tranquility will not be restored before a bloody struggle has taken place in the streets of Paris. How many victims these wretches will have slaughtered, and what a miserable spectacle we will present to the rest of Europe, this tearing each other in pieces whilst the Prussian cannons are yet pointed against our walls ! . . .

The storm indeed was about to burst over the unfortunate city, and the very morrow of the day upon which this letter was written, Palm Sunday, April 22d, saw the beginning of the civil war that was to deluge the streets of the capital with blood and leave its proudest monuments so many smoking ruins.

Its outburst was the signal for an infuriated populace to let loose its rage against the clergy, who thus had the favor of being the first victims of their anger. The arrest of the venerable Archbishop on Tuesday evening, April the 4th, that of the Jesuit Fathers of the school of Saint-Geneviève and of the Rue de Sèvres, and lastly, the visits to the houses of different religious communities, gave the alarm. At mid-day on Wednesday, April 5th, the students of Issy arrived at Paris with the tidings that the staff of the insurgents had come to take up its position in the Seminary, and that the directors were detained in the house, but that the seminarists were left a free exit.

From this moment, the danger was no longer doubtful. As was natural, those at the Seminary of Saint-Sulpice awaited their turn to receive a visit, the consequences of which, in face of the disorder and license that presided at such proceedings, it was impossible to foresee. By the advice of their directors, most of the seminarists quitted Paris the same evening. Some, less credulous of danger, or undismayed at it, were desirous to wait a little longer. Paul Seigneret, as might have been expected, was of this number, for a peril of this kind was better suited to captivate than daunt a generous heart like his. Yet the thought of those at home made him hesitate. He was advised to depart ; but he delayed till next day. The night passed quietly. Our young friend had thought the matter over, and resolved that in spite of all the repugnance he felt at the idea of leaving, he would do so, because it was his duty to spare his parents all reason for disquietude on his account. Besides, his indecision of the preceding day had been in reality without any bad result. At the moment when he should have started, if he had decided so to act, it was impossible to leave Paris without a passport, and a want of this important paper had obliged several of his fellow-students to return to the Seminary. This incident brought back joy to him again. "Come what may now," he said, "at least my heart will not be weighed down by the thought that I have been the cause of the uneasiness of my parents."

On the morning of Holy Thursday, at the solemn office of that day, the youthful levite had the happiness of receiving his God, and serving for the last time at the altar, in that church of Saint-

Sulpice, where the beautiful ceremonies, the chant of the choir, and the organ's notes had so often ravished his soul, and where he was never more to appear, unless crowned with the halo of martyrdom.

Towards one o'clock in the afternoon, he went with one of his fellow students to the Prefecture of Police for a passport. They were both in clerical dress. This proved a mishap. But was it an imprudence on their-part? Most certainly, if we are to judge now after the event. But if we simply look upon the state of things at that moment, and take into account the manner in which they were viewed by all, perhaps we might see in this step only one of those ordinary proceedings, which we do not think of taxing with temerity, until some disastrous consequence has opened our eyes. The persecution against the clergy had begun, but the persecutors appeared only to aim at persons more eminent in dignity than simple seminarists, who could scarcely dream of being detained as hostages by the Commune. It is besides certain that, at this moment, many priests still appeared in the streets in *soutane*, without being otherwise molested than by receiving greetings, perchance somewhat coarser and more frequent than usual, from some bands of drunken Communists whom they chanced to meet on their way. On the other hand, assurance had been given at the *Marie du sixeme Arrondissement* that the students of Saint-Sulpice who did not live at Paris, would receive passports without difficulty ; and that very morning one of them had obtained one under his title of student of Saint-Sulpice.

Under such circumstances it was easy to commit an indiscretion of this kind, nor could one reasonably expect to become the victim of a useless and monstrous abuse of power, such as was practiced upon our young friend and his companion by the functionaries of the Commune. With our ordinary ideas of every-day life, it requires time and experience to make us realize the thought that laws no longer exist, and that we are completely at the mercy of the first one we meet, who has a few armed bandits at his command, and is ready to execute whatever whim may seize him.

However this may be, the arrest of the seven young ecclesiastics who, together with several of their directors, represent the share that the Seminary of Saint-Sulpice had in the persecution, is one of the most curious and sad features of this era of liberty, and one which gives the best idea of those men whose domination Paris had to undergo for more than two months.

Having arrived first at the Prefecture of Police, Paul Seigneret and his companion took their place amongst the crowds that were collected at the entrance of the offices. Every one showed himself eager to forego the advantages of the Commune, by quitting Paris as soon as possible. All at once they were accosted by a national guard, who asked them politely what they wanted, and offered to be of service to them. Convinced of his sincerity by the kind attention he displayed, they followed him, when invited to do so, without the slightest suspicion.* They were introduced by him into a room, where an officer of the National Guard, with a woman at his side, was finishing his breakfast upon his desk. Empty glasses and bottles and the smell and smoke of tobacco, gave the room the appearance of the lowest tavern. The officer allowed the young men to make their request, then suddenly, as if seized by an attack of maniacal rage:

"Cowardly *calotins !*" he cried, "sluggards ! who think only of flying when all good citizens are rushing to arms ! Stop ! I will give you a passport.—You shall have a writ of detention and shall be shot ! I also have a relative a priest : I wish I had him here : he would not have long to live. Never," he continued after giving vent to all kinds of insults, "never could we pay you back all the injury you have done us ! "

The two seminarists had heard in silence this explosion of rage, provoked by the sight of their cassock : for it is the privilege and the honor of the priestly dress that it excites the anger and fury of men such as those. To these last words Paul Seigneret replied gently :

"What, is it to young people like us that you speak thus ! " It was indeed the most odious, as well as the worst chosen insult imaginable in the present case. Cowardly ! that valiant heart which

---

* Almost at the same moment, at another office of the Prefecture of Police, two other seminarists of Saint-Sulpice, wearing likewise their clerical dress, were invited in the same way by a functionary to follow him, and received from him passports which permitted them to leave Paris without any hindrance or trouble whatever.

leaps with joy at the sight of every noble and heroic sacrifice! Accused of doing evil, he whose soul only lived on the thought of doing good! This simple reply reminds us that in his repertory, at the word 'Persecution,' he had given the foremost place to the following passage of the Gospel narrative of the Passion :

" And when He had said these things, one of the servants standing by gave Jesus a blow, saying : answerest thou the high-priest so? Jesus answered him : If I have spoken evil, give testimony of the evil ; but if well why strikest thou me? (S. John xviii, 22, 23)."

This is where the disciple of Jesus Christ learns to remain calm under insult or bad treatment, without betraying any weakness, however, and without renouncing his right of condemning the unworthy conduct of his persecutors.

After a few moments the two prisoners saw with horror two more, and then again three of their fellow-students enter the same room, drawn there by the same perfidious invitation, and fallen like themselves into the same snare.

They remained here several hours, and the whole proceeding, and the only one entered into against them, which nevertheless sufficed to send one of them to death, consisted in drawing up beneath their eyes a writ of detention that would keep them as prisoners in the Prefecture of Police. These first hours of captivity were full of anxiety.

" What moments," writes one of the young prisoners some time after, " what moments were those we passed together in that horrible office ! Those writs of imprisonment beneath our eyes, the gaol in perspective, a dark impenetrable veil over the future, the looks of those armed men, as they passed to and fro, continually vomiting forth their blasphemies, and, above all, the distracting thought of the affliction of our poor families, which made us share in their anguish—was not all this too great a weight upon our poor hearts ?"

They were at length conducted to their destination, and, as the cells were all occupied, they had the happiness of remaining together, and were cordially received in the room where they were to be to detained by six Jesuit Fathers of the school of Saint-Geneviève, who had been sent there three days before. These Fathers did them the honors of the prison which they shared along with several of their brethren and servants.

There they began a new kind of community-life, over which no doubt incertitude about the future cast a gloom, whilst the numerous privations the body had to undergo rendered it still harder to bear ; yet faith taught them to accept it as coming from God, and paternal charity and friendship made it even happy and agreeable.

They performed together their exercises of piety in that place, whose echoes alas ! were so seldom awakened by the voice of prayer. An hour's meditation in the morning, the noon-day's examination of conscience, the rosary and evening prayers served to unite the prisoners at intervals in the presence of Him who gives us force to sup-

port the trials of life, and, if need be, courage for
the supreme trial of death.

Paul Seigneret was there such as he had been
everywhere—simple, kind, forgetful of self, full of
pleasing gaiety, the heart overflowing with those
generous and serious thoughts which constituted
for him his very life. On Good-Friday, the morrow of his imprisonment, he addressed to his
spiritual director a few lines to tell him not of his
resignation, but of his joy and exultation at what
had befallen him. To be in prison on Good-Friday, in hatred of the cassock, what greater happiness could be desired ?

He wished himself to be the announcer of
these events to his parents, and on Easter-Sunday
he wrote them the following note, in which he
communicated to them in all simplicity his dispositions at that moment.

"After having for a long time hesitated to
impart to you news destined, no doubt, to throw
you into consternation and cause you great anxiety,
I think that I can no longer be silent concerning
my present situation. On Thursday last, April 9th,
upon advice received from the 'Mairie' of Saint-
Sulpice, I presented myself at the Prefecture of
Police, in order to obtain, in quality of stranger, a
pass-port, but I was arrested with six of my companions, who came likewise in their turn to
make the same request, and were arrested in like
manner.

" We are, at present, all together in a spacious
room at the Prefecture of Police—twenty-six in
number, Jesuits, priests, and ourselves, seminarists,

the small fry. But life here is a real retreat : it passes amid our different exercises of piety and in the calmest joy.—I am well. I make up for the scanty pittance of the prison by the little comforts that we are able to procure. We love one another, and watch over one another, like brothers. For my part, I experience a tranquillity of mind and a peace of soul, such as I have not felt for a long time past: these are excellent conditions for my health. Sleep alone flies the hard prison pallet, or is disturbed by the deep snoring to which I have not yet been able to accustom myself. My only sorrow is to think of you, and of your anxiety ; happily I was arrested when making my last efforts to spare you such disquietude. But then, we have probably nothing to fear.

"Farewell, my dearest parents. "*Haec dies quam fecit Dominus exultemus et laetemur in ea.* May God give you this joy which will raise you above all the sadness and sorrows of this world ! "

He was therefore happy in his prison, though the manner of life there and the diet must have tried him more than any other ; yet he never complained, but, on the contrary, found that everything was ordered for the best. It was necessary that his companions, who knew his delicate state of health, should watch over him and oblige him to accept the little comforts that it was possible to introduce into the prison-life. The sleepless nights of which he speaks were a result of his habitual ill-health ; there lay a flame within which consumed the body too rapidly. His countenance, the mirror, as we have said, of his soul, put on from this moment that peculiarly interesting and sympathetic appearance which his companions then remarked, and which, later on at the Roquette, struck so forcibly those who had the happiness of seeing him.

Those feelings of brotherly love towards his follows, which were always so strong in him, were heightened by the circumstances in which he was now placed, and he experienced the sweetest consolation in the society of those students who were prisoners along with him. In a letter written some time later from the solitude of the prison of Mazas, he recalls the happiness of those days:

" I leave you to imagine how we loved and encouraged each other in our common captivity at the Prefecture of Police. There was M. Dechelette above all who had for each one of us, and for me in particular, that kindness which you might imagine would be shown by a heart like his. God alone knows the happiness we enjoyed together, and all the good he did me. O how friendship helps us to love God! We knew that our hearts were filled with the same desires and beat with the same love. And all this inspired us with such affections as this life can never satisfy —they must be continued and perfected in God. But *illum oportet crescere me autem minni.* That is what I desire for him, as well as for all those whom I esteem and love."

This true brotherly love, which knit the seven young captives so closely to each other, struck every one who saw them ; and a Jesuit Father told them one day that he recognized there the stamp of Saint-Sulpice.

Our young seminarist loved, whilst in prison, to substitute serious and instructive conversations for the study of which he was then deprived, and he was ever eager to take advantage of the opportunities he had of improving himself in the society of those men, distinguished by their learning, who had received him and his companions with so much kindness at the beginning of their captivity. With them he spoke of literature, philosophy and above all of scripture. One thing that he longed much to have with him was his notes on Holy Scripture : he had left them at the seminary and now feared that they would be lost.

"His imagination," says one of his fellow-students, who was oftenest with him during these eight days, "his imagination lost nothing of its freshness or sprightliness ; and I remember well how much he felt the loss of the sun's rays, whose beauty he loved to admire. One morning at dawn, a little bird came to sing at the bars of our single window : its song filled his heart with delight, and gave rise to the most pleasing reflections."

But there was one thought which occupied the first place in the minds of those who had been thrown into that prison with so much cruelty and with expressions of such bitter hatred : what would be the issue of all that had happened to them. No doubt the piety and charity of the captives had transformed the dark and dismal prison in which they were confined into a place to which joy had found its way. Sometimes, too, gathered round **one of the Fathers,** who had always an inexhaustible **store of** charming tales to tell, they **would** give vent **to their** happiness in **a** manner **that** astonished **their keepers.** Still the **thought that** they were in prison, **and** the uncertainty about how or when they **would leave** it, **came** back after those moments **of** forgetfulness and pleasure, to make their hearts **sink** again.

"You shall be **shot**" was **the threat that** had **been** uttered against them, and they **had** seen **enough to make** them **feel** that these words might **be more than an empty menace.**

Besides, when **one has** heard **the** bolts turned **upon him,** and finds **himself** shut up in a room **into which** the **light of day** scarcely penetrates, his **fears increase and** dangers **seem** more imminent. Such **was the case** with **our** prisoners, and **the** prospect of **death was** continually presenting itself **to them, as if in spite of** them—death which is **so little thought of, and seems so terrible to youths of twenty years of** age.

The conduct of Paul Seigneret **when,** during **his captivity, the** thought **of** death **was** before him, **bears upon it the** stamp of supernatural heroism.

The best description **we can give of it** will **be found in a** passage from **Henri Perreyve on** *The Persecution.*

"**When the hour of danger is** come, fill your **mind with sentiments** of **true apostolic** faith. With **one vigorous effort** bring back **again the** spirit **of the Christians** in the catacombs. Accept death, **and do** not propose terms to your conscience. **Be guilty of no** imprudence. The church allows us, and even obliges us to fly, when certain heresies would have forbidden us to do so. But if prudence can no longer avail, if all is lost, then don't hold back, fear nothing, speak out loudly and with firmness. Do not take death with resignation merely ; such a measure is dangerous. Receive it with enthusiasm, with joy, with transport. This is much more in accordance with the instincts of our nature. In 1793 a certain young female, who could not have resigned herself coolly to death, rushed to the foot of the scaffold singing the Salve Regina. This is in harmony with the genius of Christianity and the French character, and lastly, in such days as these put no bounds to our confidence in God ; trust that he will help us to overcome our own weakness and misery, for it is He who will answer for us, who will act for us who suffers and dies with us."*

We do not know if our young seminarist had meditated this passage in particular. · But what Henri Perreyve here wrote, Paul Seigneret accomplished to the letter. He not only reconciled himself to the thought of death ; he longed to die, and asked this from God as a favor. His peace of mind increased, and his countenance became gradually more radiant, as he saw the chances of deliverance disappearing one by one, and the awful hour of death approaching, and when his doom seemed fixed, the thought of the beauty and the grandeur of the sacrifice he was about to offer, roused his generous faith more and more, and

* Henri Perreyve, by the Pere Gratry.

changed his speech, which till then had always been firm and energetic, into a real song of gladness. It is God alone who could have given him the grace to die thus.

At the very beginning of his captivity, he often expressed to those with whom he could speak without reserve, how enviable seemed to be the fate of those who were put to death through hatred of God and his priests ; " Ah ! if we could be shot," he used to say "what a beautiful death that would be."

But we must not suppose that nature offered no opposition to so much generosity. Faith had the mastery in his courageous soul ; but his feelings lost nothing of their natural vivacity, and it was in struggling against them that he was to prove the merit of his sacrifice. That which tried him most, and caused him greatest pain was, as he himself often said with that tenderness of heart which no one could fail to notice in him, the thought of his dear family and the cruel anguish which would torment them when thinking of him. "Ah" he said " if we were alone in the world, how small a thing it would be to sacrifice our lives. But I trust that God will pour down, upon my parents, graces and consolation without measure." We will see in the last letters he wrote, that the thoughts of the sorrow which he would cause his family is still mingling bitterness with the joy he felt in being able to offer up his life in so noble a cause.

But it was not only at the thought of his family, that Paul Seigneret felt those struggles between nature and grace, which the most perfect souls often experience, and which only help to show better how the strength of God can triumph over our weakness. Though our young seminarist always preserved a sincere desire of being selected as a victim, yet the thought of that death which was nevertheless to be his, inspired him with the deepest horror. He was not afraid to die, but the idea of being butchered caused him an abhorrence such as he could not surmount without the greatest difficulty. His imagination was continually representing to him in the most lively colors those scenes of blood, where men take advantage of disorders, in order to pursue their enemies, as wild beasts hunt their prey, and are only satisfied at last, when they can vent their rage upon them by tearing them to pieces. This made him tremble and he spoke of the dread he felt for such a death, with as much simplicity as he declared the joy that the hope of martyrdom brought him. He returned repeatedly to this subject in his conversations with his companions in captivity; and when in prison at the Roquette, only a few days before the bloody tragedy took place in the Rue Haxo, where he himself would witness and suffer that which he so much abhorred, he said with his ordinary childlike and touching openness, that he had been trying for a long time to brace himself to this thought, but that it had required a great many prayers to make him reconcile himself to the idea of being massacred.

By leaving in him this proof of weakness, God, no doubt, intended to make him feel that it was from the Almighty that he derived all his strength, and consequently it was He Whom he ought to thank for the generosity with which his heart was inflamed. And this modest youth, far from taking the glory to himself, and growing proud in consequence, did not even seem to suspect that he said or did anything worthy of notice, and he would have been astonished to see any one testify admiration at his courage.

Nearly an entire week had now elapsed, and yet the position of the prisoners still remained the same ; nothing gave them any grounds to conjecture what would be their fate. The beautiful feasts of Holy Week and the Easter solemnities were over, and, though the captives had not let them go by unnoticed, they were for the first time deprived of the happiness of witnessing those grand ceremonies of the church, and condemned to pass that great week in the solitude and nakedness of a prison.

A few little incidents, however, came to break the monotony of their weary life, and drive away for a moment the gloomy clouds that hung around them. On the evening of Holy Thursday, the day on which they had been imprisoned, the seminarists of Saint-Sulpice had had the happiness of receiving the benediction of his Grace the Archbishop of Paris. And again, when this venerable prelate learned, as he was being transferred from his place of confinement in the Prefecture of Police to a cell in the prison of Mazas, that seven of the students of his seminary had been seized, he showed his solicitude for them by telling them, through one of the keepers, that he blessed them as his children.

On Easter Sunday a bundle of newspapers and a letter reached them from the Seminary. It was a great relief to the prisoners to know at last something of what was taking place around them, and above all to feel that communications were again established between them and Saint-Sulpice. Now they were assured that they were not abandoned and alone, and this was a great consolation.

Wednesday, the 12th of April, was a day of still greater excitement. The little community lost that day those whom it looked upon as its guide. The Jesuit Fathers recovered their liberty. They were set free with all their servants, after undergoing an interrogation which seemed to be made, only in order to save appearances. This event, as was natural, inspired the young seminarists with the greatest hope. They too, in their turn, would be questioned, and questioning in this case meant liberty: what could any one have against them? and besides, those who had laid aside their prejudices sufficiently, to be able to listen to justice, and release the Jesuits, could not detain others who were mere seminarists, and of no importance whatever.

Every one then began to arrange his plans for the moment when he would be set free from prison. There arose a question amongst them, which caused Paul Seigneret to declare, in a decided manner, what conduct he thought an ecclesiastic should follow with regard to the Commune. There was reason to believe that, at the same time as liberty was offered to them, it would be proposed that they should enroll themselves amongst the national guards, and thus be obliged to serve in a cause which they detested. What reply should they make to such a proposal? Would it be lawful to shun the question by giving an evasive answer?

Paul Seigneret protested energetically against the adoption of such a measure. Such conduct might be tolerated in the case of laics, but they, who had the honor of wearing the cassock, ought not to let the dignity of the priesthood be sullied. The thought of exchanging the costume of the priest for the uniform of a soldier of the commune was insufferable to him. He declared that such an act was an apostasy. He did not even allow that one could remain silent if the proposition was made:

" I will profess what my opinion is," he said "even if I were shot for it!"

But this was not the first time that he made known his sentiments with regard to this matter. The very evening before his apprehension, whilst he was yet in the seminary, he asked one of his masters the following question:

" Sir, whether is it better to die or serve the commune?"

" It is a thousand times better to die than take up arms against one's country," the professor answered, smiling at his ardor.

"Of course! I thought you would say so, and now I know what I must do."

And only a few moments before leaving the Seminary to go to the Prefecture of Police, he

said to some of his fellow-students : "Let us resolve rather to die than let ourselves be enrolled
amongst the national guards !"

The noble youth, however, had not the occasion of manifesting his patriotism, or showing
the aversion he felt for the insurrection that was
dishonoring his country. The interrogation so
ardently longed for by our captives never took
place. It was a mere caprice that had made their
persecutors commence a regular procedure. Another caprice broke it off. The prison which had
been open for a moment, was now closed again,
and only seemed more dismal to those who had
not had the good fortune to get free at that moment of light.

On Monday the 13th, at one o'clock in the
afternoon, it was announced to the seminarists that
they would soon be removed from the Prefecture
of Police. "I think," said a keeper who had not
been watching his prisoners during eight days,
without perceiving some of their worth, or without
taking an interest in their fate, "I think that you
will be transferred to Mazas, but I cannot say so
with certainty." Whatever might happen, they
felt that nothing good was in store for them ; and
in their uncertainty, in order to be prepared for
any emergency, they threw themselves at the feet
of a priest who still remained amongst them and
received from him absolution.

"This was the most solemn moment of our captivity," said one of them afterwards, speaking of this
scene ; " the future for us seemed dark and heavy,
and we knew that this might be our last absolution."

They had scarcely left the room in which they had been confined before they found themselves in the midst of a great number of ecclesiastics, hostages of the commune, who, like themselves, were on the point of being removed to the prison of Mazas. The youthful appearance of the seminarists drew the eyes of all upon them, and Monsignor Zurat, vicar-general of Paris, said to them with much kindness: "I can understand very well why we see here priests who have grown old in the ministry; but you who are merely seminarists! It is however an honor and a glory for you that you have to share the trials of your superiors in the ecclesiastical order."

Yes, it was the will of God that along with their chief pastor, all the orders of the hierarchy should have the honor of bearing a part in the persecution.

The transfer of the prisoners to Mazas was effected in those cellular prison-vans, which have left such a painful impression on all the hostages, and of which one of them has written: "My greatest humiliation during our whole captivity was to find myself in that prison-van. To be locked up in one of these boxes, with scarcely air enough to breathe, when the slightest motion jolts you against one of the four boards which hold you a close prisoner—this is like feeling one's self buried alive.

A few days before, the archbishop of Paris had undergone similar treatment. His miserable persecutors were determined not to spare him this humiliating and needless piece of cruelty.

From the moment of their entry into the prison-van, the seminarists of Saint-Sulpice were no longer to be captives together. They were to be torn asunder and deprived of the assistance and encouragement their union had brought them in bearing their hardships, in order to begin a life of sequestration and loneliness in the felon's cell.

The heavy vans soon passed the threshold of the prison of Mazas.* Each prisoner, as he stepped out, was conducted separately to a cell, shut up alone, to wait there till the cell was assigned to him, where he was to pass his last days, and whose fatal number was to be henceforward his only name and title. The prisoners did not see one another whilst they were waiting in these cells, but they were able to hear each other's voices. One of Paul Seigneret's companions distinctly recognized his gentle voice, as he sang some verses of the Te Deum and then, immediately afterwards, as by way of defiance at his persecutors, hummed the refrain of the " Marseillaise."

Cell No. 19 of the third division fell to the lot of our young friend. It is there that we shall see him for the space of six weeks making his solitary prison a place of perpetual delights. When at length he goes forth to the prison of the condemned, his soul will be still more ravished with God, and will yearn with a stronger desire of giving

---

* One of our young prisoners has told us that, on entering this moving tomb, he had the singular curiosity to look and see if communists had inscribed upon it the device they put up everywhere, and he assured us that he had really been able to perceive from the box in which he was locked, the three great words: *Liberté, Egalité Fraternité.*

himself in sacrifice to Him. And, strange to say, his weak body itself will be gifted with new strength, his face will be as it were transfigured, and will reflect with gentle lustre the perfect serenity, the calm, unspeakable joy that reigns at the bottom of his heart.

We have seen enough of this exceptional and privileged soul, to be able to understand the secret spring of its happiness and peace. What we shall now relate of his life at Mazas will enable us to verify this and penetrate still further into its workings.

It would seem that this youth, gifted as he was with the sense of nature's beauties, and so often ravished at the sight of God's wonderful works, whose happiness it was to pour forth his impressions into some soul like his own, would have found the prison-cell, with its system of isolation, particularly repugnant and trying. But it is no less true that he knew better than any other how to do without such enjoyments. There was within him a deep interior life which was far beyond the reach of passing emotions. He possessed Jesus Christ, the true joy of hearts, and grace had taught him to appreciate highly the unspeakable happiness of such society. Everything else might fail him, but nothing could alter the peaceful felicity which reigned within. "Let the world retire from us if it will," was his cry, "with Jesus Christ we shall ever be partakers of sovereign joy."

At the sight of him thus absorbed by the thought of the love of Jesus Christ, we seem to perceive at times the celestial figures of those virgin martyrs who, whilst tyrants sought to win them over by the world's most brilliant promises, or to frighten them by their threats, appeared always to gaze upon some invisible object which charmed them, so that they could speak of nothing but of Jesus Christ, their only lover, the bridegroom whose beauty and riches are unequalled, who possesses and gives with profusion precious stones and jewels inestimable.*

Jesus Christ was thus his all-sufficing consolation in captivity, and the treasure from which he drew all that his needs demanded. Hence those continual expressions of joy and that liberty of heart with which he speaks, though without regret, of the privation of all he cherished most upon earth.

But let us leave him to tell his prison-thoughts and impressions in his own simple language. On the 23d of April he writes to his parents : " Well! my dear parents, it is then from prison, from the prison of Mazas, that I write to you, from a cell out of which each day a thousand thoughts find their way to you."

Then, in doubt whether his first letter had reached home, he gives another short account of his arrest and of his stay at the Prefecture of Police, and adds :

" It was on Thursday of Easterweek that we were transferred to Mazas. Here I found a nice little cell with a small window, through which my thoughts take their flight to heaven, a pallet

* Office **of St. Agnes—***Roman Breviary.*

which has brought sleep back to me once more,
the chance of studying again, and silence, together with exterior and interior peace.   I scarcely
dare tell you that I live here happy, free from anxiety, completely at God's disposal.   I enjoy a
tranquillity of soul which recalls to me the sweetest
moments of my life.   My only sadness springs from
the thought of your anxiety, and the struggles of
our poor country.   Still it is much less painful
to hear in prison the sad rumors afloat.   One
seems thus to take part in the common sufferings,
if indeed the peaceful days that I spend here can
be said to bring me suffering.   I have now found
again my great consolation, study.   I have already
come to the end of a long study upon St. Paul,
that I had been always intending to make : I await
my Bible, and when once that is in my possession,
it seems to me that I will be able to defy ennui
to seize upon me for many long years to come.
Four days ago I discovered that my neighbor,
in the cell on the left hand side, is one of my best
friends, he who had been so full of kindness to
me during our captivity at the Prefecture of Police.
We greet one another in the morning and at
evening by three slight raps on the wall, and this
would help to lighten the weariness of solitude, if
at times it threatened to overwhelm us.   I endeavor to be as reasonable as possible in trying to
better our prison-fare by some little purchases.
But, I confess, it is not without a pang that I do
so : I should be glad to content myself with as
little as possible.   I am afraid I should never be
able to keep my own house.

" You see, then, I am happy and in peace, so I trust you will not be over-anxious about the length or issue of this imprisonment. We cannot doubt that better times are in store for us, nor can we suppose that men have been made to be for ever at war with each other. The joys with which I have been favored for the last fortnight, lead me to believe that God reserves for you also like graces of confidence and peace. This is the daily prayer which I make with all the fervor possible."

This letter was followed by one to his spiritual director, to whom he thus lays open the secrets of his soul :

" It appears to me only just that the first letter which I ventured to send from here, after that to my parents, should be to you. I remember that your last words to us, as we were going off to the Prefecture of Police, expressed your wishes for our success. You little thought that your desire would be so well realized.

" No doubt you have blessed Divine Providence, as we also have done, for the small favor He has bestowed upon us :—not assuredly that our present situation is a great source of merit. We are only too happy, and our only regret is that we have nothing to suffer. But after all, this life of close union with God, and the reflections suggested by our position here, make us feel that we belong entirely to Jesus Christ, and that He alone is sufficient for us. Let the world shut us out ; in Him we shall find our sovereign joy. Or let Him take us to Himself ; we shall only be too glad to go.

"Thus the shadows of the past vanish, and our

entire life is summed up into one complete whole
to be offered to Him, to whom we feel ourselves
joined in life and death, for time and for eternity,
ad commoriendum et ad convivendum.   Oh! what
force those thoughts give us, what pledges they
are of the future!

"What a source of perpetual consolation during life!   How I thank God for having made me
feel so keenly the reality of my attachment to
Him!   It seems to me that, later on, at the happy
day of my subdeaconship, of my priesthood, and
of my death, I shall be able to remind our Lord
of these former joys of my love, contrast the
remembrance of them with all the regrets of the
past, make use of them, in fine, as so many motives
urging me forward to the altar or the tomb, with
greater readiness and resignation.

"Perhaps you will find it somewhat strange to
hear me talking thus of happiness in these times
of bitterness and anguish.   But then, can those
be selfish joys which are drawn from the heart of
Him who, whilst He brought along with Him His
heavenly peace and joy, was Himself the most
compassionate of men; can they be selfish when,
far from making us indifferent about present disasters they have only rendered our hearts more
sensible to sorrow!   "Ah! *si scires donum dei!*
Poor humanity, that fights for happiness with
sword and cannon, and spills its life's blood in the
struggle, and yet is far from finding it there where
it sought after it with so much passion.   Time
passes like a dream.   I have found a delightful
occupation in my New Testament, which I have

been exploring under many new and interesting aspects.

" Those who have our welfare at heart are, no doubt, far from believing that we are so happy. Be good enough to tell them how well we are in every way. I follow you often in spirit amid the splendid scenery on the banks of the Loire, with its rich verdure and delightful sunshine. Sweet peace, and blissful harmony of nature! What a bitter contrast this offers with the discord of men. Do not forget to thank God for us at times, for the graces He bestows upon us."

" You see that we are not much to be pitied," he writes the same day, " our only real privation here is, as you say, that of the Holy Mass, but to this we are fully sensible ; we offer, however, this sacrifice to God every morning, with the prayer that, in return, He may grant us the grace never to assist at it in future with negligence and distraction.

" Every moment now makes us appreciate the incomparable happiness of the Christian and the priest, to whom our Lord lays open the inexhaustible and tender inventions of His love. I will not try to tell you again all the joys I have found during the last month in searching into my New Testament in every possible manner and under the most varying points of view.

" This very evening I have received the whole Bible, and I know not how to tell you the happiness I feel at the prospect of launching myself adrift upon the swelling sea."

It was indeed in the Bible especially, that he knew how to seek out and love Jesus Christ. This sacred book, with which he had been charmed in his novitiate at Solesmes, and at the seminary of Saint-Sulpice, filled the solitude of his prison with delights. When this precious treasure arrived he could not refrain from a cry of gratitude and joy:

"At length I possess my dear Bible," he wrote immediately, "and I know not how to thank you for it. You should have seen how I threw myself upon it and pressed it to my heart. *Sint castæ deliciæ meæ.* And now the commune may have me to grow mouldy here, as long as they like."

The days he passed at Mazas, where generally the prisoners long to see them end, appeared to him henceforward too short, and he lengthened them accordingly by rising at four o'clock and going to rest only at ten. As a consequence of this, his notes and commentaries on "his dear Bible," at the end of his captivity, attained considerable proportions. How his soul must have poured forth its best and choicest sentiments on these pages! and how we regret that we cannot edify ourselves by the perusal of these his last effusions! But all efforts to recover these notes, which he had with him at the Roquette, have proved useless, and there is but little doubt that they perished in that detestable pillaging of the dead, which, with the emissaries of the commune, generally succeeded each execution.*

---

* After the massacre, the assassins robbed and despoiled their victims. During the night which followed the execution of the 26th of May, as after that of the 24th, the cells of those prisoners who had been shot were pillaged. The money and everything else of any value was carried away and the rest was burnt.

In this incessant and almost exclusive intercourse with God by means of his exercises of piety and his study of Holy Scriptures, the longings of Paul Seigneret after immolation and self-sacrifice became ever more and more intense. Such desires, it is true, were habitual with him, but they seized hold on his soul more firmly, whenever Providence seemed to furnish him an occasion of laying down his life in a great and holy cause. The present occasion was so manifestly providential, that his heart could not but be overwhelmed with joy. We are ignorant, however, of all his secret communications with God during his long hours of converse with Him. But a few burning words have escaped from his heart, they are stamped with his usual simplicity and sincerity, and discover to us the desires that filled his soul:

" I hope," he wrote one day, " that I will be the last to leave Mazas, or, if victims are required, that I will be amongst the first."

About the beginning of their captivity at Mazas, the superiors at the Seminary thought that they would succeed in getting the young seminarists set free, for their detention seemed absurd, viewed even in the light of the communistic theory of hostages, which the insurgents put forward as the motive that urged them on to make so many arbitrary apprehensions. When Paul Seigneret heard that others entertained the hope of being able to deliver him soon, his first thoughts did not turn to the happiness of being at liberty again ; it was the longing after self-sacrifice that was uppermost in his mind. And he did not consent to be set free except on certain conditions. Thinking, that some other might be delivered in his place :

He writes to the director of the Seminary, who was then making every effort to liberate him and his fellow-students : " I know that you are doing all in your power to release us, and I feel very grateful for so much kindness. But I would ask of you to remember that, by my own free choice, I belong to the diocese of Paris, and consequently I cannot think of leaving prison, as long as our archbishop remains shut up there. And if heaven requires a victim of expiation, is it not better that I should die than one of those venerable priests who could as yet gain so many souls to God ? I beg of you to think well of this, as I myself have thought well over it, before writing this letter to you."

There was another circumstance which called forth a fresh manifestation of the sentiments which animated him whenever he caught a glimpse of martyrdom in the distance.

By the newspapers which reached them, the hostages were able to learn what was the disposi- tions of the communists with regard to them, and what were their chances of safety. The day after the column of Vendôme had been thrown down, they read the violent harangues spoken by the " citizens " Miot and Ranvier after this absurd act of destruction had been accomplished. The threats of death that were hurled against the hos- tages gave those speeches that flavor which *the people* then relished so well.

The young seminarist felt his heart beating

with joy and hope as he read them. The newspapers quoted these words : "The vengeance of
the people is terrible when they fall upon their
enemies at last. Wo to them who provoke and
irritate them till their just fury can no longer be
restrained."

" Till now we have vented our rage on material things, but the day is drawing near, when we
shall exact an awful retribution from those, who by
their detestable influence, are undermining and
seeking to destroy us."

Between those two sentences Paul Seigneret
introduced these few simple words, which are the
expressions of the first thoughts that came into
his mind : " Te Deum, my dear fellow ! " and then
sent the newspaper by a jailer to his friend in the
next cell to him, whose love had inspired him with
new strength and afforded him great consolation
during their confinement at the Prefecture of
Police.

" I have still before my eyes those memorable
words," that friend wrote some time later, " and
after so long an interval I still experience, when
reading them, many of those impressions which
they produced then. I remember well that in my
emotions I threw myself upon my knees, and asked
God to give me some of those beautiful dispositions which my saintly friend possessed."

It was then, too, that, under the influence of
those thoughts, he wrote those beautiful words
which have often been quoted since, and have
drawn the attention of men highly distinguished,
and most qualified to judge of nobleness of lan-

guage. These lines,* which have thus thrown around his name a glory which he no doubt little expected, though others have deemed him worthy of it, run as follows : " You have without doubt seen the speeches that were spoken at the Hotel de Ville after the column of Vendôme had been thrown down. The provincial newspapers have not failed to give a copy of them. Our poor families must be in consternation. It is they whom you must pity, and not us.

 " As for us, the commune, no doubt, does not imagine that its threats made our hearts bound with hope. Is it really possible that, at the very outset of our lives, God should dispense us from passing the rest, and should judge us worthy to offer Him this testimony of our blood in a death more fruitful than a thousand lives ? Blessed be the day on which we shall see these things, if indeed it is possible that they should ever come to pass ! I cannot think of so happy an event, without the tears coming to my eyes !"

In the same letter he adds :

" Since I know that you can communicate with the provinces, the thought of writing to my parents has often come into my mind. But I always put off doing so, for I feel that I should have to condemn myself either to speak of topics and use phrases that are in the mouths of every one, or run the risk of lighting upon subjects that are

---

* These words, which are the true expression of so much generous enthusiasm, were quoted by M. Cuvillier Fleury, in the eloquent and highly applauded speech which he made at the ceremony of the reception of M. Zavier Marmier into the French Academy.

too tender to be touched. I have written to them once already ; perhaps it would be better not to do so again. They know that I am happy and at peace. Ah ! if we had not them in the world, how little attachment we would have for things here below !

"Do not trouble yourself about us. We are still alive yet and the days pass over more and more happy. May God reward a thousand-fold you and all those who have taken so much interest in us, for all the kindness that you have shown us during our captivity."

These last words give us occasion to point out another picture which strikes us in the life of this youth during his imprisonment. As we have already said, with his Bible in hand, where he found Jesus Christ and saw Him as he was, he could dispense with everything else, and prepare himself for martyrdom. But the solitude of Mazas was not unbroken, and the relation that he still kept up with some of those whom he loved allowed our young captive to testify once more those feelings of affection and gratitude, which lay like a rich treasure at the bottom of his heart.

It was not any benefit accruing to himself that he sought after in his intercourse with others ; that which delighted him in these relations was the result of his disinterested happiness at finding in others some of that kindness and charity of which he himself had conceived the ideal. Though he was now a victim to the wickedness and hatred of men, he forgot all those who had injured him, or wished evil to befall him, and turned with love and gratitude to those who tried, by their kindness, to bring him consolation in the midst of his misfortunes. And it was by this heroic Christian charity, coupled with the thought of God and the secret hope of martyrdom, that he succeeded in turning, as he himself says, his prison-life "into real days of happiness."

His first and greatest joy was in the much valued, but imperfect intercourse, which he still managed to maintain with that one of his companions to whom he was most closely attached. On the day after they had been thrown into prison, the two young friends discovered that their cells were next to each other. From this moment they formed a system of communication by rapping on the wall that separated them. In this way they gave new life to the solitude of the prison, and were able also to begin again a sort of community-life. In the morning, at noon and in the evening, they interchanged friendly salutations, and they gave each other the signal for their different exercises of piety. But it was above all when the day was disappearing, when they knew that the devotions of the month of May were going on in the church of Saint-Sulpice, that the two friends united in spirit to taste the sweet joy which they experienced in abandoning themselves for life and death to the protection of Mary, the queen of heaven.

They could see each other every day for a moment, as they were taken out in their turn for the solitary walk which was allowed to all the prisoners. They could smile to each other at a distance and exchange a mark of affection. These little things are highly prized by him who passes his life in a lonely cell, and they did not fail to give great joy to our young prisoner, whose heart was so tender. When he was afterwards transferred to the prison of the Roquette, he spoke to that one of his fellow-students, who was conveyed there along with him, of the "delightful" days of study and prayer, that he had passed at Mazas with his friend in the neighbouring cell.

The many letters that he addressed to the directors of the Seminary, who were still free, and were making efforts to deliver their students, and in the mean time strove to bring them consolation in the midst of their misfortunes, are full of expressions of gratitude and joy:

" You are really spoiling us," he writes to M. Tire on the second of May; " good fortune is coming to us from all sides. You can imagine what happiness your letter gave us. We often thought of you, and we knew that your thoughts often turned upon us. It is certain that in prison one gains, from his affections, in intensity of pleasure, whatever they lose in frequency of communication. And then our cells begin to be filled with all those whom we love and who think of us. We live on in this way, united in heart, whilst the sweet reminiscences of the past make us forget the sorrows of the present. We would, however, be much happier to see you in person, if that were possible, for then we would be able to thank you for always having us present in your mind and for all the efforts you have made to help us."

One of the directors of the Seminary, Mr. Hogan, succeeded twice in reaching the prisoners, and saw each one of them. Paul Seigneret received these visits with a heart overflowing with delight, whilst tears of joy rolled down his cheeks. He did not speak of himself, and it was not without difficulty that he was forced to give a few words of reassurance with regard to his heart. But his tongue could scarcely find expression to declare his gratitude for all the kindness that was shown him. In those precious moments, he liked above all to speak of France, of Paris, which was still dear to him, of those whom he loved, of his absent friend, and most of all, of those whom it had pleased Providence to subject to the same trial as himself, who lived at his side though he was not able to see them.

But the consolation that he derived from the visits of his friends was of short duration. The "citizen" Garreau, who had lately been installed at Mazas as director of the prison, forbade the eccleiastical prisoners all intercourse with their relations. - The Abbé Amable, a priest of the parish of Quinze-Vingts, who lived near Mazas, had undertaken to provide the seminarists with all that of which they stood in need. He sent to them every day, through a charitable female, food sufficient to supply what was wanting in the prison fare. Those services, which they received from persons with whom they were connected in no other way than by the ties of Christian charity, made a deep impression upon the heart of Paul Seigneret, and forced him to cry out one day :

"The longer our captivity is prolonged, the more we are astonished at the marks of kindness without number, which we receive: if we leave this place it will only be with our hearts inflamed with an intense love for men."

A few short notes, addressed to M. Amable, express in a most happy and playful manner the gratitude with which he was penetrated, and at the same time modestly make known the simplicity of his tastes and the fewness of his requirements.

"I am happy, Sir," he writes on the 7th of May, "I am happy to know at last the name and address of the person who foresees all our wants, and so delicately provides what we need, and who proves to us that outside these walls there are heart's that kindly watch over us. . .

"I beg of you beforehand not to be astonished if I do not often require your kind services. You must not think, however, that it is because I am unable to appreciate your goodness in all that you do for us. No! but I need little, and with your good chocolate in the morning, together with what we get here, I find that I have abundance. There are so many others who suffer at this moment!

"We have just received all the nice things that you have sent us. We are confused and deeply touched at so much kindness, and it is so sweet for prisoners to be able to express their gratitude, that I cannot deprive myself of the pleasure of thanking you.

"We do not grow tired of telling you our thankfulness any more than you do in showing your charity. You send us enough of food to

frighten a Prussian. I assure you we are a subject of scandal to the whole prison, and we will
never be able to leave it, we live so well here.
We think every day of the great trouble your care
of us must cause you in your household arrange-
ments, and we are ever more and more touched
with your delicate attention for us. Oh! how
happy we are to feel that, notwithstanding all the
miseries through which we are passing, there are
still left men of heart in the world.

"Be assured, Sir, that my fellow-students and
I will never be able to forget all that you have
undertaken to do for strangers who were altogether
unknown to you."

It was thus that his love for God and man,
which had been the merit of his life and that which
attracted all to him, still threw over his last days a
blissful peace, such as the uncertainty about the
future could in no way disturb.

The hopes that had at first been entertained
for the deliverance of the prisoners soon faded
away. Only one, M. Raynal, was yet free, and he
owed his liberty to the special influence of his
friends.

In the meantime the Seminary of Saint-Sulpice had witnessed the outburst of another storm,
in consequence of which only one of the directors
of that house was able to keep up correspondence
with the captives. It was to him that Paul Seigneret wrote on the 15th of May, the following letter, which shows him to us more radiant and calm
as the catastrophe drew gradually nearer:

"I am very thankful to you for the new mark

of affection you have just sent us : your proofs of sympathy are felt all the more keenly as they become more rare. But then, you may be sure it does not need a letter to persuade us of the lively interest you take in our trials, and of the frequent visits you pay us in spirit. There exists, thank God, a secret intercourse between souls, which cannot be interrupted by any human agency, and by which the absent can converse with one another though they be not in each others presence. In it our affections are more disinterested, and therefore more pure, and the joy that they give us make up for all the distractions of the outer world.

"You need not therefore be anxious about us. The days succeed each other here like real holidays : weariness and sadness are unknown. What has happened seems only destined to throw an unbroken serenity over our whole life. We thank God for it from the bottom of our hearts, with nothing to fear and everything to hope for, the future presents itself to us under the most favorable of aspects.

"I live all day long plunged in my Bible in presence of the Eternal Beauty, which, thank God, has ravished me for ever.

"I am exceedingly grateful to you for offering to write to my family, but I do not see that there is any pressing need. May God grant my dear parents that confidence and peace with which I beg Him every day to inspire them. The thought of their anxiety is the cloud that perpetually hangs over our life at present.

"I thank you also for what you send us. Your

kindness prompts you to heap so many good things upon us that it will be long before we feel the pressure of want.

" We are exceedingly thankful to the commune for having sent our good Mr. Hogan out of Paris : he was only exposing himself for our sakes, or at least underwent excessive fatigue in order to help us. We would wish to hear that all we love were along with him.

" Farewell, my dear M. Sire, I sing the *Te Deum* all the day long. You see I am scarcely to be pitied. Alas ! whilst I live on quitely here, how many are there suffering in every possible manner ! "

The victim was evidently ready for the sacrifice and God was about to call him to the altar to be immolated according to his heart's desire. On Sunday, the 21st of May, the troops of Versailles entered Paris. The Commune, hunted down almost to the death, wished at least to keep its victims in reserve. On Monday, the 22nd, towards four o'clock in the evening, the 'Committee of Public Safety, sent to the directors of the prison of Mazas orders to *transfer immediately to the Great Roquette (prison of the condemned) the archbishop, all the priests ; Bonjean, senator ; the detectives and policemen ; in fine, all the hostages of any importance.*

A first list was in consequence drawn up, and the name of Paul Seigneret was there inscribed along with that of M. Gard, one of the other seminarists of Saint-Sulpice, who were prisoners of the commune. These two young men were not priests, nor could they well be looked upon as *hostages of importance.*

But the men who put these orders into execution, as well, no doubt, as those who gave them, did not trouble themselves with such reasoning. To wear the cassock or be a priest, was all one to their blind hate, and *all priests* were condemned by the very title they bore.*   That was their crime and it is this that renders glorious before men, and precious in the sight of God, the death of those victims, so truly sacrificed in hatred of religion and the priesthood.

The eighteen hostages, whose names were upon the first list, were conveyed to the Roquette in two railway-vans.   There the two seminarists found themselves again side by side, after a separation of six weeks.   He who escaped from death has described to us the deep impression produced upon him by the sight of Paul Seigneret during this sad journey.

He was very neatly dressed, his face beamed with contentment and had put on a healthy look, such as it had not worn for a long time before : there was a peculiar lustre in his eyes and a smile upon his lips ; in a word, his whole appearance betokened a peaceful and modest joy—he seemed to be at the Seminary on one of its feast-days.

* Every one knows the odious language of which these men love to make use. Such words, with others of a similar kind, were repeated by the Director of the Roquette to M. Evrard, hostage of the Commune: "*as for priests, there shall not one remain ; they shall all have the same fate.   They have been hampering us for the last fifteen hundred years.*"   SOUVENIRS D'UN OTAGE, by M. Evrard, p. 66.

" I had never seen him like that before," says his companion ; " something seemed to go forth from his person which inspired those who drew near to him with a lively sympathy in his regard. I felt my heart moved and filled with new force ; at his side, my courage could not fail me. I should have liked to have been shot at that moment."

The two friends embraced each other and then began to talk, as was natural, about their situation. Paul Seigneret gaily assured his companion that he did not fear death. The latter profited by the presence of a priest to make his confession.

" And you," said he, when it was over, " are you not going to confession ? " " Why no ! " he replied smiling, with an expression of the most perfect calm.

He spoke little during this painful journey ; he seemed not to feel the need of talking, even after the long silence of Mazas. Besides, there was quite a new sight before his eyes, and this absorbed his attention. Scarce were the hostages outside the gates, than a hideous crowd, composed principally of women and children, rushed forward and made their utmost efforts to reach the vans, rending the air at the same time with clamors for the death of those within : " Ah ! there they are ! Shoot them ! Down with the *calotte* ! Cut off their heads ! To death with them, to death ! "

A frightful train of wretches was then formed, who followed the prisoners, vociferating furiously against them, and every time an occasional jolt would throw aside the leather curtains which closed the vans, and let them catch sight of a priest, the shouts and insults were redoubled. Paul Seigneret sat at the extremity of the wagon, his eyes riveted on the horrible scene before him. What must have passed at that moment in his innocent soul which, of itself, could never have believed such things possible. But there was one thought uppermost in his mind: his dream was about to be realised. This hope could be read upon his countenance, which still preserved its calm and wore its usual smile. It must have been with looks like these that the glorious martyrs of the heroic ages gazed upon the leopards and tigers that were ready to devour them.

At length at eight o'clock in the evening the vans rolled over the threshold of the Roquette, and the massive gates of the prison of the condemned closed heavily behind them.

Need we now ask how and why it came about, that Paul Seigneret and his friend had the honor of being amongst the first chosen for the sacrifice, and associated at that dread moment with the most illustrious victims that fell during this short reign of terror. As far as man is concerned, it was in all likelihood owing to a mere whim, or to one of those insignificant reasons which it imports little to know. But it is far easier to see here the hand of Providence, which is ever presiding at what men love to call chance. Our young friend had desired, in all the ardor of his heart, that, if victims were needed, he should rank amongst the foremost, and God heard his prayer.

If he had remained at Mazas until the gloomy

vans had returned to convey fresh victims to
death, he would not have been transfered to the
Roquette, and would thus have lost the palm of
martyrdom. It was about eight o'clock in the evening that they returned to make a second transfer
of prisoners. Two other seminarists of Saint-
Sulpice, MM. Dechelette and Guitton, after having gone through the usual formalities at the
clerk's office, had already taken their places in
the van which was to carry them off to the Roquette. A third, M. Barlequot, was passing in his
turn. Along with Cantrel, the clerk, there was a
man girded with a red sash, whose duty it was to
see that the prison was well provided for the day
of the massacre. The seminarist's youthful air
drew his attention.

"Your profession," he demanded gruffly.

"I am a seminarist" was the young man's
reply.

"I must have victims more serious than
that," he said, turning to the clerk; "Let me
have a policeman in his place.

M. Barlequot observed that he was not the
only seminarist in the prison.

After some further observation on the part of
the two officials, the man with the red sash ended
by saying; "I will have it so:" the clerk was
therefore obliged, much against his will, to modi-
fy his lists: the seminarists were conducted from
the van and locked up again in their cells. The
same individual had been there, when the two
young men, whose fate was now considered worthy of second thought, had passed through the

office : he had seen them inscribed as seminarists of Saint-Sulpice, and had made no opposition to their removal. It required the appearance of a third to awaken his whimsical and cruel compassion, which, in sparing these victims, still wished to have the number completed by others. It was thus that these men decided upon life or death.

But as regards the two seminarists already removed to Mazas, in spite of the observation and solicitude of their companion, they were left to their fate. Two victims too many, or too few, made little difference to these men of blood.

It was only on Thursday, May 25th, that a clerk from the prison office of Mazas* having gone to the Roquette, noticed upon the list of the hostages who had been removed there, the names of MM. Gard and Seigneret, which he recognized having often had at Mazas to control the correspondence of the prisoners. Upon the list of the doomed, six names were already marked with a red cross, viz., those of Monseigneur Darboy and the five hostages shot along with him on the preceding day. The clerk from Mazas pointed out to the one at the Roquette, that M.M. Gard and Seigneret were simple seminarists, and that they had been removed by mistake : and begged him to take his remarks into consideration. The latter replied that if it was so, a new order was required

* M. Casareto, who held a modest post under government, had during the Commune, accepted a place in the prison office of Mazas, with a view of being of use to the hostages. It is to his written relation of the whole that we owe this account of the incident relative to the removal of two seminarists to the Roquette.

before they could be sent back to Mazas. On his return, the clerk demanded the order in question, which Cantrel, in the absence of the director, did not dare to refuse, fearing that upon the arrival of the Versailles troops, who were rapidly advancing, a denial of this kind might serve as a new charge against him. Unfortunately, however, the names of the two prisoners were not upon the paper; there was only question of two seminarists. The director of the Roquette refused, on that very account, to receive the order. Once more the clerk of Mazas made the journey between the two prisons, which the fighting began now to render dangerous. At ten o'clock in the morning he obtained from Cantrel the following note:

" Order is hereby given to the Director of the prison of the condemned to send back to Mazas those detained bearing the names of Gard and Seigneret (Paul Joseph Claudius,) who were removed by mistake on the 22nd of the current month to the wards of the prison of the condemned.

In the Director's absence,

CANTREL, Clerk."

But at the moment when this order should have been delivered, the struggle had so far advanced as to render another journey impossible. After several fruitless endeavors, the good clerk to whom we owe this account, in spite of his desire to rescue the prisoners, had to abandon them to their fate.

Thus did God render more manifest the special choice he had made in conducting surely to the altar of sacrifice the noble victim who looked upon death and desired it as something really worthy of envy : *Et mori lucrum.*

CHAPTER VI.

· HIS DEATH.

The days that the prisoners passed at the Roquette were like a foretaste of the agonies of death. The emotions they experienced were most violent. At one moment they were sustained and carried away by a glimmer of hope, and at the next they were crushed by the certainty of death. Those who have gone through the anguish of these days have described it with a vividness and truth, which render more than useless any account that we could give. But it is our duty to point out in that group of victims, which the Commune had selected in order to vent all its fury upon them, him whose life has awakened in us so much sympathy and interest. We must now reverently gather together his last words, and relate his last acts, finishing thus the beautiful picture which his history has presented to us.

The first moments at the Roquette were moments of extreme anxiety. The prisoners were thrown into a large low-roofed room, as the night was slowly wrapping all in darkness. They waited there for more than an hour, without knowing if the next was not to be their last. His Grace, the Archbishop of Paris, was there in the midst of his priests, seated on a miserable bench ; his countenance was changed by suffering ; he was now pale and sick-looking, but resigned, calm and firm in these awful trials.

" When I saw all that boundless misery," say, as seminarist, who had looked upon him at that moment, " I could not restrain a cry of sorrow: What ! you here, my Lord ! "

Insult had attended the venerable prelate up to his entry into this dismal place, and even then he was not sheltered from it. When some one had unwittingly let drop the word Monseigneur, my Lord, " There are no longer any Seigneurs here," cried out, in a drunken tone, a young guard of eighteen, " there are only citizens now."

The prisoners were at last conducted, in the dark, to the first story of the fourth section of the prison. Each one took by chance the first cell that he found open : the door was then closed and all was over. The jailers did not know which of the prisoners occupied the different cells. A bed, formed of a mattress with one blanket, was the whole furniture of each compartment. It is true, the captives had but a short time to stay there.

Paul Seigneret was separated from his companion in the midst of the disorder, which was consequent on seeking their cells. He was put into No. 18, and it is there that he passed the last four days of his life, enjoying a peace of mind which nothing could disturb.

We know our young seminarist well enough to be able to guess how he spent those hours of preparation for death. Whilst he was there in his cell, with his Bible for his only companion, when he saw that now all hope of life was passed, and that there was nothing but death before him, with what love he must have united himself to Our Lord, how frequently he must have renewed the offering he had made of his life to Him whom he loved to call his Heavenly Father : *Pater, veint hora,* Father, the hour is now come.

But we are not reduced to simple conjectures, and the veil that is thrown over this last period does not hide all from our view. In the conversations which he had during those last days with his fellow-student, from Saint-Sulpice, he made known the religious turn he had given to his life at the Roquette.

In this prison the light is thrown through a single window into two cells, which are only separated from each other by a partition. Between the partition and the bars of the window there is left a small open space, through which the prisoners of two neighboring cells can communicate with each other. The saintly Abbé Planchat was next to Paul Seigneret. They could therefore pray together, and on Tuesday evening they even addressed their application aloud to God, during several hours.

" I heard them reciting together the prayers for the dying," says one of the hostages, "and I was deeply touched by it." *

They prayed so long and loud, that they even drew the attention of the sentinel who was keep-

---

* Souvenirs d' un otage, by F. Evrard.

ing guard outside below. The latter began to shout angrily at them, but he did not disturb them, for they continued until the other prisoners, who were awakened out of their sleep, had asked for silence.

In the morning the Abbé Planchat made the meditation aloud. During the course of the day, they read a chapter of the Imitation, or performed some other exercise of piety ; in the evening they recited the rosary.

As these two saintly souls had been united in their preparation for death, so too it was natural to suppose that they would not be separated when the last hour arrived. The Abbé Planchat was massacred with Paul Seigneret, at Belleville, on the 26th May.*

---

* The assassination of this venerable priest is one of the most detestable crimes that the Commune has committed. He had no sooner been ordained than he left those wealthier classes of society, for which the high cultivation of his mind and his previous life seemed naturally to mark him out, in order to devote himself, without reserve, to the service of the working population. From that minute the sad condition of these men and the endless misery of which he was a witness, did not leave him a moment of rest. He was ever going about doing good. At one time he was beseeching his friends to come to his help, at another, he was even impoverishing, with his alms, his charitable family, in order to be able to hold out a helping hand to all : that he might come to the assistance of his apprentices, provide for his orphans, and relieve a multitude of poor people of every description. His zeal never grew cool. And yet it was after thus consecrating twenty years of his life to the service of the people, depriving himself in the mean time of rest, and denying himself every pleasure, that the Commune ordered him to be arrested in the midst of a population of which he had ever been the protector, and which, nevertheless, let him be seized, and then be conducted to the Rue Haxo, and at last be cruelly massacred there.

We do not know if our young levite had the happiness of receiving Communion before he died, which was a joy accorded to many of the victims. Our Lord Jesus Christ was present in the adorable Sacrament in that prison, where only criminals condemned to death were confined. He was resting on the breasts of many of His ministers just as, at the period of the general persecutions, He reposed on the bosoms of His martyrs, and there too occurred scenes such as had taken place in the Catacombs.

We do not think that we shall be wandering from our subject by relating the happiness that M. Eard, a seminarist of Saint-Sulpice, and companion of Paul Seigneret, experienced in receiving, what he then believed to be, his last Communion. We follow the account which he himself wrote after he had escaped from death.

On Tuesday the 23d, about nine o'clock in the morning, Father Ducoudray, who occupied the next cell, called him to the window, told him that he had the honor of bearing upon him the body of Our Saviour, and then promised that he would give him the Holy Communion on the following morning. "Prepare yourself," he said to him, "adore Our Lord, and you in your cell unite your adoration to mine. Let us keep ourselves in retreat. Can we not say, too, that the two months which we have just passed have been a true retreat? What an honor is conferred upon us! We are treated as the priests of Jesus Christ, as our Archbishop. We may feel at ease : the prosecution is without doubt *in odium fidei*, in hatred of the name of Jesus Christ. We shall never have a better occasion to offer up our lives . . ."

Deeply touched by the revelation that was made to him, the seminarist threw himself upon his knees and remained there, turned towards the wooden partition, which he now looked upon as one of the sides of the tabernacle ; he adored the God Emmanuel, God with him in the prison. "Our Lord is there," he said in his faith, "and I did not know it : *Terribilis est locus iste !*"

Every hour of the night, as he was awakened by the awful noise of the struggle without, and by the glare of the light from the fires that were devouring Paris, he thought of this first Communion in prison, which was to be at the same time his viaticum.

"At six o'clock," he says, " Father Ducoudray rapped at the partition with that hand which was then the hand of a priest, and which, that evening, would be the hand of a martyr,—he gave me Communion. I put my head as close as possible to the bars at the corner of the window, and the priest of God deposited upon my lips a particle of the sacred Host, a particle which was small, it is true, but which was all Jesus Christ. I then drew back into my cell with this treasure, this companion of the prisoner. I fell upon my knees and with my face towards the partition I prayed, I adored Jesus Christ who was present within me, and in the cell of the Father. I had now nothing more to look for upon earth ; I had my viaticum, and I was ready to go on. Those who have received the Body of Our Lord with fervor, will

understand what it is to communicate in a prison-
cell, in spite of all the rage of godless wretches at
whose mercy we are."

If the Abbé Planchat received, as is not un-
likely, a particle of the Sacred Host from some
one of the priests who bore the Holy Eucharist
upon him, the same scene must have taken place
in his cell and in that of Paul Seigneret. We
cannot help thinking that Our Lord would have
accorded this last visit to a soul that loved Him so
tenderly, to one who had found the sweetest and
best joys of his youth in the Holy Communion.

Whatever may have been the case, God clothed
the gentle and timid seminarist with force, for
He wished to show in him that love is stronger
than death, and that one can take the words of
the Gospel, literally, and rejoice, yea, thrill with
delight, in face of a persecution which demands
the last drop of our blood: *Gaudete et exultate.*
There were many who saw his happiness, and
they have assured us of it.

We know that in this ante-chamber of death,
there were moments when the prisoners experienced the sweetest consolation. Such for instance were the times at which they were allowed
to see each other, and converse together. One
recreation that they had every day, in common,
united the hostages of all the different sections of
the prison, and in each section the doors of the
cells were left open for some time. The captives
had thus the liberty to pay their visits and talk
with one another. These were moments of in-
conceivable relief, which came to break the long

hours of unutterable anxiety, during which they had to listen to the noise of the struggle that was going on without, at one time sustained by hope, as they heard the army of order gradually approaching, and thus hastening the hour of their deliverance ; at another, startled by the rough voice of the executioner, who came ever and anon to call out the names of those who were marked as victims for death.

Paul Seigneret has left the same impression on all those who saw him during those days of terror, and they all make use of the same expression in conveying what they felt : *the angelic* appearance of their young companion in captivity, struck them so forcibly, that they can never forget it.

There was another, besides his companion from Saint-Sulpice, whose society he sought more particularly. He loved to be often near M. Perney, a venerable missioner, who had likewise fallen into the hands of the barbarians of the Commune, after having preached the Gospel to barbarians less cruel and fierce than they. This worthy priest has told us how much he was edified by the modesty, delicacy, piety, and ardor of our young seminarist, whom he then saw for the first time. In their very first conversation together he remarked how full Paul Seigneret's mind was of sentences of Holy Scripture.

In their interviews, the pious youth loved to make that which was uppermost in his mind the theme of their discourses.

—" Come, Father," he would say, " tell me

some stories about your young martyrs in China!"

—" That makes your teeth water, does it not?" said the missioner one day, smiling.

The following is the account that M. Perney gives of the good impression he made upon his mind. After having sketched in a few lines the qualities of each one of the victims chosen for death, he adds:

" But what shall I say of that *angel of Saint-Sulpice!* what openness! What purity of soul! What modesty! He used to come and sit down upon my pallet and talk with me about the martyrdom of our Chinese neophytes. His modesty was so great that he could scarcely bring himself to tell me that his happiness was at its height in finding himself *here.* I am sure that this good youth dreamt of nothing but martyrdom during his sleep.*

A distinguished member of the University, M. Chevriaux, principal of the Lycée of Vauves, shared with the ecclesiastical hostages their prison and their dangers. Paul Seigneret introduced himself to him as being the son of an Academy inspector, and he liked to speak with one, who brought back into his mind the thought of his father. M. Chevriaux was astonished at the angelical serenity which shone on the countenance of this victim, and he has pointed him out as remarkable amongst all the others. He could not at first believe that the assassins would have

---

* Deux mois de prison sous la Commune, p. 186

chosen this youth, who seemed so gentle and in-offensive ; and his murder appeared to him particularly odious, and filled him with the greatest indignation.

Paul Seigneret had also occasion to speak several times with another hostage, M. Evrard, Sergeant-Major of the 106th battalion, whose ac-quaintance he contracted, both on account of the vicinity of their cells, and because he was drawn by the charm a soul full of energy had for him. M. Evrard, in his ' *Memories of a hostage,*' has given a portrait of him, which will be easily recognized by those who have known the young Martyr :

" Amongst all my fellow-prisoners, he whose courage and resignation I most admired, was M. Seigneret. This charming youth, so gentle and modest, sacrificed his life with truly wonderful courage. I was struck when listening to him, with the force which faith gives to a pure and virtuous heart. He was of good stature, above the middle height ; his rich chesnut hair set off well a face remarkable for the regularity of its features. There was in him something quite angelical and captivating. He entertained no hope of escape from the doom which awaited him, and seemed de-tached from life, which, however, at his age seems to be full of charms and attractions. He awaited martyrdom with pleasure, regretting only the afflic-tion his death might bring upon his family. He seemed proud that Providence should have placed him amid so many noble victims, and have chosen him to share their happy lot, and showed his joy at not having to undergo the vicissitudes of a long life. Great was his surprise when I told him that I would sell my life dearly to those miserable assassins."

But this last testimony, and all those that precede, are summed up for us and completed by that of his companion of Saint-Sulpice, whom Providence allowed to accompany him up to his last moments. Everything in his friend's modest person and heroic behavior made a deep impresion upon him and did not fail to inspire him with courage. "I was with him," writes M. Gard, "eight days at the Prefecture of Police : I was his companion on our sad way from Mazas to the Roquette ; at the prison of the condemned we were side by side for four days, during the darkest hours of our captivity ; I saw him at the moment of the fatal call before the massacre ; on Monday, at the Rue Haxo, I was able to gaze upon his corpse, as it lay extended upon the ground, covered with his blood, amongst fifty others, and again on Tuesday evening I saw him sleeping tranquilly in his leaden coffin in the Church of Saint-Sulpice. After all this, I must say that not only none of my thoughts or impressions concerning him are sad or painful, but on the contrary, I feel a vague yet real joy, whenever I think of him. Never shall I forget that gentleness and serenity, or his calm and steady courage !

"What he was at the Seminary, ever tranquil and firm, that he was also during the long days of imprisonment, that he appeared to me in the prison van, when he replied with a smile, that he did not see the necessity of going to confession ; and he was the same when the name of Seigneret was called out, and I shook his hand upon the threshold of eternity !

" One would have said that for him captivity had no pang, and death no sting. In prison he went about modestly, silent and peaceful, always smiling, as it were at something invisible. Never any bitterness or regret, never a complaint, or action which could lead one to suppose that he had lost his self-possession. His gentle mien excited the sympathy of all, and every one asked who this young man was.

" Several times I went into his cell, and seated on his bed, we would talk together, confirming one another in simplicity, in faith, and in our expectation of heaven or of liberty. He often called to mind the days passed at Mazas in peace, recollection, study and prayer. He spoke also of the Holy Scripture, and the study of it : all was good and beautiful.

" I would like now to have penetrated more deeply into his interior and to have discovered better the dispositions of his soul, that I might be able to make them known to his parents, friends and masters. But how could I foresee that we should be separated in death, and that I should remain, when he would take his flight to heaven ! "

The first two days, however, at the Roquette had passed as quietly as the moment and place would allow. More than one amongst the prisoners had cherished the hope that the Commune would draw back before the perpetration of a crime which would be without any advantage to itself. But on Wednesday evening, May 14th, the barbarous execution of Monsieur Darboy, along with five of the principal hostages, cruelly dispelled all these illusions. Next morning Paul Seigneret told M. Gard how, from the window of his cell, he had seen the sad cortege pass. One of the assassins having caught sight of him, levelled his rifle at the Archbishop, and looked with a sneer towards the window, as if to announce what they were about to do, and the hope they entertained of being able soon to recommence their work. Our young friend, then more than ever persuaded that ecclesiastics were chosen, in preference to so many others, to be the victims of despairing rage, was therefore confirmed in his hopes and longings after martyrdom, and awaited in peace the hour of sacrifice.

On Thursday morning, Jecker, the banker, was summoned to undergo his doom, and was despatched, no doubt alone, in some corner of the prison. Roused by apprehensions of a like fate, Paul Seigneret could not help declaring anew to his companions, how terrified he was at the thought of dying alone in some spot apart, or falling into the hands of a furious rabble, to be butchered in a general and indiscriminate massacre ; adding that he had asked God not to allow such imaginations to come and disturb his present peace of mind.

The same day, the two seminarists of Saint-Sulpice passed a part of the walk, which the prisoners were allowed to take together, in the company of M. Bacuez, a director of the Seminary and hostage like themselves, but belonging to the third section. They walked up and down the prison court-yard just as they had done two months before in the walks in the garden of Saint-Sulpice, but the recreation took a grave and solemn turn : they conversed on death, eternity and martyrdom. Paul Seigneret said, with his usual courage, and simplicity, that he counted upon being amongst the first summoned, and that he looked upon going to God as a great happiness. Then they embraced one another and parted :—it was their last interview.

A happy chance has brought to light, when least expected, a note containing Paul Seigneret's affectionate farewell to his family. It is dated from the Roquette, 25th May, and, along with another letter likewise written from that prison, on May 23d, to his friend and fellow-student M. Déchelette, his neighbor at Mazas, it reveals the tenderness and generosity of his heart, and his winning, childlike simplicity.*

It is easy to recognize in these lines the youth who, throughout life, has always appeared to us pure, delicate, and disinterested in his affections, who is true in his heroism, and detached from things of earth, raises himself towards God with ease and gladness. We seem now to see him, as the last moment approaches, leaning thoughtfully against the prison window, with serenity in his

---

* This note was written on a page of a pocket-book found at Versailles, among the numerous objects that were brought forward to convict the perpetrators of the crime of the Rue Haxo. It is probable that Paul Seigneret had this pocket-book upon him at the time of his death.

looks, his eyes turned towards heaven, smiling at
death, offering to God the sacrifice of his two
dearest earthly joys, and writing in all his candor
of soul this double will, dictated by filial love and
friendship.

" MY DEAREST FRIEND,

" I do not know if you are still at Mazas; yet,
I let my letter take its chance. How glad I
should be to learn that you are still there.

" We are here at the Roquette, the prison of the
condemned. I bless God for it from the bottom
of my heart. Everything falls out in accordance
with my desires. I had so often asked that, should
some mishap come upon us, it might fall upon
me and not you. My wish seems upon the point
of being crowned.

" Oh, my dearest friend, whether I remain or
whether I am taken away, how much we will always love each other, be it here below, or there
in heaven above! God knows all the joys you
have brought me, and all the good your friendship
has done me for the last two months. I hope to
make you some return by a more entire affection
on my part. If God takes me to Himself, I will
watch over you as a brother, and I will endeavor
to send you a hundred-fold the good blessings,
graces and joys I should have desired for myself.

" Farewell, my very dear friend. Our lodging
here is once more of the very simplest description,
—a straw mattress served for our bed, as at the
Prefecture of Police, and I am writing to you
against the window.

"I saw M. Gard in the van yesterday. He is the only one of us all, thank God, who has changed prison along with me. It is impossible for me to express to you the joy I here experience.

"Once more good-bye. If we do not see each other again, tell all those that we love that my thoughts are often with them. May God have you in His keeping! I should die so happy if I knew that you were safe and sound.

"I embrace you with all my heart,

"Paul Seigneret."

"My very dear Parents,

"I am unable to write a letter, but perhaps this pocket-book may find its way to you, along with the few things I have with me.

"I thank you, dear father, and you, my dear mother, for the unbounded kindness you have always shown me. I die sad at the thought of the sorrow that awaits you, and of the little I have contributed towards your happiness, but glad at being able to efface by my blood whatever I have done to offend you.

"My sole regret is that I have not a thousand lives to offer to God, in atonement for the least of my offences against Him and my fellow-men.

"I now bid farewell to my dear uncle, to Alexander, to Charles and to my dear little sister. Their happiness has always been much dearer to me than my own. I trust that God will give them in His bounty all graces and joys, and a future such as I might have asked for myself.

"Tell all those that I love that the thought of

them has **not left** me **for a single** day ; and will yet accompany me beyond **the** limits of the world.

" I leave you for a better life, **in which you** know that I long ago placed all **my hopes** and **all** my joys. May you, therefore, **be able, even** in the midst of your sorrow, to rejoice **at least a** little **over my** lot. I shall **die singing the** *Te Deum.* **We** shall **soon be** reunited, **to** love **one** another **for ever.**

" Good-bye to all you **whom I love** ; you **have given** me a thousand **times more** than I **have ever given you.** Let **us** hope **that** in heaven I shall **be able to love you as** I desire.

" **I embrace you all,** whilst my **heart** is over-flowing **with gratitude.** Rest assured that our separation **will be merely** material, and that, as **I** hope, only **for a short time.**

"**Your Son,**
" **Paul** Seigneret."

The morning **of the day on** which this letter **was** written, Friday, 26th May, was the **day** of his martyrdom. Towards half-past **five in** the evening, another **call** was made, as all **the** cap-tives expected.

The **brigadier** Romain, who did his **sad task** in **a cruel, off-hand,** cynic fashion, presented him-self **with a list, and** gathering around him all the prisoners **of that** fourth section, **which had already** furnished the first victims ; " *Gentlemen*," he said, "*pay attention ; reply to your names when* **called.** *Fifteen are wanted !*" Fifteen ! and there **were** only some thirty remaining. "This savage declaration," says one of the hostages, "sent a shudder through all there present.

The name of Paul Seigneret was called out. He ought, it would seem, if we are to judge by his age, to have remained the last of the hostages. But God was answering his desires, and wished to crown His work in him.

Like all the others whose names had just been called, Paul Seigneret stepped forward, and modestly took his place in the ranks of the doomed. God only knows the sentiments with which he was animated at this solemn moment; but it seems to us, that he must have taken this step as he would have done that of his subdeaconship. He embraced M. Evrard, saying simply: "We shall meet again." He then passed before M. Gard, who only shook his hand, not doubting for an instant that he would be called likewise, and wishing to march on to death at the side of his noble friend to whom he would say farewell when the last moment arrived. But there were no more names upon the list, and the victims descended immediately without betraying any weakness, and without any ostentation. As Paul Seigneret passed by the half-open cell of M. Petit, Secretary to the Archbishop, he saluted him, bidding him good-bye with a bow and a smile, as if nothing at all had happened.

At the door of the prison, a band of twenty-five policemen and soldiers was added to the number of the fifteen hostages. And then before that painful march from the Roquette to the extremity

of Belleville, of which we know so few details.
We should like to have been able to follow
the victims, step by step, on their long and painful way, to have heard their prayers, to have
listened to the last words they addressed to one
another, to have witnessed how they exhorted
each other to courage and resignation, amidst
the yells and cries of death, which were breaking
upon their ears from all sides ; we should like
to have contrasted the calmness of their counte-
nances with the looks foreboding evil, which were
stamped upon the faces of their assassins ; we
should have wished, above all, to have penetrated
into their hearts, and have seen there the force of
grace which can raise man, notwithstanding his
weakness, far above the apprehensions of death.

But how can we distinguish each one of the
martyrs amidst that hateful multitude of armed
ruffians and unnatural women thirsting for blood,
who swell and roll about like an impure wave?
They alone could have told us the charity with
which they opposed the cruel hatred that was
vented against them, with how much patience
and gentleness they received all the injuries,
insults and blows that were heaped upon them,
with what unflinching steadiness they looked upon
their massacre which was now inevitable. But
death has imposed an everlasting silence on them
all.

Paul Seigneret must have been like a gentle
lamb in the midst of these ferocious beasts.
We can see him now marching steadily onward,
praying in union with Our Saviour on his way to

Mount Calvary. His bright and eager look bespeaks the exultation of his soul, and yet he is still simple and modest, and his features tell us of that peace and serenity of which death itself could not rob him.

The place chosen for the completion of the detestable crime, which was about to be perpetrated, was in the Rue Haxo, a street of the *Cité Vincennes*, which was the last retreat of the expiring Commune, and which is now deserted and desolate like some spot over which there lies a curse.

Scenes of horror took place there. The hostages were left at the mercy of a rabble mad with rage, and thirsting for their blood. This, too, was the kind of death that our our young friend abhorred, but God, in whom he put all his trust, gave him, without doubt, strength to overcome himself, and to suffer all without losing any of the joy he felt in being able to sacrifice his life.

If we are to believe those accounts which, we are told, come directly from eye-witnesses, the suffering of Paul Seigneret, must have been particularly painful.

According to these reports, he was cruelly struck to the ground, at the opening of the avenue that leads to the Rue Haxo, for having presumed to help to raise a venerable priest at whose side he was going to death, and who had fallen under the blows that he had received. The murderers turned all their fury upon their young victim. They showered their blows upon him, threw him down, and dragged him along the ground to the end of the enclosure where the execution took place.

The same witnesses tell us that during his agony he was heard distinctly pronouncing some words of love for his family and of forgiveness to his murderers. But soon, exhausted by fatigue and the cruel treatment he had undergone, he lay stretched out motionless upon the earth, whilst the assassins, thinking that he was dead, hastened on to the perpetration of other crimes. But at the end of the execution, one of these monsters perceived that he was not yet dead, and discharged at him the last shot that was heard in the *Cité Vincennes* on that evening of terror.

We will not, however, present all these details as absolutely certain. The state in which the body and the clothes of the young martyr were found after his death, make us hesitate about admitting them. But that which is certain is, that it was a ball which pierced his breast that gave him his death blow.

We do not, however, find any difficulty in believing that in his last agony, his thoughts should have turned on the anguish which would afflict his dear parents. Had he not written from prison that it was the thought of their troubles which invariably cast its dark shadow over his life.?

We may be sure, too, that there were no other feelings in his heart than those of kindness and charity, and that, if his lips did open, it was only to speak words of forgiveness to his murderers.

When we picture to ourselves this youth, full of nobleness and goodness, in the hands and at the mercy of bloody assassins, and at last shot down by their balls, a feeling of indignation and anger first rises in our soul, and we are tempted to cry out: *Revenge, O Lord, the blood of thy saints which has been shed.* But faith covers, as with a veil, the crime of the murderers, and discovers to us only the charity of the victim who forgives them all, and the fruits of his glorious death. Paul Seigneret, as we have seen, was burning with the desire of doing good, and he could not understand how God had given him such irresistible aspirations, whilst he had left him scarcely any hope of satisfying them. But we see now that he was able, as he desired, *to die usefully*, and we cannot doubt that, besides the merit of the sacrifice he made, a death, which has brought to light so beautiful a life, has been a thousand times more profitable to souls than would have been the few short years which he could have consecrated to God and the Church.

It was thus that the longings of his generous heart were satisfied. That which he had scarcely dared to think possible was granted to him :

At the very outset of his life God dispensed him from passing the rest, and judged him worthy to offer to Him the testimony of his blood in a death more fruitful than a thousand lives.

On Monday, 29th May, the day after the last combat had taken place, M. Sire, a director of the Seminary, and M. Gard, the companion of Paul Seigneret during his imprisonment at the

Roquette, went in search of his precious remains. It was only at the prison that they learnt that the last massacre had taken place on the heights of Belleville, which had thus become, like Montmartre of old, the field on which the martyrs gained their crowns. When they arrived at the *Cité Vincennes*, a most heartrending spectacle presented itself to their eyes. About twenty bloody corpses had already been drawn out of the hole into which the murderers had thrown their victims, and people were endeavoring to get out the others. Those who had come to look for the body of Paul Seigneret had no difficulty in recognizing him amongst the rest that were laid out upon the ground. He was there, his eyes shut, his face without a wound, without a blemish, without a contraction, and white as alabaster. Death had robbed his pleasing features of all their liveliness, but decomposition had not yet set in ; his look still wore some of that serenity which had struck every one during the last days of his life. His clothes did not bear the marks of any violence that might have been used. His cassock was saturated with blood from the wound in his breast, and was pierced at the bottom by several balls. His rosary-beads, the little office of the Blessed Virgin and his New Testament, which he prized so highly, were found upon him.

In the evening, the body of the young seminarist was conveyed to the church of Saint-Sulpice, and on the following day it was religiously inclosed in a triple coffin by the hands of his friends and masters. On Wednesday a solemn

service was celebrated for · him in the church.
That was the last touching meeting of the priests
of Saint-Sulpice and the students, who had
been witnesses or victims of the recent disasters.
The fellow-student of Paul Seigneret, who had
likewise been his companion at Mazas and the
Roquette, assisted at the altar, whilst one of the
directors of the Seminary offered up the Holy
Sacrifice. And he himself, the chosen one of
the Lord, was there, too, in all the glory of his
death; he was on earth by his sanctified body,
and he was present also, no doubt, in soul before
the altar and before the throne of God.

When the office was finished the venerated
relics were deposited in the vaults of the church of
Saint-Sulpice, until the place had been chosen
where they should definitely rest.

One happy proposal easily satisfied the wishes
of all. The place where the body of the young
levite martyr should be laid, was at the Seminary
of Issy, in the crypt of the chapel of Our Lady of
Loretto, which might be called the Holy of Holies
and the heart of Saint-Sulpice.

But a whole year had to elapse before this de-
sign could be put into execution. It was first necessary to raise this beloved sanctuary from its ruins.

At last, however, on Thursday, 27th June, 1872,
a few days before the vacation began, the ceremony of translation took place at the Seminary of
Issy, and we are sure that those who assisted at it
will never forget it.

The directors and students of the Seminaries
of Issy and Saint-Sulpice were gathered together

in the court yard, and there received with religious love and marks of the greatest respect the body of him who had been chosen out from amongst them as the victim most ready to be sacrificed. There were none there but friendly hearts, and in all the name of Paul Seigneret awakened the sweetest reminiscences. The priest who officiated at the ceremony was the uncle of Paul, he to whom the latter, when he was young, had so often laid bare his soul in those beautiful letters which we have read. Those who stood beside him, assisting him in the sacred functions, were the fellow-students of the young martyr, some of whom had shared his captivity, and others had contracted close relations with him during the years of his Seminary life. Besides the friends who had come from without, to pay the tribute of their love to him whom they had formerly known, there were also present many priests and laics who had gone through a part of his trials, and who had witnessed the serene joy of his countenance, which even death was not able to take away from him.

In conformity to the rules prescribed by the liturgy, the customary prayers were said, and a *Requiem Mass* was sung in the chapel. The ceremony, however, was rather a triumph than a dirge, and those who had been invited to come and pray around his coffin, which was covered with the white surplice of the levite, and strewn with lilies and roses, felt more joy than sorrow in their hearts.

No doubt it was only the cold clay that was left ; his body now was only a broken vase from

which the soul, that had left such happy impressions upon all, had escaped ; but all bitterness
was taken away by the firm belief that this soul,
once disengaged from the fetters that held it captive here below, had flown straight to heaven and
had found in God its glory and its rest.

The ceremony took a still more touching character, when, at the end of the Mass, the body of
the young martyr was borne from the chapel of
the Seminary to the tomb which had been prepared for it in the crypt of the chapel of Our Lady
of Loretto. It was then immediately perceived that
a true affection for him, whose memory all were
trying to honor, had guided those who had been
charged with the preparations for this feast,—for
such we must really call it. The walks of the
garden and park of the Seminary were strewn with
leaves, and made ready as if for a triumphal
march. Garlands of evergreens, into which were
woven red and white roses, symbolical of purity
and martyrdom, formed at short distances from
each other graceful arcades, under which the venerated remains were to pass.

Every one was filled with gentle emotions.
Those two long lines of levites, clothed in surplice,
who walked slowly up the avenue singing the
canticle: *Benedictus Dominus Deus Israel:* that
coffin adorned with flowers, that assistance of
pious sympathizing friends who wore so recollected a look,—all presented a spectacle well calculated to touch the hearts of those present, and bring
back to their minds the thought of those grand
solemn translations of the bodies of the Saints,

which our forefathers celebrated in the ages of faith.
When the body had been laid in the Chapel of
the Sacred Heart, by a sudden inspiration the
hymn of thanksgiving was entoned, that *Te Deum*
which Paul Seigneret had sung in prison and in
the presence of death; all voices took up with joy
the song of triumph.   It did not come in the per-
formance of the ceremony, but was the true and
spontaneous expression of the sentiments which
filled all hearts at this moment.

The body of Paul Seigneret now rests under
a slab of white marble, ornamented with those em-
blems which are often found on the tombs of the
martyrs in the catacombs.   On it is the following
inscription :

Hic quiescit
Paulus-Maria-Joseph-Claudius-Seigneret
Clericus.
Seminarii Sancti-Sulpitii **Alumnus**
Qui Puer ingeniosus et sortitus **animam bonam.**
Vitam brevem
Sed caritate in Deum et Homines eximiam
Constantique Crucis Christe Desiderio flagrantem
Sanguinis Effusione
Gaudio exultans complevit
Parisiis Die XXVI Maii An. D MDCCCLXXI Ætatis XXVI
M odium Religionis Frucidatus.
Desiderium cordis ejus tribuisti ei Domine
(Ps. xx. 2).

Here lies the body of Paul Mary Joseph Claudius
Seigneret, cleric, student of the Seminary of Saint-
Sulpice, who, being a youth of talent, and possessing
a soul enriched with every virtue, completed, by
shedding his blood with great joy, a life short
indeed, but made glorious by his charity towards

God and man, and by the burning love with which he ever sought the cross in union with Christ, being shot at Paris on the 26th of May, in the year of Our Lord 1871, in hatred of his religion.

Thou hast given him, O Lord, his heart's desire.

(Ps. xx. 2).

The Seminary of Saint-Sulpice will cherish with love this precious treasure. When the young aspirants to the priesthood go, according to the pious custom that prevails in the Seminary, to pray at the chapel of Our Lady of Loretto, they will gladly descend to kneel likewise beside the glorious tomb of Paul Seigneret. It will recall to them the grand and striking outlines which this life of a true priestly soul has revealed to them, and which may be summed up in three sentences.

Have always noble and high objects in view.

Love with passion Jesus Christ and souls.

Find your happiness in constantly immolating yourself by pursuing generously your duty, and, if it be God's will, by shedding even your blood.

Mihi vivere Chistus est, et mori lucrum.

Philip, i. 21.

THE END.

www.ingramcontent.com/pod-product-compliance
Lightning Source LLC
Chambersburg PA
CBHW031041120726
47905CB00007B/2273